RENT
TO
BE

RENT TO BE

A Novel

SONIA HARTL

Owned by Bonnier Books

embla
books

Sveavägen 56, Stockholm, Sweden
Copyright © Sonia Hartl, 2023

A CIP catalogue record for this book is available from the British Library.

ISBN: 9781471415753

This book is typeset using Atomik ePublisher

Embla Books is an imprint of Bonnier Books UK
www.bonnierbooks.co.uk

FSC
www.fsc.org

MIX
Paper from
responsible sources
FSC® C018072

To anyone who has ever cried in a public laundry room
because you had a dryer full of wet clothes
and your last quarter was Canadian

This one is for you

CHAPTER ONE

I hadn't expected to spend my Friday night banging a block of ice against a concrete corner while I wore four-inch heels and a little black dress that barely covered my ass, but these were desperate times. I was supposed to be on a date with a hockey player for the Griffins who miraculously still had all his teeth. Never mind that he listed amateur gynecologist as one of his hobbies and named Elon Musk as his personal hero in his bio. A nice smile went a long way.

Instead of circling the same block five times to find a free parking spot near Founders Brewery, I was sweating through my date dress while trying to get my hands on the card I'd literally frozen last month. I'd paid the minimum balance a few weeks ago, freeing up five dollars of available credit. I had two dollars and sixty-three cents in my checking account. Between my debit and credit cards, I'd be lucky to squeak by with enough to transport the boxes I hadn't been able to fit into my tiny Corolla. My wine-stained futon and dresser with the missing bottom drawer would have to stay on the street, but the fate of my frat house furniture was the least of my worries.

I lifted the block of ice over my head and slammed it down with enough force to bounce it into the bushes separating the sidewalk from the road. Between the blunt force and the sticky Michigan summer heat, a few more solid whacks broke the ice in half. My credit card slipped against my numb fingers as I wedged it free. I stood and wiped the sweat from my brow with the back of my arm. The cheery yellow curtains on the third floor shifted before quickly closing again. I glared up at my former apartment.

Earlier in the day, I'd gotten the news that I'd been passed over for a promotion. Again. By a guy who had the same qualifications but way less seniority than me, but who had a first cousin in upper management. Again.

I already had my date scheduled and had big plans to drown my sorrows in too much beer, followed by sloppy car sex with the hockey player. Then my roommate Vera texted me and said I was needed back at the apartment immediately. Nothing else. No explanation. When I arrived, I found the boxes on the sidewalk. Vera and Quinn had packed up my stuff, changed the locks, and pretended they weren't home rather than face me. Cowards.

And okay, I hadn't paid rent in over three months, but it wasn't for lack of trying. Thanks to a tight housing market, the cost of living in Grand Rapids had gone through the roof. I could barely afford to eat, let alone pay my bills on time.

When I graduated a year ago, I took the only job I'd been offered, an entry-level position as a business data-entry analyst for Cornerstone Enterprises. The salary wasn't great, but I made ends meet for the first six months. Then the repayment on my student loans kicked in. Since a good chunk of them were private, I couldn't get a deferment. Two months after that, the transmission went out on my car. I'd been playing catch-up ever since.

I thought my MBA was going to open doors for me. After I'd entered the job market, it became clear those doors also required social skills, connections, and the ability to kiss ass on command. Things that no amount of education could buy me.

So here I was.

I gave the third-floor window the middle finger, just in case Vera and Quinn were still watching, and pulled my phone out of my purse to request a taxi. Fifteen minutes later, a van pulled up to the corner. Though the driver almost took off when I explained I really only needed him for transporting my belongings, he relented after I assured him that I'd do all the loading and unloading myself. I made quick work of stacking up the remaining boxes—lovingly labeled "Isla's Shit" by my former roommates—and gave the driver my brother's address. I got in my car and followed close behind, in case he decided being a makeshift mover wasn't worth the hassle after all.

Sebastian's condo was only a mile away. His job had sent him to London for the next month, which gave me plenty of time to hide out in his guest room while I figured out my next steps. Asking my parents for help was out of the question. Up until two hours ago, I'd lived with my only friends. Everyone I knew from high school and undergrad had either moved away, or we'd drifted apart. It wasn't Seb's job to bail out his screwed-up younger sister. The only person I could count on to get me back on my feet was myself.

The taxi stopped in front of my brother's building, and I unloaded my things, as promised. The total "move" had cost six dollars and fifty cents. I'd made it. Barely. When I had all my boxes stacked on the sidewalk, I handed the driver both of my cards, explaining how to split the charge. My shoulders hunched as his expression shifted from polite disinterest to curled-lip disdain. It was the same look I'd gotten from the clerk at the Shell station when I tried to buy gas with three cans and a sticky nickel I'd dug out of my console, and the last thing I needed on an already shitty day. He didn't know me. He didn't know the kind of stress I was under from trying to make a single pack of Dollar Store ramen stretch between two meals.

I was out of college, dammit. I was supposed to be past these days.

As the driver peeled away from the curb, I shook my fist like I came straight out of the "Old Man Yells at Cloud" meme. "I have an MBA!"

It was all so pathetic. No one gave a shit about my degree. Not my boss, not my former roommates, not the Shell station clerk, so I had no idea why I expected a random taxi driver to care. The only person who seemed to think my overpriced education mattered was Sallie Mae, and that's only because she wanted her money back. With interest.

Huffing out a breath, I gathered my sable-brown hair into a messy bun, securing it with the tie on my wrist, and grabbed a box off the ground.

My parents lived and died by the belief that nothing worth having would ever come easy. My dad drove a truck, and my mom did hair in our basement. They were "pull yourself up by your bootstraps" and "earn your keep" kind of people. The most common phrases in our house had been "walk it off" and "suck it up." They didn't add *buttercup* on the end because they thought it might make us kids soft. My mom used to say they had to be hard on me and my brother because people would take one look at our large gray eyes, heart-shaped lips, and apple cheeks, and think they could step all over us. As a result, I always felt like I had to show my parents how tough I could be. I didn't cry when I skinned my knees after falling off my bike, or when Toby Booker dumped me at the prom because I wouldn't suck his dick, or when my grandma Jane died, and I got a birthday card from her the day after her funeral.

I wanted to cry now.

My nose started running, and my eyes felt itchy, but no tears. I hadn't cried since I was a toddler. Part of me wondered if my tear ducts had closed up from disuse, the way the holes in my ears did when I hadn't worn earrings in four years. Though my body managed to compensate by giving me the sniffles. The bane of my existence. I really would've preferred to cry like a normal person in times of distress.

When it appeared I wouldn't be having the sidewalk break-down I deserved, I took a deep breath and got on with the business of moving my stuff. I gave one of Seb's neighbors a tight smile as I marched through the entrance of the building. No one who saw me now would think anything was out of the ordinary. Just bringing a few boxes over to my brother's place.

Thank God he had given me a spare key for safekeeping. It would've been really embarrassing if I'd gotten caught breaking into his condo. Seb had majored in engineering and did something in tech or with security or with numbers or something. He explained it to me often, but I still had no idea what he did for a living. Though I did appreciate that whatever he did ended up sending him to London for a month so I could stay at his place without telling our parents I'd been kicked out of my apartment. While they'd probably let me move in with them, they'd make me pay for it. Not in money. They just wouldn't be able to resist comparing my situation to that time I tried to sell Mrs. Brisbane flowers I'd picked from her own garden. Or when I'd posed as a Girl Scout troop leader to get a discount on campsite fees in high school. Or when I'd been kicked out of the freshman dorms for underage drinking when I'd been caught skinny-dipping in the courtyard fountain. They'd shake their heads, like they saw it coming the whole time, and chalk it all up to another Classic Isla moment. Their nonstop jokes and comments would chip away at my confidence until I had no choice but to move out again to save what little self-respect I had left. Which made Seb's empty condo my only option.

I took the elevator up to the tenth floor, balanced a box of pots and pans with one arm while I dug out the key, unlocked the door, and pushed it open with my butt. My brother's condo always smelled like apple cinnamon, and the familiar scent warmed me down to my toes. His enormous leather couch, vintage tin advertisements, and scattering of family pictures and travel mementos gave his place a homey, lived in look, even with the cold and impersonal lines of his industrial finishes.

If I'd had a fraction of my wits about me, I would've noticed the lights on in the living room and registered that I wasn't alone. Sadly, I'd never been blessed with the ability to see the things right in front of me. So when my brother's best friend, Cade, came out of the bathroom down the hall, wearing nothing but a towel and the leftover water from his shower, I flung my box of pots and pans at him and screamed. A slight overreaction on my part.

He jumped out of the way to avoid the clattering cascade of kitchen supplies, and in the commotion, his towel came loose. It dropped to the ground at his feet. We both froze.

Holy shit.

Cade Greenley—the guy who had once put crickets in my room and told my boyfriend I had lice—was standing fully naked in front of me. I tried to avert my gaze, but I was caught in the penis headlight and couldn't move or blink or do a damned thing other than stare. A light dusting of dark hair over hard pecs, with a trail down the center of his sculpted abs, leading to . . . I gulped. He was unfairly perfect everywhere, and I. Could. Not. Look. Away.

I licked my lips, a completely involuntary and subconscious response, and his cock twitched. Oh God. Pulsing heat spread through me, and I did my best to extinguish it.

What was even happening right now?

This was Cade. While he'd always been hot, it had been in a peripheral sort of way. I understood Cade's hotness the same way I understood that the sky was blue and the grass was green. It just was. No further explanation needed. But now that I'd seen the full picture, how could I look at him and not see this, every time, for the rest of my life?

"Isla. My eyes are up here." The warm humor in his voice brought me back to reality.

I snapped my gaze up to his face, and his smug expression was nearly enough to earn me a spotlight episode on *Why Women Kill*. I had no one to blame but myself, though. I knew better than to give Cade ammunition for his ego. He'd never let me live this down. Every time we crossed paths from now on, he'd have that smirk. The same one he'd worn for months after I'd walked in on him having sex with Crista Martin on our basement couch, and he knew I watched for at least a few minutes before creeping back upstairs. Except this was worse. Back then, I'd been able to say it was dark in the basement, and

I couldn't really tell what they'd been doing under the sleeping bag, but this time I had no excuse. I'd totally been checking him out.

That didn't mean he always had the upper hand. Being raised in the Jane household meant I'd learned to give back better than I got. When Cade put crickets in my room, I put mealworms in his grilled cheese. When he told Rob Cattrall I shaved my toes, I told Alyssa Garrison he waxed his back. It was almost as if he liked getting his ass handed to him.

Now we had this thing between us that was going to change everything. And as much as I regretted seeing Cade naked, both of us knowing I could never unsee it, I couldn't find it in myself to be sorry either. I was officially doomed. Forever stuck in the penis paradox.

When it came down to it, I had no choice in my next course of action. It was the only thing I could think of to put us back on even ground. I grabbed the top of my little black dress, pulled it down, and flashed him my boobs.

CHAPTER TWO

"Jesus Christ, you win, okay?" Cade yanked his towel off the floor and held it bunched in his fist in front of his waist. "Put those things away before you hurt someone."

"They're just boobs, you big baby." I pulled up my dress and made the proper adjustments. "I know for a fact you've seen your fair share of them before."

Though his aggravated expression amused me, it still didn't feel like we were anything close to even. His towel covered up the problem but didn't make it go away. I was aware of his bare chest, hard stomach, and everything he was working with behind that flimsy piece of terrycloth in a way I'd specifically and purposefully *not* been aware of before.

I didn't have a single Cade-less memory from childhood. He was always around and always poking his nose in my business, but for the first time in our twenty-two-year history, it felt like he had an edge over me. I hated it.

In an effort to restore balance to the universe, I trained my gaze on his face. He kept his silky black hair trimmed corporate short. He had lightly tanned skin, his square jaw dotted with just enough end-of-day stubble to leave a light burn on soft skin, and his striking blue eyes looked like they could see into your soul. Or at least know the color of your underwear. He also had a small scar above his lip from the three stitches he'd had to get when he was eight, after I hit him in the face with a Frisbee. Though the overall package was appealing, Cade would never be accused of being pretty, or even handsome, any more than a volcano would be described in those same terms. He was too rough, too imposing to be anything other than . . . hot.

I mentally fanned myself. Good Lord, that was enough awareness for the day.

"How do you know how many body parts I've seen? Have you been keeping a close eye on who I've dated in the past?" he tsked. "Some might say that's a sign of jealousy."

I rolled my eyes. "If only I thought about you half as often as you think about me."

"If only." He nodded at the pots and pans spread around our feet. "What's with the box you threw at me?"

"The . . .?" Oh. Oh, shit. Thanks to our impromptu game of Naked Chicken, I'd totally forgotten about my boxes. I hoped no one had stolen them. At this point, I couldn't afford to replace a gum wrapper. "I'll be right back."

He gave me a quizzical look, but I didn't have time to think up an explanation. I rushed out the door and took the elevator back down to the first floor. As I stepped outside Seb's building, I breathed a sigh of relief. All of my boxes were still right where I'd left them. I chewed on my lower lip as I glanced up to the tenth floor. I had no idea what Cade was doing here while my brother was out of town, but it didn't surprise me that he had a key too. It threw a wrench in my plans, though. If I started dragging all my worldly possessions into the guest room, Cade would know something was up, and he'd absolutely tell Seb. I could see exactly how that would play out. Seb would feel compelled to fulfill his role as the Good Kid by telling Mom and Dad that Isla screwed up again, and I'd have to answer questions about why I couldn't just grow up and take some responsibility for my life.

I didn't need Cade or my brother or my parents to make me feel like a failure. I was already doing a stellar job of that all on my own.

What I needed was a believable excuse for all the boxes. My first thought had been to tell Cade my apartment had flooded, but it would've been just like him to point out that my stuff was dry. Maybe I'd say I was downsizing. Cade didn't have to know this was everything I owned, and it was no secret my former apartment was the size of a teacup. I could bring up my stuff, stash a change of clothes in my car, and go . . . somewhere. I'd figure that part out later.

By the time I smoothed out my story in my head and brought another box upstairs, Cade had changed into sweatpants and the Lions jersey I'd gotten him for Christmas last year. He didn't even root for the Lions, which I found out after the fact, but he still kept the jersey for some reason, even when I offered him the gift receipt. And yes, he spent the holidays with us. Though I couldn't blame him for that.

His dad, Trent Greenley, had been a musician who spent ten months out of the year traveling, chasing gigs. I remembered next to nothing about Cade's dad, other than the few times I'd seen him weaving around his backyard in a drunken haze on those odd weeks he'd make it home to see his wife and kid. He died when we were in high school, and we all went to the funeral, but Cade hardly knew him either. The saddest thing about it was how sad it hadn't been.

I remembered Cade's mom well enough, though. Meadow Greenley owned a new-age shop and had thought a lot more about her crystals and dream journals than she'd ever thought about her son. She had a vacant, not-present air about her, as if she lived a whole other life inside her head. She could also be incredibly fun and energetic and saw beauty in everyday things. Being around her was like being caught up in a tornado of flowers and sunshine. It was bright and pretty, but still left behind one hell of a mess.

On her good days, she'd sing and dance and turn embarrassing moments into celebrations, like that time she bought ice cream and streamers and threw a small party for Cade's first zit. On her bad days—and she had a lot of bad days—she'd get lost in her own world and forget to do basic tasks, like feed her son. Cade usually wandered over to our house, where he had a place at the table whenever he wanted, and because he never went hungry, his mom simply didn't notice. She wasn't a bad person on purpose, but that excused nothing because she'd never made much of an effort to be a good one either.

Cade had his bare feet kicked up on the coffee table, with a bowl of Fruity Pebbles balanced on his chest, and *Schitt's Creek* up on Netflix. "You've been gone a while. Did it really take you that long to come up with whatever lie you're about to tell me to cover the real reason why you're moving into your brother's condo?"

Damn him. And damn me for forgetting Seb's living room faced the street.

"I'm not moving in," I sniffed. "I'm downsizing. You know my apartment is small."

"Downsizing. Right." He took a bite of cereal and chewed slowly, as if he had additional thoughts on his mind. Which he'd no doubt share in due time.

"What are you doing here anyway? Can't you annoy the residents in your own building?"

"I'm having my kitchen and bathroom renovated. They're both completely unusable for at least a month. Seb said I could stay here while he's out of town."

Of course he'd be staying here for the entire month. Because the universe couldn't ever cut me a break. I lifted my chin and stared him down with what I hoped passed for casual indifference. "That's fine by me because I'm not moving in."

Cade raised a single eyebrow. It always bugged me that he'd been able to do that without looking like he was having a stroke.

"I'm not." I crossed my arms. I didn't want to keep talking about this. The more I said, the easier it would be to stumble over my half-baked story and walk into whatever trap Cade was surely laying at my feet. "It's Friday night. No hot date?"

"Who says I don't?" He gave me a cocky grin. "Ever heard of Netflix and chill?"

"I hope my brother has this place fumigated when he gets home." I turned on my heels and slammed the door behind me, though I could still hear his chuckle through the walls.

I returned with my first box, and Cade offered to bring up the rest for me, but I turned him down, telling him this was all part of my new exercise routine. I didn't want him involved in this any more than absolutely necessary. Plus, once I traded out my heels for flip-flops, it didn't take long to bring the rest of my things up. Aside from books, clothes, and a few personal items,

I didn't have a whole lot to my name. It had been a long time since I'd been able to buy anything for the fun of it. Honestly, I'd hoped to drag out the process a little more, since I didn't have anywhere to go. On the other hand, I really wanted to get out of there before Cade got to the "chill" portion of his evening.

I stacked the last box in the guest room and dusted off my hands. Seb kept it sparse in there, with an IKEA dresser and the double bed with a blue plaid comforter from his childhood. My stuff now took up over half the room. Cade was sleeping in there, but he'd have to deal. I had just as much right to the unused space in my brother's condo as he did.

As I headed into the hall, I slung my purse over my shoulder. "I'm going now."

"I was kidding about the Netflix and chill." He took his feet off the coffee table and turned down the TV. His serious expression had me inching toward the door. "I don't know what's going on with you, and I'm aware that you'd rather chew glass than tell me, but we both know you're not really downsizing. So why don't you stay, Rainbow Bear?"

My heart skipped at the nickname he'd given me years ago. When I was eight, I woke up one night to the sound of crying. There was no crying in my house. It freaked me out, but it also piqued my curiosity. I snuck out of bed and crept downstairs to find Cade curled up on our couch, crying in his sleep. Trent was on the road and Meadow hadn't come home that night, and he woke up scared and alone in an empty house, so he came over to our place. I didn't really understand what was happening at the time, though. He hadn't been there when I went to bed, and he usually slept on Seb's floor when he stayed the night. Watching him hug himself while his entire body shuddered with sobs had hurt down to my core. All I wanted to do was make it better, but I was a child and completely out of my depth, so I did the only thing I could think of at the time. I dragged my comforter downstairs and covered him up, then tucked the teddy bear I slept with every night under his chin. As soon as his eyes fluttered open, I ran back upstairs. Neither one of us mentioned it at breakfast the next morning.

A week later, my teddy bear reappeared on my bed. On its plain white stomach, a rainbow had been painted with painstaking care. Not a single smudge between the colors.

We'd didn't acknowledge the hard stuff or the serious stuff, preferring to keep our interactions light and somewhat antagonistic. But every now and then we had these Rainbow Bear moments. Little pockets of tenderness that happened so infrequently, I often wondered if they'd ever happened at all.

He patted the cushion next to him. "Come on. I'll even let you pick a movie."

I had to leave, but I couldn't seem to get moving. Even though I knew it wouldn't be wise, I actually considered sinking in next to him on my brother's soft leather couch. My feet and my heart were sore, and his offer was tempting. It had been a rough day. All I wanted was a few hours of peace, where I could forget about my housing woes and my dead-end career and the fact that I was hanging on by my fingernails.

But then I glanced at a family photo on Seb's bookcase. They'd all been so proud of me when I graduated. My parents had been certain I'd never be capable of following in Seb and Cade's more admirable footsteps, which only drove me to show them otherwise. Spite would forever be my greatest motivator. At my graduation, they went out of their way to remind me that I'd finally shed my reigning title as the family screw-up, but it came with the implication that they were keeping the crown polished. As if it was only a matter of time before I'd be wearing it again. That was just a year ago. Not nearly long enough for me to be sick of my family's respect yet. I couldn't risk it.

I pulled my keys out of my purse. "I need to go back to my apartment."

"Okay. If that's how you want to play it." His lips thinned, and something like disappointment passed over his face. "Whatever you plan on doing tonight, be safe."

My spine stiffened. He wasn't my brother, and it wasn't his job to look after me. I wasn't a hundred percent sure where I would go yet, but I was resourceful. I'd been in tighter jams. None that I could think of right then, but that wasn't the point.

"I'll be fine. At my apartment." I stepped into the hall and closed the door.

I might not have had a place to sleep worked out yet, but there was one place I could go for now where I would always be welcome.

*　*　*

"You need to leave."

I peeled open one eyelid and looked up at the woman who had doe eyes, golden-brown skin, and a thick mane of dark hair pulled into a high ponytail. She wore a pink cardigan and a "don't fuck with me" expression. Neeta Sharma. My favorite librarian and promising future bestie. I was ninety-nine percent sure she hated me.

The West End Library was my favorite place in the world. It had a pyramid-shaped fountain out front, three levels with a giant iron staircase winding up the center, and a wall made entirely of multicolored glass. My parents used to bring all of us kids here on rainy days when they needed a few hours of quiet and couldn't send us outside. Seb and I would put on hilarious puppet shows in the children's section while Cade watched with a sullen-faced glare.

They had extended hours in the summer for the speaking events and reading programs they put together. The week before last, I'd been swarmed by a bunch of junior high kids who were there all night for a lock-in. It was too bad they didn't have one of those tonight. I could've signed up to volunteer and slept in a maintenance closet.

I picked up my phone from my chest to check the time. "You don't close for an hour."

"We don't, but you've been lying here for forty-five minutes, and we've reached our weirdo capacity for the day. So you're going to have to go now."

It had become a weekly ritual for Neeta to find me to lying down in the business aisle of the library, which annoyed her to no end. Rightfully so, if I was being honest. I couldn't even explain to myself why I did this, but I found it incredibly soothing to be surrounded by the wisdom of people who had found career solutions and passed those along through the written word. Books centered me. Lying down and letting all that knowledge tower over me gave me a strange kind of comfort in a world that otherwise felt like it was spinning out of control.

I sat up. "What if I'm looking for a book recommendation?"

Neeta eyed me suspiciously. "I guess it depends on what you're looking for."

"A book that gives practical advice to women, like where to go and what to do when their roommates kick them out of their apartment and they can't go to their family for help and their career has already stalled out before it can really begin."

17

She gave me a long-winded sigh. "If you leave now, I'll let you stay for an extra half an hour next week without argument."

"I'll take it." I jumped to my feet, eager to get out of there before she changed her mind. "Just out of curiosity, what would happen if I didn't come in anymore? Do you think that's when you'd realize you've enjoyed my presence here the whole time?"

"We've already picked the celebratory cake we're getting when you stop coming in."

One of these days I'd grow on her, but today wasn't going to be that day.

After I left the library, I drove around the city for a while, then parked at a Target when I started to get low on gas. I was beginning to run out of options and hope in equal measure. I couldn't go back to my brother's place or my parents' or the library. I supposed I could always sleep in my car, but that seemed like a real easy way to get murdered, and I wanted to live through this night. Mostly so Cade couldn't say "I told you so" over my casket.

It wasn't until the lights dimmed inside the store and the last employee drove out the parking lot that a viable solution occurred to me. I had a key card to the building at work.

Cornerstone Enterprises made the majority of us salaried, so we all had twenty-four/seven access. Overtime was strongly encouraged. In fact, I suspected the reason why I hadn't been promoted—when people with the same level of education but less seniority than me had already moved up—was because I wasn't willing to donate more than an additional five hours of exploited time a week, while everyone else looking for a promotion put in an extra ten to fifteen unpaid hours. I couldn't bring myself to do more than five.

Every week I tried to look for the positive, something to keep me motivated, but there wasn't a lot I liked about my job. Even before I'd started working there. It had never been my dream to do data entry for a multinational corporation. I'd sent in my CV to Cornerstone as a last resort, and they'd been the only place to give me an interview.

When I first started college, I wanted to be a librarian. I loved books. Everything about them, from the feel to the smell, to the escape they provided when it felt like the world was forever on fire. But my mom said it wasn't practical, and my dad said it would never pay me enough to make a dent in my loans, and I wanted to make them proud more than I wanted my own dreams. When I took the GMAT to decent results, I decided to pursue the same degree as Cade, and by the time I figured out I'd still be broke with an MBA, just miserable on top of it, it was too late. I couldn't afford to take on any more debt. This was my life now.

I used to vent to Quinn and Vera, but they told me to get a new job and blew off my problems, so I stopped talking. They never would've understood anyway. Their parents paid for their college. They didn't know what it felt like to lie awake at night in a cold sweat with the constant fear of being one emergency away from total financial ruin. And they didn't get how finding a new job wasn't an immediate solution either. I wasn't the top of my field or in demand. My internship hadn't panned out, and I was terrible at networking. I'd graduated from a middling college and had one year of work experience. At best, I'd be able to make a lateral move to another corporation exactly like Cornerstone Enterprises, where the only difference might be better tea selections for the breakroom Keurig. My options were limited. If I didn't stay somewhere long enough to move up, I'd be stuck in the endless loop of entry-level hell forever.

So I kept working. I put in my extra five hours, begrudgingly, and hoped one day I'd be lucky enough to trip over a corner of loose carpet and fracture something serious, so I could sue the ever-living shit out of them and somehow scrape my way out of the chokehold my student loan debt had on me.

That was my new dream.

As of now, I'd settle for having a place to crash for the night, and my cubicle would have to do. The only alternative I could think of would be to order a cup of coffee at Denny's and hope they didn't kick me out when I fell asleep in one of their booths. That sounded infinitely less appealing than curling up under my desk. If I got caught on one of the security cameras—which never got checked unless something had been stolen—I could just say I fell asleep while working late on Friday. The big bosses would love that. Maybe I'd finally get a raise.

With my decision made, I drove through the deserted lot and parked my car as close as I could get to the entrance without taking one of the spots reserved for the higher-ups. Just in case. I didn't expect to see anyone in the morning, though. While it took some seriously deranged working habits to move up the ladder at Cornerstone Enterprises, even the overly ambitious drones who worked sixty hours a week took Saturdays off.

I grabbed my backpack and stuffed it with one of Cade's old shirts (that I sometimes slept in because it was soft and comfortable), a change of clothes for tomorrow, some bodywash, deodorant, and my makeup kit. Might as well freshen up in the morning and really sell the lie that I'd spent the night in my apartment. I also grabbed my pillow and comforter, though sleeping on the hard floor was going to suck no matter what.

Before I let myself into the building, I looked around, as if I was waiting for someone to jump out of the bushes and stop me. Ridiculous. There was no one here. I was completely alone. With a shake of my head, I swiped my card and pushed open the door.

Walking though Cornerstone at night was like exploring a large and boring cave. Every step I took echoed, and the only light came from the eerie blue glow of the computer screen savers. I tiptoed around the open office, careful not disturb other people's work areas, and made a little nest in my cubicle. As I stared up at the underside of my desk before I fell asleep, I wondered if what people said about rock bottoms was true. If there really was no place to go but up. Or if there were still endless ways to fall.

CHAPTER THREE

I woke to the sound of someone yelling. That wasn't anything new. I rubbed my eyes, wondering if it was Quinn shouting about how I put hamburger grease in the garbage disposal, or Vera complaining about me stealing her shampoo again. I blinked at the wood-grain pattern above me and turned my head. A sharp pain shot down my neck. I wasn't in my apartment. I didn't have an apartment anymore. I'd spent the night on the floor under my desk.

It all came rushing back to me at once. Getting kicked out of my apartment, seeing Cade naked, being told someone who started a month ago got the promotion I'd been hoping for, seeing Cade naked, vaguely wondering if the amateur gynecologist with the nice smile found someone else to have awkward car sex with, seeing Cade naked. In about that order.

The woman who had woken me got louder, and I bumped my head as I sat up. No one was supposed to be here. It was Saturday. At least I was pretty sure it was Saturday. I swear, if this turned out to be like that freaky *Groundhog Day* movie, where I had to live Friday all over again until I made better life choices, I was going to be seriously pissed.

I crawled out from under my desk and peeked my head over the row of glass above my cubicle. Alice Bishop paced in front of her office on her phone. She had a stack of files tucked under one arm. Her sleek blond hair was held back in an elegant clip, and she wore a tailored suit with expensive shoes. I immediately ducked down again. Alice was my boss's boss's boss. She got to have a real office with a door and windows. Cornerstone Enterprises didn't cluster their executives on the top floor, preferring to spread them out like dukes and duchesses watching over their flock of peasants. It was supposed to build morale, and I supposed it did give some in the cubicle farm the far-reaching belief they could one day occupy Alice Bishop's office by proximity alone. I didn't have that kind of fruitless optimism. I preferred to drink instead.

After retying my sloppy bun, I quickly changed into white cotton shorts and a mint T-shirt, hoping I could sneak out while Alice was occupied with whoever was trying her patience on the other end of the line. I moved between cubes, ducking and rolling with my arms full of my bedding, backpack, and purse, like I was in the worst *Call of Duty* game ever. I nearly made it to the exit hall without being seen. But then I did the smartest—or dumbest—thing I could've possibly done in that moment. I listened in on her call.

"I understand, Mary." Alice stared at the ceiling as if she not only didn't understand, but she was barely keeping her urge to yell again in check. "No, your granddaughter's birth is very important. I'd just hoped you could help me with a suitable replacement since my flight is leaving in . . ." Alice glanced at her diamond-encrusted watch, and I found myself briefly hoping I'd one day be the type of person who wore a watch. "It leaves in two hours. I should be at the airport already." A frustrated pause, then, "Who else is going to make sure my dog is walked and my plants are watered and keep an eye on my house?" Another pause. "The cleaners won't do that. And I can't hire a service on such short notice during vacation season."

There was a season specifically dedicated to vacations? We didn't get that life in the cubicle farm. But something she'd said piqued my interest. She had a service to walk her dog and water her plants and watch her house? I didn't have a lot of expertise, but I could do that. In fact, I'd do it for free if it meant endearing myself to my boss's boss's boss, especially because I didn't stand a chance of getting out of the entry-level loop on my work ethic alone.

Alice ended the call with a sigh. It was now or never.

I stashed my bedding and backpack in a nearby cubicle and approached her with caution, like she held a weapon, rather than my career, in her hands. "Hi. Isla Jane." I pointed at myself like I could really be talking about anyone else. "I work over there." I waved at the general vicinity of my desk and willed my hands to stop doing things. "I couldn't help but overhear . . . I didn't mean to listen, but I was here . . . um . . . getting some extra work done."

Alice looked over my outfit. My cotton shorts and T-shirt weren't exactly Cornerstone approved, and she gave me a single eyebrow raise. Which made me think of Cade, which made me think of Cade naked, which made heat rush to my cheeks. In front of my boss's boss's boss. Every day it became clearer that I wasn't cut out for the corporate world.

"I figured we could be more casual on Saturdays?" When she didn't respond, I plowed ahead. Because, honestly, how much worse could it get? "Anyway, my parents have dogs." Ceramic ones my Aunt Betty sent us every year, but it's not like she was going to call them to ask. "I'm an excellent dog walker, and I can water plants. If you need someone. If not, I totally get it—I'll just get out of your way, and—"

She held up a hand to stop me. "I need a house sitter. Do you know what that is?"

"Yep." No clue. But if I could learn how to pierce my own belly button from YouTube, I could learn all about house-sitting. "I can start immediately."

As she studied me, she tapped a finger to her cherry-red lips and managed not to smudge her lipstick. How? "I'll pay you, of course. You can still work during the day. You'll just need to be in by night."

She reached into her Gucci purse to pull out her checkbook, and the blood drained from my face. Her purse looked somewhat similar to mine. The way a mangy alley cat resembled a panther. Where mine was plastic, hers was made of genuine leather, and her clasp had a gold "G," while mine had a "C" made from cheap nickel. I'd bought my Cucci knockoff at a purse party for twenty bucks a few months ago. Back when I still thought the term *disposable income* existed for people like me. I might've worked on the same floor as Alice Bishop, but we were an entire world apart.

I tried to hide my purse behind my back, hoping she wouldn't notice, but she had probably already cataloged it and filed me away as a loser. The shame tightened my throat, and my nose began to run. It felt like I'd been caught cheating. Like this was the consequence of daring to want something nice, even when I knew it would never pass.

"You don't have to pay me." My voice wobbled as I kept my gaze on the ground. And on her real Louboutins. At least she hadn't caught me in my date-night heels, the ones I'd bought from the clearance bin at Walmart and painted the bottoms red. "I'm happy to do it for free."

"Really?" She looked up from where she had her pen poised over a check. "The service I was going to hire would've charged me five hundred dollars for the week."

My heart flipped over in my chest, and I was pretty sure I'd let out a gasp. Five hundred dollars? I could've been making very close to what I made now by walking a few dogs and watering some plants? And I wouldn't even have to pay rent because I'd be staying in someone else's house? What had I gone to school for, again?

"That's Isla Jane." I pointed to the line on the check. "It's spelled I-S-L-A." I mean, sure, I wanted to endear myself to my boss's boss's boss, but I wanted five hundred dollars more. And truth be told, I probably wouldn't be getting promoted anytime soon anyway. I lacked the proper sense of masochism. "Did you . . . um . . . want to do a background check or whatever on me first?"

"Not necessary." She ripped off the check and handed it to me with smile that promised certain death if she came home to find a single knickknack out of place. "I know where you work, and I'm betting that means I can also find out where you live."

As of last night, those two places were one and the same, but there was no reason for Alice to know that. I thanked her and wished her safe travels. As soon as the elevator closed, taking Alice one step closer to her destination, I did a little spin and hugged the check to my chest. Five hundred dollars! I'd be able to put gas in my car and buy something to eat other than Ramen and give Quinn and Vera a small portion of what I owed them for back rent.

Maybe there really was no place for me to go but up.

*   *   *

Since I had a feeling Alice would *not* appreciate it if I borrowed a few outfits from her closet for the coming week, I needed to stop by my brother's apartment to get some clothes. Which meant running into Cade. Maybe this was a good thing, though. The sooner I faced him after the Dropped Towel Incident, the sooner he could start being fully clothed in my mind again. Not that I spent that much time thinking about Cade, clothed or otherwise.

I unlocked the door to my brother's condo. "Hello?"

No one responded, but I didn't trust that for a second. I walked in with my hand over my eyes. Better safe than sorry. I stumbled over Cade's giant clown shoes in the entry but righted myself before I fell over. As I passed through the living room, I gripped the couch to get my bearings, then reached out in front of me, feeling my way through the room.

When I hit a wall of flesh with my palm, I uncovered my eyes and took two full steps back as I glared at a shirtless Cade. "Was that fun for you?"

"Absolutely." Amusement danced in his bright eyes.

He must've just gotten back from the gym. A sweaty T-shirt was draped over the back of the armchair, and he wore a pair of loose basketball shorts that left nothing to the imagination. My breathing turned shallow as I took in the bulge outlined by the silky material, knowing exactly what it would look like if he pulled his shorts down. Why was my mouth watering? I'd seen

27

Cade's penis exactly one time. That was not enough for me to have a conditioned response to it yet.

"Isla." His voice was rough and scratchy, and I involuntarily shuddered as the way he said my name poured over me like warm honey. "You're staring again."

I gazed at him with wide, startled eyes. As if I'd just woken up mid-sleepwalk and wasn't sure how I'd gotten here. "It's not what you think."

"I'm pretty sure it's exactly what I think." He gave me the kind of self-satisfied smile that made me think he could read every single dirty fantasy I'd had about him since yesterday. "This is starting to become a habit."

"What's wrong with me?" I scrubbed my hands over my face. "It's not like I'm the only one of us who got an eyeful yesterday. Why isn't this a problem for you?"

Maybe he didn't find me attractive. Which was fine. Preferable, even. We'd practically grown up together, so there was no way anything could happen between us, but I'd be lying if I said I wasn't a little offended. I had great boobs. They were worth an inappropriate thought or two.

"Steel trap." He tapped his temple.

I narrowed my eyes. "What's that supposed to mean?"

"It means I can recall any image, in perfect detail, while holding the thread of a conversation and keeping those two things separate. It's an incredibly useful skill."

"Don't think about my boobs."

He grinned.

"Stop it." I pushed past him and went into the guest room.

Cade leaned against the doorframe and watched as I dug through my boxes, pulling out and discarding various clothes. "Where did you stay last night?"

I gave him a look that I hoped said "none of your fucking business," but aloud I replied, "My apartment."

"Liar." The silky tone of his voice was like a finger trailing down my spine. "Why are you packing up a week's worth of clothes if this is all stuff you're giving away?"

"I'm not giving anything away yet, so don't take my boxes to the thrift store because you think you're being funny." I keep my back to him as I dug out my swimsuit. Alice probably had a pool. I stuffed it into the small suitcase I'd bought at the Women's Career Expo. Because then I'd thought I'd have career that would let me travel to somewhere other than the countywide swap meet.

"Wouldn't dream of it." He rubbed a hand over his stubbly jaw. "Have you talked to your parents, though? Maybe they can help."

I snapped my suitcase shut and leveled him with an unamused look. "We both know that's not true, so please don't pull a Seb and call them on my behalf. I'm fine."

"Yeah, okay." He put a gentle hand on my arm, bringing me to a stop as I moved past him to leave. "Just so you know, you can come to me if you're ever in trouble. You don't have to do everything on your own."

"Yes, I do." I shook him off, dragging my suitcase with the squeaky wheels behind me.

I went down to the parking garage, got in my car, and planted my face against the steering wheel. Maybe I'd gotten in over my head, but I was fixing it. I didn't need Cade's help. If I could make this house-sitting thing work, I'd be back on my feet before Seb got home, and no one in my family had to be any wiser.

CHAPTER FOUR

When pulling up to Alice Bishop's home, I became of aware of two certainties. One, a person three rungs ahead of me on the corporate ladder made a hell of a lot more than three times my salary. And two, if anything happened to her dog while I was here, I'd be using that five hundred dollars to buy her a new one, hoping she wouldn't know the difference. Because she absolutely had the means to make me disappear.

Before I left Seb's parking garage, I'd done some research on house-sitting. To prepare myself in case I'd signed up for something freaky in the fine print. I really had no reason to worry. House-sitting was like being a living scarecrow, but instead of guarding corn from birds during the day, I was guarding houses from burglars at night. Truthfully, any burglars would probably laugh themselves hoarse and rob the house anyway once they got a look at me, but if Alice wanted to drop five hundred dollars on my services, who was I to argue? This was way better than paying rent to two roommates who barely tolerated me. I should've looked into something like this sooner.

I pulled up to the gate, where a man wearing a gray wool uniform and looking like he hated life had to let me into the neighborhood. I had no idea why anyone living here thought they needed walls and a gate when they were already so far removed from the rest of us, or why any of them would require a house sitter for that matter, but those weren't things I was being paid to consider. I was just here to water the plants.

Alice had sent me a text, from the plane, telling me to eat whatever I'd like, when to expect the cleaners, and which bedroom I'd be sleeping in. I didn't ask how she'd gotten my number. I slipped my phone into my Cucci purse, stepped out of my ten-year-old Corolla, and stood in the circular driveway with the perfectly manicured hedges in the shorts and T-shirt I'd gotten from the five-dollar clearance rack at Old Navy. I'd never felt more out of place in my life. And I said that as someone who once showed up to a regular keg party in a nightie after Quinn told me it was sleepover themed.

The house was large enough to cast a shadow out to the street. There were only two stories, but it had the presence of a high-rise. Soft gray siding paired with navy shutters across the expanse of windows on the first and second floors. The severe roofline jutted the structure skyward. It was the kind of house designed to intimidate.

A pile of rocks near the front had been arranged in a way to look both artful and natural. The smallest one on top of the pile was fake, which I never would've guessed if I hadn't been told. Using the code Alice gave me, I released the latch under the fake rock to retrieve the key and unlocked the front door.

The ornately carved wood looked like it should've been heavier, but the door glided open with airy ease, as if I'd crossed the threshold of the blessed. The foyer had eighteen-foot-tall ceilings. If I yelled loud enough, maybe I'd hear my own echo and feel a little less alone, which just made me unnecessarily sad.

The inside of Alice's house was pretty, but cold. I had a hard time picturing anyone living there, let alone a person who owned a pet. It looked like it had been staged to sell.

I walked through the sunken living room, where the couch cushions didn't even have an indent to indicate they'd ever been sat on. Tall vases of colored glass twisted in elegant shapes decorated the enormous fireplace. The open kitchen had gleaming copper pots hanging over the island that looked like they'd never been used. The dining room table had an ornate rose-and-lemon centerpiece, even though no one would be home to have dinner. Museum displays probably got more everyday handling. I already felt sorry for her dog.

With that thought, a tiny pile of yarn plopped down by my feet and turned its creepy orb-like eyes up to me. It had a flat yet circular body, stubby clawlike legs, and a nose that looked like raw beef. It might've been a dog. Or a grisly old Roomba. It was hard to tell.

I crouched to get a closer look, and a black spotted tongue lolled out of its hell mouth. Yikes. "You must be Bitsy. Aren't you the strangest-looking thing?"

Bitsy thunked her head forward and clamped down on my big toe. I yelped, but as I stood to shake her off, I realized the sensation of her chewing on me tickled more than anything else. The poor toothless beast.

"Want to go for a walk?" Seeing as she was a dog, I hadn't expected a response, but I'd hoped for some sign of life. A happy bark, a tail wag—anything, really. Instead, she stayed firmly suctioned to my toe as I dragged her toward the door and leashed her up.

I stepped outside and drank in the scent of freshly clipped grass and sun-warmed concrete. Alice's neighbors must've been having a party. Cars lined the street four houses deep in each direction. I dragged Bitsy along the sidewalk like I used to do with my stuffed animals. Not much of a walker, this one. At the end of the cul de sac, she found a nice leafy bush for doing her business, then flopped down again, and I dragged her back to the house.

As soon as we got inside, I unleashed her, and she waddled down the hall. Probably in search of the portal to the dimension where she actually belonged. Next, I went around to the side of the house and dug through the shed until I found the plastic watering can that was supposed to be on the third shelf but was tucked behind some tarp on the bottom shelf. Once the plants had been taken care of, I had the rest of the afternoon to myself.

I opened the refrigerator to see what kind of food Alice had on hand. I left a streak of fingerprints behind on the stainless steel, and felt very much like Pig-Pen bringing my cloud of dust into this pristine palace. I had no idea how I was going to stay here and not feel like I was leaving it in a state of chaos just by existing.

Cool air drifted over my skin, and it surprised me to find things like strawberry jam and block cheese and pickles in Alice's refrigerator. Rich people—they were just like us. Except not.

She had hummus, which I loved and had not had in months; bacon, which I also loved and had not had in months; and an already opened bottle of champagne I'd be more than happy to finish off for her. If I didn't go up a dress size by the end of this arrangement, I was going to be disappointed with myself.

The fancy fruit basket on the counter held a variety of apples, oranges, and bananas on the lower level, and a small cache of avocados on the upper level. That was the one food item I did eat with some regularity, because it was the only way I was able to treat myself anymore. According to some millionaire (because it was always some millionaire), I could've had a house of my own by now if I had just quit eating avocado toast. Though I was no mathematician, I was pretty sure the three dollars and fifty cents I spent a week on avocados and the one dollar and nine cents I spent on bread from the last-chance sale rack didn't add up to a monthly mortgage payment. No wonder I'd never been all that great at budgeting.

I munched on an apple while I poked around the rest of the house. Still no sign of Bitsy. I really hoped she hadn't wandered off somewhere to die. There was no way I'd be able to replace a dog that looked like it had been made from the spare parts of other animals.

In the hall closet, Alice had an actual fur coat. I'd only seen fur coats in movies as the clichéd garment of the rich and famous. I'd never seen someone wear one in real life, though— not even in the winter. I ran my hand down the soft fur and inside the silk lining. It felt amazing.

Last, I checked out the guest room where I'd be staying. It had an understated sunflower theme. Butter-yellow walls, dark walnut furniture, a few sunflower throw pillows, a couple of candles with sunflowers baked into the wax. Nothing too gaudy or overdone. I loved it.

I set my backpack on the bed and changed into the hot pink bikini I'd had since high school. Though I'd filled out a bit more since then, I couldn't justify the expense of a new suit when this one technically fit. I grabbed my phone and planned to head out to the pool, but paused at the hall closet. She had said to make myself at home . . .

With one last stop at the kitchen to grab a glass of champagne, I stepped out to the sunny backyard in my bikini and the fur coat. It was hot and ridiculous, but it was one hundred percent worth it for the few hours I'd get to pretend that this was really my life.

My phone buzzed, pulling me out of my temporary fantasy. I frowned at the picture that popped up on my screen, but answered it anyway. "Hey, Mom."

"Are you busy?" It was one of those trick questions I hated answering because it could go either way. If I was busy, then I could be accused of not making time for my parents, but if I wasn't busy, then I was lying about and not doing anything productive with my time.

"Sort of?" I hedged.

My mom let out a deep sigh. I didn't know what that meant, so I didn't say anything. "I just got off the phone with Sebastian."

"Oh?" Did that mean I was in for another exciting run-down of all the ways Seb was the superior child? He was only a year older than me yet had somehow managed to become an adult while I was still floundering. A fact my mom could never resist rubbing in my face whenever we spoke. "What did he have to say?"

"He said he might stay another month in London."

"Really." I sat up, careful not to slosh champagne down the front of Alice's fur. If Seb was staying in London for two months, it would give me that much more time to save up enough money to find a place of my own by the time he returned. "That's great news."

"Why is that great news for you?" The suspicion in my mom's voice had me grinding my teeth together. "You aren't thinking of freeloading at his condo while he's gone, are you?"

"No, Mom." I sounded as tired as I felt. Leaning forward, I rested my forehead on my knees. "Why do you always ask if I'm freeloading or running some kind of scam?"

"Suck it up. I was just joking."

I was always the one who had to suck it up. My feelings were never allowed to be hurt, because it was just a joke. My fault for not being able to take it. "Okay, but you do remember that I have my own apartment, right?"

"Don't you pay rent and share that apartment with two other girls? Not exactly your own." She hadn't outright said, *"Why can't you buy someplace nice and get on with adulthood, like your brother?"* But the implication was there anyway.

"I don't actually share an apartment with two other girls anymore." Fuck. I squeezed my eyes closed and bit my lips together. I needed to look into getting my jaw wired shut. "What I mean is, I might be buying soon. I, uh, got a promotion."

Oh God. I'd really just said that. I couldn't take it back now.

"Honey! That's wonderful news!" The joy in her voice rang through my ear and dropped like a lead weight on my chest. And yet, through the lie, I was grateful for the praise.

"Yeah, it's great." I sounded like I was on my way to a funeral. "Anyway, that's why I'm so busy right now. I've got to go. But it was good talking to you for a minute."

I hung up before she tried to invite me home for dinner to celebrate. Trying to keep up the fake cheer while talking about a job that continued to be out of my reach would be too much. Even though I really had no choice now. I had to keep the lie alive. Which meant I'd need to earn enough money from house-sitting to make it look like I'd gotten a promotion. Solid plan. I could see no way in which this would inevitably backfire on me.

Though if I wanted to have any chance of succeeding, I needed to look like a legitimate business. I opened the internet browser on my phone. It seemed like most of the house sitters online got up and running through a combination of Facebook and Instagram ads and word of mouth. If I did a good job this week, maybe I could ask Alice to recommend me to some of her friends. That meant keeping Bitsy alive. I really needed to find that dog.

This wouldn't solve my immediate problem of where I'd be staying between gigs, but I could make this work. Sleeping under my desk hadn't been all bad. More importantly, I could keep my family from finding out what a complete and utter failure I'd become.

I'd sold my laptop already, so I'd have to do everything from my phone, which I managed to keep by being on the family plan. I still had an active website from my book-blogging days. Something else I'd given up when I realized being a librarian just wasn't in the cards for me. I hadn't reviewed a book in four years. An old hurt squeezed at my heart as I glanced over the work I'd put in. I supposed I could've kept blogging, but at the time I'd thought it better to shut that part of myself off. It was how I'd fooled myself into believing I didn't want it as much anymore.

Instead of wiping my blog clean right away, I copied and pasted my reviews over to my email. Just in case I ever needed them again. Then I reworked my website to read "Isla Jane: Professional House Sitter." I decided on my rates based on what Alice had paid me and what the other house-sitting services charged. I undercut the local competition a little, hoping it would encourage the other Cornerstone executives to use me. There weren't many competing house sitters, though. This was a niche market, and I didn't want to house-sit for just anyone who filled out my contact form. I had serious doubts about being able to continue living rent-free for very long, but Alice had said this was vacation season. If she'd recommend me to her rich friends, maybe I'd be able to get by for a few months. And if I wanted that to happen, maybe I shouldn't sweat my way through her silk-lined fur coat.

As I shrugged out of the fur, my gaze caught on a man standing on the balcony of the house next door. A man who some (not me) might say reminded them of a volcano. A man a little too rough to fully blend into the corporate world he seemed to be excelling in anyway. A man who was currently giving me the kind of grin that made my toes curl while my gut churned with fear. After what could've been a second or a year of us staring at each other, Cade turned toward the French doors behind him and went back inside.

CHAPTER FIVE

I jumped to my feet and threw the coat off, but there was nowhere to hide. I mean, I could've gone inside the house and locked the door, but it was a little late for that. I had no doubt Cade was about five seconds away from making his way down the stairs next door and crossing between the cypress trees that had been planted along the property line for privacy.

What was he doing at the house next door? He wasn't quite as out of place as me in this neighborhood, but pretty damn close. Had he also gone into the house-sitting business? I shook my head at the absurdity. Cade didn't need to house-sit. He actually liked being a cog in the corporate machine and had moved up in his company with an ease that alluded me.

Even though I'd been expecting him, my heart leaped into my throat when he came wandering into Alice's yard, hands in his pockets, like he was out for a little stroll. Only someone who really knew him would recognize the predatory gleam in his eye. I attempted to swallow, but my mouth had gone dry.

"What brings you to the neighborhood?" The casual humor in his voice didn't match the razor-edged sharpness of his smile. He was pissed.

"It's none of your business what I'm doing here." I crossed my arms, pushing my boobs into dangerous territory with a seven-year-old swimsuit a full cup size too small. His pupils flared as his gaze dipped to my chest, and I immediately dropped my arms. "As much you'd probably like to think otherwise, you're not my brother, and it's not your job to look after me."

"Believe me, I know damn well I'm not your brother." The slight growl in his voice and the heat in his eyes made everything tingle, and I was really starting to hate the thinness of the material covering my nipples. "If you don't tell me what's going on with you right now, I'm calling Seb. Maybe he can talk some sense into you."

"Running to my brother to tattle?" I approached him and cupped his cheek. "And what are you going to tell him? I caught your sister enjoying a glass of champagne by a pool. Seems suspicious. Think you better come home from London for this one."

He caught my wrist and lowered it to my side. "I didn't tell him you moved your stuff into his condo when I talked to him last night. Don't make me regret lying to my best friend."

I tilted my head in confusion. Cade had lied to Seb? But he didn't lie to Seb about anything. The two of them had been closer than brothers since the day Cade toddled into our back-yard, wearing nothing but a pair of gray underpants and a Sponge Bob inner tube. Meadow had plunked her four-year-old in a kiddie pool, then gone inside to meditate, and had forgotten about him. It was a wonder he'd managed to stay alive before he found our family. He'd been a skinny kid, raised on a questionable diet by an absent-minded mother and a just plain absent father. And he'd been painfully shy. That's what I remembered most about Cade from when I was a little girl: how he tended to hover in corners like a living shadow, always watching but very rarely participating.

He didn't come out of his shell until freshman year of high school. That's when puberty hit. He filled out and grew six inches overnight, at which point he'd been able to stand up for himself. But my brother had stood by Cade all through elementary and middle school, when he wasn't the cool kid and it had been hard for him to fit in. Seb had broken Charlie Thompkins's nose in the third grade for calling Cade a freak; then he yelled at me for disrespecting Cade by giving Charlie Thompkins a hand job in the tenth grade.

But I couldn't entirely blame my brother for that one. He was a Scorpio. It was in his nature to hold a grudge until the end of time.

That was the kind of bond Cade had with my brother, though. They were ride or die for each on a level most people didn't understand. I got it because I'd grown up with both of them, and saw how and why that bond had been formed, so it completely took me by surprise that Cade would outright lie to Seb, just to protect me. What was I to him? Other than a nuisance who'd been around for his entire life.

"Why?" I blinked against sun and shielded my eyes.

"Why what?" As he shifted his stance, uncertainty clouded his eyes. I'd hadn't seen him this visibly uncomfortable since the fifth grade, when his mom had sent him to school in a hand-knit sweater that was two sizes too small, and all the boys on the bus had called him Belly.

"You know what I'm asking." I lowered my voice, even though we hadn't been anything close to shouting. It was as if something had changed in the air around us that required hushed, serious tones. "It's not like you to keep things from Seb."

"I don't tell him everything." His words felt like an electric current running along my skin, drawing out little goose bumps in its wake. He cleared his throat. "At least I didn't tell him this particular thing because I'm still not sure what you're up to, but I'm trying to help. No matter what else *you* might think."

I'd never really learned how to ask him for things. No matter how many times he offered. We gave each other shit all the time, and we pushed each other's buttons for no other reason than that we were bored, but we rarely did deep conversations. The last time had been three Thanksgivings ago.

* * *

He came into my parents' house late after making his obligatory, after-dinner visit to Meadow. He punched a wall, then got out a fifth of Jack Daniels and drank a quarter of the bottle in one swallow. He didn't know I was sitting at the dining room table in the dark, having an existential crisis about the path I'd chosen for my education and already feeling like I was trapped. We passed the bottle between us that night, revealing more of our insecurities and the things we refused to acknowledge while sober.

"What are your fears, Rainbow Bear?"

"All of them?" The whiskey had begun to set in, and I tilted to the side, my shoulder bone digging into his bicep as I attempted to sit upright. "Or just my top ones?"

He wrapped his arm around me and held me tight against his side. He took the bottle and tipped it back. His Adam's apple bobbed as he took a deep swig. "Your choice."

"Let's do top three. Tornados. Meat in ball form." I ticked them off on my fingers.

He gave me a lopsided grin. "Really?"

"It's gross." My tongue drunkenly scraped the back of my throat just thinking about it.

"As amusing as that is"—he gave me a little nudge—"tell me something real."

His tone was gentle yet probing. As if he genuinely wanted to know. A warm buzz from being the center of his focus made my limbs loose and my head light. His serious expression made me want to dig deeper until I pulled up the most personal thing I could share simply because he asked for something real.

Maybe it was the whiskey, or the way he looked at me, but I wanted to be honest with him and share the things I hardly dared to admit to myself. "I don't want to go into business, but I have no idea what I'm supposed to do with my life. I'm terrified I'm going to get to the end of it and feel nothing but regret."

He stared at me for several long seconds, his gaze trailing over my face as if he had all the time in the world to study the exact contours. "Want to know my top three?"

"Please." My voice cracked on the syllable.

"June bugs. Conversations with my mother when she's high." He glanced to the side and grimaced, as if he could see through the walls to the house next door. When he turned back to me, his gaze dipped to my lips. "Although, after tonight, I think my biggest fear is going to be never finding the courage to go for what I really want."

I held my breath as a bead of sweat rolled between my breasts. He was going to kiss me. I was so certain. But after a beat of silence, he tucked me back against his side, passed the bottle of Jack Daniels to me, and asked what had happened to me being a librarian.

The next morning, I came to with a brutal headache and an acute sense of embarrassment over the things I'd shared the night before. I left before Cade woke and didn't speak to him for a month. The next time we saw each other for Christmas, we both acted as if that night had never happened. So, yeah. We didn't do the deep-talking thing.

* * *

"It's not a big deal. I'm just house-sitting for my boss's boss's boss." I gestured at the monstrous house behind me, as if to make sure he was extra certain I wasn't just crashing some rando's pool. "I'm trying to endear myself to her or whatever. Kiss ass. Climb the corporate ladder. All those things you're so good at."

"Bullshit." Cade tapped a finger to the bridge of my nose. "You get a little scrunch, right here, when you're lying. What's really going on?"

"What about you? What are you doing here?"

"My bosses are having a barbecue. Quit deflecting."

I shook my head. If I didn't tell him what happened, he'd either pester me until I gave in, or call Seb so he could pester me. The two of them together were insufferable, and I was kind of glad my brother was away for a minute so I could have a break.

"I started a house-sitting business." Or I would be starting one as soon as I fine-tuned my website. "It's a perfectly respectable second job."

He gave me a look like he knew I wasn't giving him the full story. "So you just decided you didn't need your apartment anymore because . . . why? Please don't tell me it's because you assumed you'd be able to live in other people's homes instead."

"Actually, my roommates decided I didn't need to live in my apartment anymore."

He tilted his head back and muttered something under his breath. "And why is that?"

"That's kind of what happens when you stop paying rent." Though I could've found a way to phrase that more delicately, I'd never tried to earn Cade's approval. Probably because he'd never made me feel like I had to earn it.

His ground his teeth together. "Jesus, Isla. What the fuck?"

Ugh. Maybe I cared about his approval a teeny bit. "It's been really tough, okay? My job pays for shit, and my student loan payments are half of my income—and that doesn't include all the credit card debt I'm carrying. I was somehow making it work for the first few months, but then the transmission went out on my car, and everything snowballed from there."

"But you have your MBA." He said that like he truly couldn't understand why I was struggling. Like my degree was some kind of financial cure-all. Like he'd also bought into the belief that all someone needed to succeed was a good education, when the reality was much different. And spending six figures on a piece of paper that said I was smart and qualified, when fifty other people applying for the same position had that same paper, probably meant I wasn't that smart after all.

I didn't respond to his MBA comment because, really, what could I have said? It's not like I hadn't been screaming that very fact at random Shell station clerks and taxi drivers for months now. "Are you going to tell Seb I got kicked out of my apartment?"

He blew out a breath. "I don't know."

I nodded. It was the best answer I could expect under the circumstances. But I didn't regret telling him. It had been foolish of me to think I could get away with the downsizing lie. As a kid, I'd made bird feeders out of milk jugs because I hated waste. I still had the same bikini from high school, for fuck's sake. I didn't get rid of things willingly.

"Unless . . ." He glanced back at the house where his bosses lived. "This is going to sound a little insane, so bear with me."

A trickle of unease slid down my spine. If the man raised by Trent and Meadow Greenley thought something was "a little insane," we were probably entering bat-shit territory here. But I was also willing to do damn near anything to get out of Seb or my parents knowing I couldn't pull myself up by my cheap plastic Cucci bootstraps. "I'm listening."

"My bosses are social and active. They host five recreational events and a gala in the summer. I always attend, but since I never bring anyone, half my coworkers want me to meet their daughter or niece or friend of a friend. They all seem to think I'm getting to the age where I should be settling down."

I snorted. "You're twenty-six, not forty."

"A lot of them are old school. And nosy." He ran a hand through his silky black hair, which fell perfectly back in place. "I don't like it."

"Do you have to go to these things?"

"No. They aren't mandatory. There are several people who don't go, and they never get shut out of opportunities. Plenty of networking is done during office hours. But it's good for morale. My bosses are big on showing us that we're valued as employees."

"That's nice." I once got a ten-percent-off coupon to the local deli in the 'Thanks for All You Do' edition of my company's newsletter.

"Yeah, well, because I always show up alone, I keep ending up partnered up in games with their daughter, Penny, who's also single."

"Oh." I hoped Penny had a bald spot and unreasonably long nose hair. "They must think a lot of you if they want you to date their daughter. That's nice too, I guess."

"They're not trying to set me up with Penny—she's the social director—and I guess she's trying to help make me more social at these things." A muscle ticked in his jaw. "But you know how it is with office gossip. I'm concerned there will be speculation about me and Penny, which could complicate things with my bosses and put the respect of my team on the line."

"I can see why that would suck." I wasn't sure what he expected me to do about that, though. "Do you want me to go over there and show her how Tinder works? Most of the guys around here are either sentient cans of Bud Light or active members of a local satanic cult, but if she's not picky, she'll find enough matches to keep her occupied for a while."

"That's not necessary, but wow, what a depressing look into your dating life." He smirked, and I came very close to shoving him and his expensive suit into the pool. He must've seen something in my expression, though, because he took a careful step back. "I had something else in mind. It might be better if I started showing up with a steady girlfriend."

"Ah, you want me to show *you* how Tinder works. I don't know if you'll find a lot of steady-girlfriend material, but you're a good-looking guy. You might match with a few people who bathe on a regular basis."

He gave me a bland stare. "Thanks for the vote of confidence, but I'm aware of how Tinder works. I'm not interested in having an *actual* steady girlfriend."

"What?" I clutched at my chest and gave an exaggerated gasp. "But you're the ripe old age of twenty-six. You've only got a few good years left before the erectile dysfunction kicks in."

"I really hate you sometimes."

"You adore me." I batted my lashes, and he huffed out an annoyed grunt. "So what's your plan? And how does this involve me?"

"I was hoping you would pretend to be my girlfriend for the summer, to cut off any rumors and get the people at work off my back." He bit out every word like it physically pained him to say it, and his tight expression promised there would be consequences if I laughed.

And because I could never resist tempting the tiger, I let out a laugh loud enough to set the dogs off two houses over. "Please tell me you're not serious."

He shrugged, which he only did when something was important to him, but he didn't want anyone to know it was important to him. "If you do this for me, I'll keep quiet for you."

All of my amusement died. I narrowed my eyes. "Are you threatening me?"

"Nope. This is a mutually beneficial exchange." He tucked a lock of hair that had come loose from my bun behind my ear, and I shivered. "I'm trading one service for another."

Yeah, right. I was not going to let him have this so easily. We wouldn't be us if I didn't at least attempt to one-up him. "And if I tell you to shove your trade up your ass?"

He shrugged again and began to stroll away. He was bluffing. He had to be. Still, he hadn't even gotten the last word and it felt like he'd won that round. Damn it.

But it wasn't like he asked me to do anything hard, like clean his toilet or wax his chest. He just wanted me to play his girlfriend for a pretty legitimate reason. There were some side benefits to an arrangement like that. It would give me a chance to witness a genuine corporate ladder climber in the wild. Observe his habits. See exactly what he said and did to make him worthy of moving up, and then I could copy his style in my own workplace. And maybe someone at these parties needed a house sitter in the future.

"Wait." I grabbed the back of his dove-gray jacket. "I might be interested."

He turned with a hint of mischief in his eyes. "Might be?"

He knew he'd won. Not that I'd ever stood a chance of resisting. But as I felt the scales begin to tip in his favor, panic wrapped a tight grip around my lungs, and I needed to bring things back to even again. "I have a few conditions."

"Of course you do."

"I want to be fed on these faux-date nights." After the last few months, the list of things I wouldn't do for free food had become uncomfortably short. "And none of that hors d'oeuvre shit. If a real meal isn't part of the night, you're required to make it up to me."

He gave me a curt nod. "Done."

"And if I need fancy clothes, that's on you too." I would not blow what little money I managed to pull together from house-sitting gigs on impressing someone else's boss.

"Says the woman who wears fur to a pool party of one."

"Are you referring to that old thing?" I waved a hand at the coat lying across the Adirondack chair. "I only wear it on laundry days."

A small smile quirked his lips. "Fine. Fancy clothes and food. Anything else?"

"Just one more." I wrung my hands and willed my eyes to stay above his neck, and not stray to his broad chest, hard stomach, and . . . lower. "Are we going to be expected to prove our relationship? In the physical sense?"

He raised an eyebrow. "I'm not going to bend you over my bosses' dining room table and fuck you raw to prove we're dating, if that's what you mean."

He was trying to get a rise out of me. I knew this. It still didn't explain why I suddenly felt like I was sunbathing in a fur coat. "I meant touching and kissing, you ass."

"I might put my hand on the small of your back, like this." He stood beside me and his hand lightly grazed my back above my bikini bottoms. My skin softened like butter, as if my body wanted to melt against him even when my mind was screaming at me to be cool. The rough pads of his fingertips were so at odds with the corporate facade. A lingering reminder of who we were and where we'd come from.

"That would be okay." Who was this Marilyn Monroe impersonator who'd snatched my body and stolen my voice box? Not me. Isla Jane did *not* get breathless over Cade Greenley.

"And I might give you a very chaste and work-function-appropriate kiss, like this." He pressed his lips to my temple, and they were warm and firm, and somehow my neck tilted toward him to increase the pressure. He grinned against my skin, and that snapped me out of this temporary spell I'd fallen under.

I elbowed him in the ribs. "I got it. You've made your point."

"So we have a deal then?"

I couldn't see a downside to this arrangement. Especially now that it included dinner service. Maybe I should've slept on it, but I'd never been one to take the time to think through big decisions, like a rational adult. Here went nothing: "Deal."

I stuck out my hand, and his enveloped mine. I didn't know what I expected. The earth to quake? The sky to rumble? Some cataclysmic event to mark the bargain we'd struck? But it was just the two of us, admitting, maybe for the first time, that we needed something from each other.

I sincerely hoped I wouldn't end up regretting this worse than I did my MBA.

CHAPTER SIX

The rest of the week at Alice's passed uneventfully. Bitsy emerged from her hiding spot three times a day, when she wanted to me to drag her up and down the street for a "walk." Every morning I refilled her dish with soft food she could gum down, but I never saw her actually eat. I assumed eating was something she did in the dead of night, like a proper creature from the underworld. Since I managed to keep Bitsy alive, catch up on *The Bachelor*, and get my website fully up and running, I considered the week a success. Apparently Alice thought so too, since she didn't stop payment on my check.

I ended up slipping under Quinn and Vera's door an envelope containing some cash and a note promising to pay more as soon as I had it. I wasn't expecting to move back in with them, but I still felt the need to make things right. My upbringing wouldn't allow me to do it any other way. Repaying debts had been drilled into my head ever since my parents gave Seb my allowance for a month after I accidently stepped on his *Mario Kart* disk and snapped it in half.

Midweek, Alice had texted to ask how everything was going, which made me feel both part of the inner loop at Cornerstone Enterprises, and ridiculous for thinking I was any closer to the inner loop than the guy who delivered her mail. I was also relieved her check-in likely meant she didn't have any of the neighbors spying on me. There might've been some questions if any of them had peeked in the windows the night I discovered the liquor cabinet. I vaguely recalled chowing down on a pint of Cherry Garcia while I danced to full-volume Taylor Swift in a ball gown. The exact details were a little fuzzy.

I'd sent Alice a link to my website, letting her know I was official. In case she wanted to pass along a referral. By the end of the week, I'd gotten a call from Jim Hinkley, who had the big office/nice view combo on the fifth floor. His vacation started the day Alice was due to return home, and because they had set up the same house-sitting service, he was also in a bind with their last-minute cancellation. So on Saturday, I packed up my overnight things and headed back to my brother's condo to do a little laundry before making my way over to Jim's.

In the parking garage, my phone buzzed, and a picture of Seb screaming in terror on the Easter Bunny's lap flashed on my screen. I answered. "Hey, loser. How's London?"

"Rainy. I hate it. Have you talked to Mom recently?" His clipped tone was something I'd long ago stopped taking personally. He was always cranky when traveling, like his whole being was wound tight until he could come home again.

"Not since last weekend—why?" I tried to call once a week and have dinner over there at least once a month, but I'd kind of been avoiding my parents ever since I'd lied about getting promoted. "Did something happen?"

"She said Dad's back has been bothering him, but like it was no big deal."

My stomach dropped. We'd long ago learned the tone Mom tried to use with us when she was upset but didn't want us to know she was upset. The tone she'd used the first time a malnourished Cade had wandered into our yard, and when Dad was temporarily laid off during the recession, and the night Grandma died. We called it her No Big Deal voice.

"I'll go over there next week and check things out," I said.

"Good." Seb paused as a clatter of noise erupted in his background. "Sorry. Having a late lunch at a local pub. Mom also told me about your promotion. Proud of you."

Yeah. My promotion. The lie wasn't the worst part. I lied to my family all the time about who I dated, how much I drank, where I spent my free time. Every time they asked me if I was okay. But I'd never lied about something simply because I wanted it to be true, because I needed to hear that I made them proud, because that was the only way I felt like I had any value at all. Just thinking it about it made my skin shrink around my bones.

"Thanks, Seb." My voice cracked. I was digging myself deeper by letting my brother believe I'd been promoted too, but I couldn't seem to tell him the truth. Not when I would've had to also admit that not only had I *not* gotten a promotion, but I didn't have a place to live either. "I've got to go, but I'll call you when I check in on them."

I hung up before I could say anything else. If I didn't tell him directly I'd gotten a promotion, I could still call it an omission, in my mind. Now I'd have to avoid calls from him too until I figured out what to do. At this point, it seemed my only option left was to actually get a promotion and act like I'd had it all along. In short, I was screwed.

I took the elevator up to the tenth floor and let myself into Seb's condo. I banged the front door against the wall as I entered, making as much noise as humanly possible without putting a hole in the drywall. There would be no accidental nudity on my watch today.

"Honey, I'm home," I called out.

The apple-cinnamon scent made my mouth water, and I was suddenly very hungry for homemade pie. Having access to fresh fruit all week at Alice's had spoiled me. I had no idea how I'd manage returning to the land of packaged soup and ninety-nine-cent microwavable dinners once vacation season ended. Maybe a nice farmer somewhere outside the city limits would let me milk cows in exchange for produce.

In the kitchen, Cade leaned against the counter. His usually neat hair was sleep rumpled, and he was shirtless, of course, but at least he had pants on this time. Bleary eyed, he nodded at me in acknowledgment. Must've been a rough night. I peered around the corner into the guest room, to see if he had a date, and immediately hated myself for it. He brought his cup of coffee to his lips as he watched me. Lips that I absolutely had not been thinking about, the shape, the warmth, the feel of them pressed against my temple.

I opened the bifold closet doors that concealed the washer and dryer, and dumped the clothes I'd worn for the week into the machine. "I'm not staying. I'm sure you'll be surprised to know that I have another job booked for this week."

"Good for you." Not a hint of sarcasm in his tone. I didn't trust it for a second.

"If this keeps up, I might never have to pay rent again."

"Sure thing, Rainbow Bear."

I slammed the lid shut on the washer and faced him with my hands on my hips. "You don't have to worry about me. I'm handling this just fine."

"Never said any different." He raised his coffee cup to me.

How dare he stand there with one ankle crossed over the other, all calm and collected, and not lecture me. He lived for moments like this, where he could play the role of concerned friend while I knew he was secretly gloating about having the upper hand. The fact that he wasn't giving me shit about my new arrangement was suspicious enough on its own, but then he did something even worse. The jerk smiled. A genuine one that reached his eyes and made the brilliant blue shine. What the fuck was going on?

I leveled a glare at him as I leaned against the edge of the couch. "Why are you being so nice and agreeable?"

He let out a chuckle that hummed across my skin and made everything tingle. "There is no winning with you, is there?"

"This is not normal behavior."

He set his coffee down and skulked toward me. The closer he got, the more aware I became of his naked chest, in a way I'd never allowed myself to be aware of before the Dropped Towel Incident. His cock was now the last thing I thought of before I went to bed and the first thing I thought of when I woke in the morning. It haunted my dreams. Most of all, it was pissing me off that my vibrator was buried in one of the boxes in the guest room, and I had no way of looking for it without Cade finding out exactly what I was trying to retrieve.

Not that I wanted to sleep with Cade. That would be ludicrous. We'd never been like that and never would be. I just had a temporary penis fixation, and I needed to get it out of my system. I couldn't even swipe through my newest batch of Tinder matches without wondering what their cocks looked like and if I'd have the same draw to them that I seemed to have with Cade's. As much as I tried to shut down any errant daydreams, I couldn't stop visualizing what it would feel like to sink down on his length, fully seated, my inner walls hugging him tight. I'd move slow at first, then faster and harder as he hit that spot deep inside me. The thought alone had me biting my lip as I barely held back a groan.

"What are you thinking about?" The jagged cadence of his voice startled me, and my cheeks instantly heated. He stood within inches of me.

I breathed in his familiar scent of Irish Spring, generic dryer sheets, and something a little muskier that made me think of strong hands and legs tangled together and making love on lazy Sunday mornings. The combination was intoxicating. I leaned in, an imperceptible crossing of distance, but of course he noticed. His amused expression told me enough.

I pursed my lips and took a much-needed step back. "I'm thinking about rescue dogs and blueberry pancakes. Why?"

He gave me a knowing look. "Those must be some damn good pancakes."

"You have no idea."

His gaze dipped to my lips for a fraction of a second, so quick I almost missed it. "I'm going to the gym." He grabbed a shirt off the back of the couch and pulled it over his head.

The second he was covered up, I felt like I could breathe again. "Gym. Good. Bye."

"If you leave before I get back, make sure you write down the address of where you're staying, so I know where to pick you up."

"Pick me up?" Had we made plans while my brain was busy short-circuiting over sex fantasies about my brother's best friend?

He gave me an exasperated sigh. "Don't tell me you've already forgotten about our deal? You can't back out on me now; I already told everyone at work that I was bringing my girlfriend."

I wished I could forget about our deal. Maybe then I'd be able to get a decent amount sleep instead of waking up in the middle of the night with my hand between my thighs while I thought about his fingers pressing into my lower back and his lips against my temple. Not to mention the image of him naked and covered in water droplets. I couldn't seem to forget about that, even if my life depended on it.

I cleared my throat, tucking that visual away as I tried to gain some semblance of control over the conversation. "I'm not backing out. I just didn't realize you had an event tonight."

He titled his head and frowned. "Did you already have plans?"

Other than gorging on the contents of Jim Hinkley's refrigerator while I took a "Which Disney Movie Matches Your Personality?" quiz over and over until I got *The Little Mermaid*? "Nope. No other plans. What's the event?"

He grimaced. "Mini golf on a party barge."

"That's a real thing?"

"Afraid so."

"How am I supposed to dress?" I hadn't played mini golf since my eighth-grade field trip to the Family Fun Center, where the softball I took to the head in the batting cages traumatized me from such places for life.

"Casual. It's mini golf, not a night at the opera."

"Can I wear my 'Lick me' ice-cream shirt?"

His jaw clenched. "Not that casual."

This was going to be a lot more fun than I had initially thought. I shooed him toward the front door. "Go to the gym. Don't worry. I'll come up with something."

"I wasn't worried until now."

"You shouldn't be." I patted his cheek. "I promise I'll make you look good."

He opened his mouth to argue, but I shut the door in his face, then went back to the guest room to pack up another round of clothes for a new week in a new house.

CHAPTER SEVEN

Jim Hinkley's house was even more elaborate than Alice's, with three floors, a one-hundred-gallon saltwater fish tank, and an elevator that was too small to be for accessibility. A pink Cadillac was parked in the four-stall garage. I had officially entered the Barbie Dreamhouse. Keeping seven bathrooms clean sounded like a nightmare to me, but that wasn't my business or my problem. All I had to do was guard the house, water the plants, and feed the fish.

My flip-flops slapped against the white marble. His home had an old-money smell to it. A blend of furniture polish, mothballs, and expensive chocolate. Since food was always my first priority, I headed into the kitchen first. Dark wood beams crisscrossed the ceiling, matching the ornate cabinetry, and white quartz countertops with a clear glass backsplash lightened up the otherwise heavy room. Jim's refrigerator was stocked with organic fruits and vegetables, which I considered a bonus. All of those leafy greens and ruby-red strawberries would go bad by the end of the week if someone didn't eat them. It was like I was doing him a favor.

On my way to the living room, I stopped in front of the saltwater tank to take a quick count of how many things I'd be required to keep alive. Neon green, pink, and purple plants rose out of volcanic rock as brightly colored fish darted in and out of little hidey-holes. Two of the seahorses were getting it on, and honestly, good for them.

Large paintings in tacky gold frames hung from the silk papered walls. Jim's living room was the size of Seb's entire condo, with a fireplace large enough to stand upright in. In the adjacent office, just one of the silver paperweights on his desk could've paid my rent for the year. Yet there had been a wage freeze for all lower-level employees due to an only five percent market gain in the last quarter, rather than the expected ten. It made me want to break something. Instead, I'd settle into his home for the week and eat the expensive caviar and drink the expensive wine he told me I was welcome to enjoy, with spite in my heart.

At the same time, I was so thankful, to the point where my frustrations shamed me. The food, the roof over my head, and the ability to pay my credit card on time gave me a sense of security I hadn't had in months. I didn't know how to reconcile that anger against my gratitude. It was the crux of living in the black hole of debt. Desperation had conditioned me to be grateful for basic necessities, as something I could one day earn, but never fully deserve.

Jim had told me I could have my pick of guest rooms on the second floor, so I took the elevator up. Because why the hell not? If there was a power surge and I ended up trapped in there, maybe he'd double my pay for the trouble.

After poking my head into four rooms with different color schemes, I picked the bedroom at the end of the hall, decorated in soft blues and muted grays that probably would've been given the soothing stamp of approval by HGTV. I set my backpack on the four-poster bed and turned to the window facing the lake. Dark blue water lapped against the grassy shore. I let the calming motion quiet my mind. I couldn't seem to swallow the white-hot ball of rage that had lodged itself in my throat, but I could acknowledge it without letting it burn through me.

I was going to be okay. Maybe not forever, but I clung to the "right now" and the few things I could control. If I tried to look beyond that, I might've started screaming into a pillow. Next week was a problem for Future Isla. For this week, I'd be okay.

My mom called, and I held the phone in my hand, staring at a picture of her as it flashed on my screen. In it, she had pink-tipped blonde spikes, an outdated hairstyle she'd since changed twice. I should've answered. After my call with Seb earlier, I should've at least made sure Dad was doing all right. But after taking the tour of Jim's extravagant house, which only ended up making the weight of my debt feel heavier, I didn't have the emotional energy to deal with my parents and whatever issues they were keeping from us. So I let it go to voicemail and promised myself I'd check in with her tomorrow.

Needing to get ready for Cade's work event, I showered, shaved, and slathered on a thick, cinnamon toast-scented body cream that I'd found on the counter. I put on a yellow cotton sundress with a hem that fell just below my knees and buttoned up the front, and a jean jacket in case it got cold on the water. I flat ironed my hair, allowing my silky sable strands to fall halfway down my back. I did a more understated version of my date-night makeup. What I'd now be referring to as my "work-function" makeup. As soon as Cade texted me, I dashed out the front door, tucking the key to Jim's house in my Cucci purse.

I slid into the passenger side of Cade's Jeep, appreciating how he remembered that I liked the seat heater on, even in the summer. While I had dressed casually as directed, Cade wore pressed gray slacks and a white button-down. He had his sleeves rolled up, so I guess that counted as casual, but he still looked like an accountant who had stayed too late at the office. I wiggled against the warm leather and pulled the mirror down to check my lip gloss.

When it became clear we weren't moving, I turned to face him, pausing at his odd expression. "What's that look for?"

He shook his head as if he were coming out of a daze, and backed out of the driveway. "Nothing." He cleared his throat. "You look nice."

"Why do you sound so surprised? Did you expect me to show up in my car-washing tank top and my cutoff shorts that have a ketchup stain on the butt?"

"No. It's just . . ." His fingers flexed against the steering wheel. "Nothing."

"No, it's not. Tell me." I poked his arm, his side, under his armpit. I'd learned forever ago that the only way to get Cade to crack was through relentless annoyance. "Tell me."

He swatted my hand away. "It's not a big deal. I just sometimes forget how gorgeous you are and it threw me off for a second. Now leave me alone. I'm driving."

I sucked in a sharp breath. If this was some sort of game and he was trying to render me speechless, he'd won. Hands down, no contest. But this didn't feel like a game, and the look on his face wasn't triumphant or smug. In fact, he looked downright mad about it.

"If it makes you feel better," I said quietly, "I never forget how attractive you are."

He whipped his head around to face me, eyes wide. His Jeep bumped along the drift lines on the shoulder of the road, and he immediately righted his steering wheel again. "We are not having this conversation while I'm driving. Actually, scratch that: we are not having this conversation at all."

"Fine by me." I crossed my arms and glared out the window, even though I completely understood where he was coming from. He was Seb's best friend. I'd known him my entire life. We had an established relationship that didn't include anything remotely romantic, and we both wanted to keep it that way. Still, I was irked he got to say it first. "Just remember, you're the one who brought it up."

He grinned and my skin warmed in response. Or maybe that was just the heated seat. "Do you always have to have the last word?"

Of course I had to have the last word. "You already know the answer to that."

"Fair enough." He glanced at me, his eyes lingering a moment before turning back to the road. "Do you want to go over some basics before we arrive?"

I let out a breath as the tension in my shoulders loosened, grateful for the subject change. "What basics? Like which fork to use when they seat us at the big kids' table?"

"I was thinking more like who my bosses are, coworkers' names, what the company does, what I do for the company. Things a steady girlfriend ought to know."

I knew he did something in sales, but I usually tuned out work talk whenever I hung out with him and my brother. "You can try, but I have to warn you: Seb's been talking to me about his work for years, and I still have no idea what he does for a living."

He let out a laugh. "No one knows what he does, but my job isn't quite that impressive. I just got promoted, so I'm now a sales manager for the Midwest region of Torres-Glasser Bass Fishing. We're the fourth largest manufacturer in the US of tackle, lures, reels, and rods."

"That sounds impressive." A lot more impressive than being one of a thousand data-entry analysts for Cornerstone Enterprises. How had he managed to accomplish so much? We came from the same neighborhood, had the same education, and were nearly the same age. Were some people just destined for great things while the rest of us clung to whatever scraps were left behind? "I didn't know you fished."

He smirked. "I didn't until I started working for Torres-Glasser."

"Is that what you have to do to succeed in business? Pretend to be someone you're not?"

"Yes and no." He frowned as he mulled over my question. "I'm in sales, so I need to use the products I'm selling to know how they work. But I also need to show that I care about the company and what they do, so my bosses feel confident about giving me greater responsibility. And I'm not saying that selling fishing equipment is going to change the world or anything, but I like my bosses. I like how they run their business and how they treat their employees."

"What if you didn't care about the company or like your bosses?"

"Then I guess I'd look for somewhere else to work."

The comment wasn't directed at me, but my guard went up all the same. It was just like Quinn and Vera had said. Find somewhere else to work, as if it were that easy. "You know, not all of us get to like or respect our bosses. Some of us work somewhere because that's the best we can do at the time, and we stay because where else are we going to go?"

He gave me the single raised eyebrow. "Feel free to retract those claws at any time. You know damn well I never said you should work somewhere else. I said *I* would work somewhere else because liking the company and the people I work for is important to *me*."

I had no idea why I was being so defensive. Or why it even mattered if Cade thought I should quit my job. Most of the time, *I* thought I should quit my job, but I didn't know where I'd even begin to apply. I'd sent my CV to a hundred different companies for a month after I graduated, and Cornerstone Enterprises was the only place that had reached out to me. I could only make lateral moves at this juncture in my career. Plus, at the end of the day I'd never be doing what I really wanted to anyway, so what was the point?

"I'm sorry." My shoulders sagged as I leaned against the headrest. "I didn't mean to snap at you. I'm having a really shitty month."

"You always mean to snap at me." He reached over the center console and squeezed my hand. "And I know you're having a shitty month."

If I'd been a crier, I might've teared up right then. I hadn't realized how badly I needed a friend until that small bit of comfort poked through the petrified parts of my heart. It had been too long since someone just listened to me without offering up patronizing non-solutions. I stared down at his hand covering mine, and felt an enormous rush of affection for Cade Greenley. Yes, he'd been a pain and a bother most of my life, but he also knew how to just . . . be there. It made me wish, not for the first time, that I hadn't snuck out of my parents' house the morning after Thanksgiving three years ago. What if I'd stayed? What if I'd let myself lean on Cade? Would I have been able to be vulnerable without feeling ashamed?

Lost in the moment of reminiscing, I covered the top of his hand with my other one. When he glanced at me, I gave him a soft smile. Not teasing or flirtatious for once. His eyes lit with surprise, and he faced the road again.

He didn't let go of my hand for the rest of the drive.

CHAPTER EIGHT

I still couldn't believe there was such a thing as mini golf on a party barge. And yet, here we were, golfing it up. The two-level, nine-hole course made it look more like a small island than a boat. It had five holes on the bottom level and four holes on the upper level, with booths spaced out next to the guard rails, and a giant bar at the center.

It was absolutely as ridiculous as it sounded, and the most fun I'd had since I graduated and entered the workforce. The air had a reedy scent to it from the lake water, and gentle waves lapped against the hull. Each hole took about twelve tries to sink a putt, thanks to the motion of the waves, but Cade and I stopped keeping score around hole two and turned it into what we did best: a one-up competition.

At the fifth hole, Cade stared down the mouth of a giant clown, lining up his shot as best as he could on a rocking boat. "If I make this, you have to do my laundry for a month."

I waited for him to pull back his swing, then I leaned over. "If you miss, you have to shave my bikini line."

He hit the ball so hard, it slammed against the clown's nose, bounced over the side, and rolled into the water. He dropped his club, and scooped me up over his shoulder. "That's it. Cheaters go overboard."

I scream-laughed and scratched at his back as he held me next to the rail. He let out a shout when I rammed my thumbnail into his armpit, then froze and set me on my feet. The swift motion caused me to stumble. I righted myself and brushed my hair out of my eyes to find two men in their late fifties grinning at us. They were decked out in full golf gear, polos, khaki shorts, argyle socks, and visors. I had to give them credit for getting into the whole act.

"Mr. and Mr. Torres-Glasser." He shook both his boss's hands with a kind of stiff formality I'd never seen in him before. Professional Cade couldn't have been more out of place on a party barge. Maybe that's why I wasn't getting promoted. I didn't have a big enough stick up my ass. He put his hand on the small of my back and gave me a little nudge forward. "I'd like to introduce you to my girlfriend, Isla Jane."

I plastered on my job-interview smile and stepped up to play my part. "It's so nice to meet you. Cade speaks highly of you both."

"Welcome. And please call me Anton, as I've been telling Cade to for two years now. Though he still won't do it." Anton Torres-Glasser clasped my hand. He had wavy dark hair, large brown eyes, and a light Cuban accent. "My husband oversees the sales department, though, so he still insists on the Mister."

"I do. But you can call me Ted." He gave me a wink. He was a head taller than his husband, with soft brown eyes and a honey-colored beard liberally streaked with gray. "We've heard a lot about you, Isla."

My skin warmed and my heart softened, which I found disconcerting since I didn't have warm and soft feelings for Cade and whatever he might've told his bosses about me. It was all part of his act. "Everything he said is true. Unless he was mad at me that day—then he's a liar."

Both Anton and Ted chuckled.

Cade wrapped an arm around my waist and gave my side a quick squeeze in approval. "Thank you both for inviting us out today."

Anton waved him off. "If it wasn't for these events, I'd never be able to drag Ted from the house. Once we finish these nine holes and have dinner, the sun should be finished setting, and then the real fun can begin."

"The real fun?" I asked. Cade had said there would be golfing and dinner. He hadn't mentioned any other extracurriculars.

"Ever been night fishing?" Ted asked.

I shook my head. I'd never done any fishing, but I didn't think it would be a good idea to mention that to the bosses I was supposed to be impressing.

"You're in for a treat. The fish on this lake get feisty in the moonlight." Ted slapped Cade on the back. "You'll show your girl the ropes?"

Cade squeezed my side again. "Sure will." When Ted and Anton headed over to the bar to get a drink, Cade leaned down close to my ear. "You were amazing."

My toes curled in my ballet flats. While my mind knew very well nothing ever could or would happen between us, my body didn't seem to be getting the message. It was throwing me off balance, and I hadn't been all that balanced to begin with. "I didn't do anything."

"You were charming and adorable. They love you." Before I could overthink his words too much, he pointed to a gorgeous Cuban woman putting at the third hole with a baby-faced blond guy who looked a little dazed at his luck in golfing partners. "That's Penny Torres-Glasser. She's the one who sets up these events. The guy she's golfing with is Jeff Crane, a recent outside hire. He's another sales manager."

"*That's* Penny?" Holy shit. She was heart stopping. With shiny dark hair that grazed the small of her back, Anton's large eyes framed with long lashes, and top-heavy lips, she was the kind of beautiful that made you do a quadruple look. "And you didn't want people to think you were dating her . . . why again?"

"I told you. It would make work complicated for me." He grabbed my shoulders and spun me around so I faced him instead. "You're starting to drool. It's embarrassing."

I gave him a light shove. "Can you blame me?"

He took my hand and pulled me toward the stairs. "Come on, cheater. We've got another four holes to do before you get your dinner."

We played the remainder of the course on the upper level, with each of our demands for missing a shot becoming more and more absurd. By the end of the ninth hole, I apparently owed Cade personalized singing telegrams for a month, a jar of honey I collected myself from a local beekeeper, and an hour-long back massage at a time and place of his choosing. It was pretty safe to say he would be getting none of those things.

After we turned in our clubs, we grabbed a booth on the upper deck, and a waitress brought us burgers and fries and fried bread covered in powdered sugar, which made the whole upper level smell like a carnival. Various coworkers stopped by to say hi to Cade or briefly talk shop with him, and he introduced me to a bunch of people whose names I'd never remember. It was all low-key and casual. No wonder Cade didn't mind coming to these events. Except he acted like it was a day at the office while everyone else acted like it was a kegger. I took his lead and didn't drink and remained distantly polite with everyone, but it was still a lot more fun than a work function had any right to be.

Cornerstone Enterprises would never host something like this. Our holiday party had been held in the basement of our building. It was cold, the cookies tasted like wood, and the only reason I'd bothered to show up at all was to collect my Cornerstone Enterprises–branded travel mug because it was free. I didn't even drink coffee.

"Are you having a good time?" Cade reached across the table to thread his fingers with mine. It was for show, of course, but it didn't *feel* like show. That was something I'd have to deal with later. Like at the end of never.

"Surprisingly, yes. Your work functions are nothing like mine." Just the thought of Alice Bishop organizing a mini-golf-party barge outing made me want to laugh. Or cry.

"Yeah, I lucked out the day I got the call from Ted." He gave me a rueful smile. "I'd gotten another offer at a software company, but Torres-Glasser sold me on their company during my internship. I couldn't see myself anywhere else. They have a genuine appreciation for open dialogue and respect the input of their entire team, not just those in upper management."

That didn't sound anything like where I worked. There was little Cornerstone Enterprises valued more than silence and conformity. "How did you move up so fast?"

"The plan had always been to move me up, but they wanted me to get a year of outbound sales experience first so I'd really understand my team."

"Ted and Anton seem amazing. I'm happy for you." I turned my gaze to the setting sun. I meant it when I said I was happy for him, but envy had a sharp edge, and I couldn't help but feel the sting as it sliced through me.

I could sense his eyes on me, but I kept my gaze on the horizon, afraid he'd see the jealousy written all over my face. I hated that I felt that way. It wasn't his fault that my job sucked or that I didn't have the drive required to move up or that I'd wasted so much money on a degree I'd never wanted in the first place.

"Do you want to talk about it?" he asked softly.

"Not really." I faced him then because I wanted him to know that what I was about to say next was the absolute truth. "I really am happy for you. You know that, right?"

"Yes. And you know that it's still okay for you to be sad for yourself, right? Just because things are tough for you doesn't mean you want any less for someone else."

One corner of my mouth tugged upward. "How did you get to be so smart?"

"College, probably." He stood and extended his hand to me. "Ready to do some fishing?"

We headed down to the lower deck, where Ted and Anton had set up a bunch of rods for everyone. Cade explained they were the latest model, just off the line, and the main reason why a lot of their work events were held on or near water. They liked to mix workplace comradery with product testing. I thought it was brilliant.

I held a rod at an awkward angle, which I'm sure exposed my noob status, but I had a feeling Ted and Anton wouldn't judge me too harshly for my lack of fishing expertise. "What's the difference between night fishing and day fishing?"

"Night fishing is a lot more active, especially in the summer." Cade wound some bait around the hook on my rod, and I couldn't help but notice how good he was with his fingers. I averted my gaze and shoved that thought down with all the other nonplatonic Cade thoughts I'd been having throughout the day. "The water gets cooler after the sun goes down, which makes the fish come closer to the surface."

"Interesting." My go-to word for when things were not, in fact, all that interesting. I stood there holding my rod, having no clue what to do with it. "So, how do I get the fish to bite into this thing?"

He came up behind me and fit his arms snug against mine and covered my hands with his own. "You'll want to push down on this button here." He placed my thumb on the reel. "Then pull back like this." He guided my arms upward. "Then let go of the button about mid-cast." He moved my arms forward in a thrusting motion, and I let go of the button. A clear wire line whizzed out of the reel and landed with a plunk in the water.

I turned my head, where he was so close my lips could almost graze his jaw. "I get this fishing-in-the-dark thing now."

"Yeah?" The heat in his eyes damn near burned through me.

"Yeah. It's just an excuse for you all to do a whole lot of touching."

He chuckled, and his thumb skimmed the inside of my wrist. "I'm not going to lie. Touching a beautiful woman in the dark is the best part of night fishing."

We stared at each other in the moonlight, our breath shallow, the air between us charged with the heavy weight of expectation. I wanted his hands on me. Everywhere. His gaze dipped to my lips, and his eyes traced the heart shape of them. My pulse beat hard and fast as he moved his head closer, and something jerked in my hand.

"Oh my God. What's happening?" In my shock, I let go of the fishing rod.

Cade grabbed it before we lost it to the lake, and gave it a hard tug before putting it back in my hands. "It looks like you got a bite. Reel it in." When I just gave him a blank look, he pointed to the lever on the side of the reel. "Crank that. It'll pull the line back in and bring your fish up with it."

Reeling in a fish was not as easy as it looked on TV. Every crank of the reel felt like I was trying to jack up a car. I must've had a monster on the line. What if it was too big for the boat? What if I was reeling in the freshwater version of Moby Dick?

"You going to quit playing with your food and reel that sucker in already?" The lilt of laughter in Cade's voice made me crank that much harder.

"Working on it," I said through gritted teeth. "This beast is putting up the fight of his life." A few second later, my "monster" finally broke the surface. It was a tiny, flappy little thing. Maybe six inches long.

Cade rubbed his chin with his thumb and index finger. "It's a beast alright. Better call the Discovery channel and let them know we've got a new contender for *Shark Week*."

"Shut it, you." I swung the fish at him with a little more momentum than I realized. And watched—as if stuck in slow motion—the slimy, wiggly body smack him across the face with a wet slap. "I'm . . ." I tried my best to hold the laugh in, but it was like a sneeze. I had no choice but to let it go. "I'm so . . ." Oh God, I was laughing so hard it hurt. "Sorry," I gasped.

Cade plucked the rod out of my hand with an eerie-like calmness and set it aside. My cheeks hurt, and I was mildly terrified, but I couldn't stop laughing. "Just so you know," he said, his voice gruff, "you're definitely going overboard now."

I shrieked and took off running. He chased me up the stairs to the second level, which had now been deserted in favor of trying out the new rods on the first level. I made it halfway past the seventh hole when Cade caught me around the waist and swung me around. My arms came up around his shoulders as he gripped my hips.

Neither one of us was laughing anymore.

We stared at each other for one beat. Two.

I don't know which one of us moved first, but we crashed against each other in a wild tangle of lips and hands and teeth smacking together. It was messy and desperate and hot. So fucking hot. His mouth moved against mine in a rush to take, feed, conquer before either of us could remember who we were and why we shouldn't be doing this. This wasn't a sweet first kiss on the doorstep between two strangers. This was a hunger that threatened to set the world on fire.

Our tongues fought and stroked like we were in a battle to make the other person feel more, want more, and both of us were winning. I arched against him, clawing at his shoulders and neck as I kissed him with a level of intensity that almost scared me. I wanted it all with him, harder, deeper—everything.

He held my chin with one hand, claiming my mouth, letting me know that I was his and he was mine, and this was all we'd ever need. This moment right here. Completely lost to each other. His other hand cupped my ass as he lifted me against the rail, stepped between my legs, and dragged me against his thick, hard length. I wrapped my legs around him and rocked, needing friction more than air. My head tipped back, and he scraped his teeth over my throat. The stubble on his jaw was rough against my sensitive skin, and it wasn't enough. I wanted him inside me, filling me up, pushing me to the edge.

Tiny tremors tickled my toes. Even with all the layers of clothes between us, I was close. Cade increased the motion of his hips, rotating them in a circle to hit just the right spot. Almost there. When, out of nowhere, he set me to my feet and backed away.

What?

The sudden loss of him threw me off, and I had to grip the railing to keep my legs from giving out underneath me. My heart hammered against my breastbone. My lips were swollen and tingly, and a foggy haze I couldn't quite shake had descended over my brain.

Cade ran a hand through his hair and gripped his scalp. He kept his eyes on his feet, like he couldn't even stand to look at me. What happened? "We can't do this."

"Um, pretty sure we just did." I bit down on my lower lip.

I'd meant for that to come out sassy, and it ended up sounding more like a plea, and I hated it. I hated that I wanted him to touch me so bad I ached for it, and he'd stopped. The rational, currently nonfunctioning part of my brain knew why, but the other, feral part of my brain that was screaming for release said we'd already crossed that line. Why not see it through?

"You're Seb's sister. We can't risk it. You know that as well as I do."

And there it was. The bucket of cold water that had been hanging precariously over my head. We couldn't risk it because we couldn't ever just be a casual hook-up. I would always be Seb's sister, and he would always be Seb's best friend, and those were the identities we'd carved out for each other before either of us had learned how to ride a bike.

"Yep. Got it." My voice sounded like the embodiment of cracked earth in an impossibly dry desert. I couldn't fake nonchalance any more than I could seem to fake being Cade's girlfriend without taking it too far.

He raised his eyes to me, the startling blue full of regret and the kind of resolve I'd never be able to chip through, no matter how many tactics of annoyance I deployed. "Are we okay?"

"We're fine." I huffed out a breath. It's not like I disagreed with him, but I had a hard time with things like logic and reason when I was that close to an orgasm. "We got caught up in the moment. It's done now." I straightened my dress and put on what I hoped was a bright enough smile to chase away the clouds hanging over my head. "We should get back to the fishing before anyone starts to wonder where we are."

He grabbed my hand as I turned away, drawing me closer, even as I wanted to walk away with some leftover dignity. "You know you're important to me, right?"

No, thank you. "I will seriously slap you with another fish."

"Sorry. Not the right thing to say. I'll let you have that last slap for free." He flashed me a grin that made the cold dark place in my heart yearn for something I knew I shouldn't want and couldn't have anyway.

We'd lost our minds for a minute. Faking it must've gotten to us both, but it couldn't happen again, for so many reasons. He was right about that. And I'd keep telling myself he was right, even when proving him wrong was a hallmark of our existing relationship.

CHAPTER NINE

The next morning, I woke up in Jim's house with a sick sense of dread. Everything that had happened on the party barge came crashing down on me. The making out, the rejection, the even more horrifying *"You know you're important to me, right?"* This was worse than that time I'd gotten drunk in college and let the school mascot fingerbang me while he was still in costume. At least back then I'd had alcohol to use as an excuse for my poor decisions.

But last night I'd kissed Cade while being fully aware of what I was doing. And there had been some definite grinding too. God, I'd nearly come from dry humping. It was like freshman year all over again. Snuggling into the goose-feather comforter, I licked my lips and gave a long, satisfied stretch before I remembered—again—that this was *not* good and I was *not* supposed to like grinding against Cade.

And if I touched myself while thinking about said grinding last night . . . well, that was last night. Today was a new day. I had big plans that didn't include thinking about Cade, like getting out of bed, watering Jim's plants, feeding his Nemos, and going for a swim in the lake.

In his saltwater tank, Jim had two clown fish that I'd named Nemo One and Nemo Two because I was creative like that. He also had a few other bright and flashy fish that hid from me whenever I approached the tank, so I didn't bother to name them, and two seahorses who liked to fuck a lot. I called them Ed and Wilbur. I hoped by forming some kind of attachment, they'd be less likely to die on my watch.

After tending to my feeding duties, I filled up a charming little tin watering can I found in the shed, and took care of all the plants. By the time I made it to the third floor, I was grateful for the elevator. Even if I still found it ridiculous.

Next, I checked on my website. I'd gotten a few hits, and some of them probably weren't bots, though the website was more for show than function. After I'd gotten an email from a guy claiming to need a house sitter for a place I'd found on an abandoned property list, I made the decision to only house-sit for people who either worked at Cornerstone or were referred by someone I knew. That left me with an extremely small pool of potential clients, and I still hadn't gotten a call about a gig for next week, but there was time. I could make this work.

Vera sent me a text thanking me for the note and money, which reminded me that I needed to make another stop at the bank for more, once Jim's check cleared. At least she was talking to me again. Though it took her three days to reply. As I scrolled through the rest of her texts, my stomach churned. Vera and Quinn had taken a long weekend to hang out at her parents' cabin and had hit the outlet mall, on their way back, to buy things for their new joint office. Otherwise known as my old bedroom. I hadn't expected an invitation to the cabin—even if they were technically my only friends, because making new friends as an adult was both painful and awkward—I knew things were strained between us because of the whole issue of me not paying rent. But I guess I thought they'd kicked me out of the apartment as a last resort. It was becoming more and more apparent to me that it wasn't really like that.

Not that I expected my friends to carry me through life—I didn't at all—but I was in trouble. They knew that. Though I couldn't entirely blame them for not offering their help when it never occurred to me to ask either. That wasn't how I'd been raised. We didn't talk about money, because it wasn't polite conversation. Not for the first time, I wondered who truly benefited from keeping the subject of money off-limits? Because it sure as shit wasn't the people who needed it. I'd never learned how to budget or balance a checkbook. No one had ever sat me down and explained to me the realities about the debt I was incurring from the money I was borrowing for school, and weighed them against the likelihood of my recouping that money in the current job market. And that was on me, I supposed. I should've educated myself and made better choices. But at the same time, who the hell made good choices at eighteen? Especially when, for all intents and purposes, getting an MBA in supply chain management should've been a good life choice.

Instead of responding to Vera's text, I deleted the whole conversation and blocked her number. Quinn's too. I'd still give them the rest of the rent money—it would eat away at me if I didn't—but I didn't have to be friends with them anymore. Friends didn't put another friend's belongings in boxes and leave them out on the street.

With that part of my life as settled as it was going to be, I had the rest of the afternoon to myself. I changed into my too-small bikini, made avocado toast topped with over-easy eggs for breakfast, and took my plate down to the pine dock to dip my toes in the water while I ate. Jim had the brown-shelled eggs I never bought because they cost three times as much. Turned out, they tasted exactly like the white-shelled eggs. The way rich people consistently found ways to throw away money never ceased to amaze me.

Once I finished eating, I set my plate to the side and leaned back on my hands. The sun had warmed the wood beneath my palms, and the air carried the same reedy scent from last night's lake. My mind drifted back to what happened after the kissing and grinding. We'd gone back downstairs to join everyone else, but there was significantly less touching in round two, which took all the fun out of night fishing. It hadn't really been weird—Cade and I knew each other for far too long for things to ever really be weird between us—but he put on the professional polish with me too, giving me a certain amount of distance. I didn't care for it. The only reason I was there at all was to be his pretend girlfriend, and he hadn't even tried to keep up his end of the act.

Probably because he was afraid I'd jump on him again.

That thought settled like a rock in my gut, though I most definitely hadn't been the lone kisser and grinder in our little moment. He'd been a full and willing participant. Still. I didn't like feeling as if he had to handle me with kid gloves or that we couldn't be the same as we'd always been, pushing each other's buttons and giving each other shit. I didn't want things to change just because we'd gotten caught up in the game we were playing for his bosses.

And that's all it had been. The act, the moonlight, the fishing. Nothing more.

Last night would probably end up being another Thanksgiving. A thing that had happened once, but something neither one of us would acknowledge going forward. Just as well. Nothing good could come of it anyway.

I stood and dusted off my hands, preparing to jump into the lake, when my phone buzzed on the dock. The picture of a young Seb screaming at the terrifying costumed bunny flashed on the screen, but I wasn't in the mood to talk. I sent it to voicemail. Little pinpricks of guilt poked at my consciousness, though. I still hadn't called my mom back. Maybe after my swim.

I jumped in the water and immediately broke the surface, gasping for air. The cold squeezed my lungs and numbed my limbs. I treaded water for a moment as I tried to get accustomed to the temperature. It was shallow enough near the dock for me to stand, and I let the lake grass tickle my toes as I bounced up and down, trying to get warm. My phone started buzzing again. If it was Seb calling back, that probably meant something serious was going on. I hoisted myself out of the water to find my phone, this time with a photo of Cade laughing on my screen. I'd taken it on the sly. It was the only picture of Cade in existence where he wasn't scowling, and it was my little secret.

I answered it and put it on speaker, leaving it on the deck. "Whatever you have to say, make it quick. I'm wet."

"Is that why you're breathing so heavy?"

I paused. "You did not just ask me that."

He laughed, and I knew we were going to be fine. Just like we'd always been. Great.

"And yes, that is why I'm breathing heavy," I said. "I'm actually trying to get a swim in, but people keep calling and bugging me."

"Not my fault. You sent Seb to voicemail, so naturally he thinks you're lying in a ditch somewhere, and he asked me to check on you."

"Call him back and tell him that instead of worrying about me, he should be worrying about . . . whatever the hell he does. Seriously, what does he do for a living?"

"Beats me. But I'll tell him you're alive and well."

"Thanks for checking in, I guess."

I ended the call, but for some reason, I didn't feel like going back in the water.

*　*　*

"And here I thought your assumption about us missing you if you left meant you wouldn't be coming back for a while." Neeta stood over me with her hands on her hips.

I rolled to my back and blinked up at her from my position on the ground. "I hope you didn't buy a cake already. That would be a tragedy."

She looked at me like I was a dog with its head stuck in a fence. "Your definition of tragedy is wildly different from mine. What brings you to the Romance section?"

"We're friends? Right, Neeta?"

"No."

Harsh, but honest. "Am I at least your favorite patron?"

"Not even close." She frowned. "I find you fascinating, however."

Fascinating. I'd take it. "Can I ask for your advice?"

"As long as that advice pertains to book recommendations."

"Sure, book recommendations. Do you have a book for someone who lost all her friends, is living in strangers' homes, and has decided to further screw up by making out with a guy who is totally off-limits, and now she feels like her life is just spinning into endless chaos?"

Neeta stared at me for what felt like an eternity, and I cringed. This might've been the point where I broke her. She was finally going to kick me out of the library.

Instead, she did something that shocked me down to my core. She extended her hand to me and pulled me up off the floor. "Okay. You win, weirdo. Let's go grab a cup of coffee, because I've got to hear this story."

"Does that make us friends?"

"Absolutely not." But her lips twitched as she said it.

I was growing on Neeta. Much like a fungus. It was not in a way she wanted or needed, but it was happening anyway. I considered it one of my greatest accomplishments to date.

We ended up going to the coffeehouse next door, where I only ordered water but still got a cup with my name spelled incorrectly on it, so it made me feel like a real customer. I took a seat across the booth from Neeta and rubbed my thumb over where the barista had written *Eyela* in Sharpie. The blueberry muffins in the display case called to me, but I couldn't justify spending that much money on a piece of bread the size of my fist when I could get a whole loaf for half the price at the grocery store down the road.

I proceeded to fill Neeta in on all my recent problems with the house-sitting business, my crappy job, my useless degree, and my Cade issues. It was a lot. Not having actual friends anymore meant I had a surplus of drama to unload, but to her credit, she didn't immediately run screaming from the building.

In fact, she looked positively delighted that I'd turned out to be every bit the train wreck she'd always suspected.

"Why not just move in with your brother?" she asked.

I shook my head. "I would rather continue to live under my desk at work."

"What about your parents?"

"That's an even worse option. My parents are . . ." How did I phrase this delicately? I didn't want to make my parents out to be cold, but they had some pretty rigid beliefs. "They're hard on me. They love me, but they have this dated way of thinking. They're all about taking care of yourself and being a positive contributor to society and so on. If I asked them for help, they would feel like they'd somehow failed."

"Geez. I haven't moved out yet. I don't know what I'd do if my parents tried to make me feel bad about it. No offense, but your situation sounds really messed up."

"Yeah." I couldn't even work up a proper defense to that because she wasn't wrong. The last few months had been eye-opening on multiple levels. "Anyway. Here I am. Sitting houses because it's the only way I can afford to live and pay all my bills."

"And you called cake a tragedy." She rolled her coffee cup between her hands. "What about this Cade guy? Why can't you move in with him for a little while?"

"No." I laughed and it came out sounding like the last wheeze of a dying cat. "I can barely keep my hands off him when we're in public, at a work function. Could you imagine the mess we'd get into if we were alone under the same roof for an extended period?"

"Sounds like a good time to me."

"You're really bad at this giving-advice thing."

"I've given you great advice." She shrugged. "It's not my fault you don't want to take it."

"I don't think I want to be friends anymore."

"Too late. You're stuck with me now."

I tried not to smile in relief. It had taken her some time to warm up to me, but I needed a friend now more than ever. Neeta had already seen enough of me at my worst, so I wouldn't be scaring her away anytime soon. And I had a feeling she would never pack up my boxes while I wasn't home and leave them outside. She was wrong about Cade, though. So wrong. "Let me show you a picture so you can understand what I'm up against here."

I pulled up the most recent picture I had. My mom had gotten us all matching sweaters for Christmas, but Cade had sweater trauma from his childhood, so she never made him wear one. He also hated getting his picture taken. I had to pester him into it. He eventually relented, but he refused to smile, so he glowered in the corner like the ghost of Christmas Past in his black button-down shirt. Still hot. In a lurky sort of way.

"Wow, I see what you mean." Neeta grabbed my phone and swiped her fingers over it to zoom in. "The reindeer sweater is cute too."

"What?" I grabbed the phone back from her and took a quick peek. "Ew. No. That's my brother, Sebastian. Cade is the hot, broody guy in the corner."

"Oh." She blushed. "He's okay, I guess."

Neeta thought Seb was cute. Good to know. I'd file that fun fact away for later. "So, as you can see, I can't very well share a shower with that"—I pointed to my phone—"without ruining my brother's most important friendship and ruining whatever I have with Cade too."

"What do you have with him? Isn't he also your friend?"

"Sort of? I'm not sure, actually." I'd always considered Cade to be Seb's friend, despite the fact that he'd been around for most of my life. Though he'd always been there for me too, and when he held my hand in his Jeep, it didn't feel like he was just Seb's friend anymore. But maybe I'd read into that more than I should've. "Anyway, I'm sick of me. Let's talk about you. Are you seeing someone?"

"No. My job keeps me pretty busy, and every date I've been on lately has felt like a psychological experiment, except I don't get paid for my time."

"I could keep an ongoing blog about my dating history." I took a very nonchalant sip of my water. "Seb's single, by the way. He's out of town right now. He travels a lot, doing whatever he does for a living, and it makes dating hard for him."

"You don't know what your brother does for a living?"

"No one does. It's not personal." Seb needed someone like Neeta in his life. Someone who would be direct with him and tell him when he was being an ass. "As your friend, maybe I should invite you out for dinner with us one night when he gets back in town."

"Aren't you afraid I'd just be using a friendship with you to get close to your brother?"

"Not unless you're afraid I'd be using my brother to lure you into a friendship with me."

"Fair." She tilted her coffee toward me. "My break is just about over, but I'm glad we did this. Trying to meet people when you're an adult is the worst."

"I've been trying to be friends with you for months."

"Yeah, but you're also the weirdo who takes comfort in lying on the library floor when you're in crisis. Forgive me for thinking you weren't great friend material."

She made an excellent point. "There should be a Tinder for friends. A Friender."

"There are a few. No one posted pics of their hot brothers, though, so I had to swipe left."

I laughed. "I like you, Neeta. I'm happy you're my new best friend."

"Whoa, slow down." She held her hands out. "I don't know if I'm ready to be the best."

"You're the only. You get the title by default."

"Really?" She raised her eyebrows, but when I nodded, she didn't comment further. She just took my phone and added herself to my contacts, then sent herself a text. "Maybe we can watch a movie together next weekend."

After she headed back to the library, I stood and tossed my empty water cup. My phone buzzed against my hip. Neeta had texted me the same meme I'd posted to Instagram last week. This best friendship was already going better than the three years I'd lived with Quinn and Vera. I followed her on all my social media platforms, with a smile on my face.

I might not have had the whole adulting thing down yet, but I'd made a friend. All on my own. At least I could still do one thing right.

CHAPTER TEN

I sat in my car outside the library. A storm was moving in. Roiling gray clouds gathered in the distance, and a light patter of rain dripped down my windshield. I loved a good rainstorm in the summer. It had always been cozy-blanket and book weather, and that warm feeling lingered, even if it had been a while since I'd picked up a book.

After checking my website for any new hits from Cornerstone employees and finding none, I had a mini-meltdown. Even though I was supposed to be taking things one day at a time and going with the flow and all that, I didn't know what I'd do if I didn't get another job lined up soon. Maybe I could make a copy of Cade's key and sleep in his condo while renovations were being done. I'd sneak out before the crew arrived to work. He'd never know. And I didn't need a working stove or running water. It would be like that time we had to do Pioneer Week in elementary school, but better because I'd still have electricity and access to public bathrooms.

Hopefully it wouldn't come to that. I still had the rest of the week to find a new client. With my worries temporarily settled, I finally called my mom. I figured it would be best to deal with family issues while I was within walking distance of my favorite emotional crutch. Though if things were that bad, Seb would've called me back himself instead of sending Cade to check on me. The thought of Cade calling me out of some kind of brotherly obligation caused the muscles in my neck to tighten in annoyance. And last night he'd had the gall to tell me I was important to him. I really should've left that fish I caught under the seat of his Jeep for that one.

My mom picked up on the first ring, preventing me from rehashing the night before for the millionth time. "At last. My long-lost daughter has finally emerged from whatever hole she must have fallen into. I'm so glad. I was beginning to worry."

Clearly, I'd gotten my flair for the dramatic from the maternal side of the family tree. "I've just been busy with work stuff this week." Between the house-sitting and the Torres-Glasser function, that was technically not a lie. "You know how it goes. How is Dad?"

"Oh, he's fine." Seb was right. It was the No Big Deal voice. "Just a little trouble with his sciatic nerve. Nothing you need to worry about."

Any time Mom said we didn't need to worry, that was when we needed to worry most. Guilt gnawed at me. I should've called yesterday. "How bad is it bothering him?"

"Not bad now that the doctor gave him some medications. He should be good to go in a few months or so, but he can't drive on the meds, so he's taking a little time off, is all."

I pulled the phone away from my ear and swore under my breath. My dad got some vacation and sick time, but it wouldn't cover two months, and they relied on his pay. The hair salon my mom ran out of their basement wouldn't cover half their mortgage. I couldn't afford to help them either—not when I could barely afford to help myself.

"Isla, honey. You still there?"

I fumbled with my phone and brought it back up to my ear. "Yeah. Sorry. Are you going to be okay on bills while Dad is off?"

"We'll be fine. He has short-term disability." She bit off each word, like it cost her a significant portion of the pride she valued so much to admit they needed help. As if being shown concern was a mark of their shortcomings. It didn't come as a surprise when she changed the subject. "You should come over for dinner soon."

"Sure. That'd be nice." There was no point in trying to press the issue when my mom made up her mind not to talk about something. I'd just have to wait and see my dad for myself. "I need to go. A storm is starting, and I'm still in my car."

I ended the call and tossed my phone on the passenger seat. At least they could get short-term disability to cover their mortgage. They'd be fine. I glanced at the library. The familiar urge to surround myself with books welled up inside me, but I had a feeling Neeta wouldn't appreciate seeing me again so soon, even if we had become friends.

On the way back to Jim's house, I stopped at the grocery store for the things someone else's house couldn't provide. Namely, hygiene products. I'd been living off whatever I could steal out of the broken ladies' dispenser at work for the last few months, but it was time to suck it up and sacrifice the eight dollars for a box of Tampax. And while I'd been using a toothpick to dig out the dregs of my travel-size Secret for the last week,

I strongly suspected the tiny pills of dry deodorant I managed to extract weren't doing the job anymore, and people had just been too polite to tell me. As much as I hated spending money on those things, I had to admit I now had room in my budget thanks to Jim's well-stocked refrigerator.

I swept a hand down my hair, shaking off the rainwater. The elderly gentleman who wielded the discount sticker gun groaned as I gave him a little wave on my way through the produce section. We were old friends. Every week we'd play this fun game where I would snag one of his stickers and place it on a loaf of bread that wasn't half stale, and he would tell his boss and try to have me banned from the store. Good times.

He stiffened as I approached the regular priced bread, and stared in shock as I walked by without pausing. It was so damn satisfying. This must've been what the hot girls felt like every time they breezed past the line at the club. Add in the fact that I was now able to afford a proper stick of deodorant, and I had to believe that things were finally looking up. I'd get another job by the end of the week. I just had to keep putting positivity out into the universe.

*　*　*

Positivity was bullshit. Looking on the bright side had only lured me into a false sense of security about my future, when I should've been preparing for the worst. My time at Jim's had passed too quickly. It had been easy to be positive when I had a full week of house-sitting ahead of me, but that slowly trickled to unease as the days ticked down and I still hadn't booked another job. Cade hadn't let me give anyone my web address at the Torres-Glasser mini golf outing—because he claimed it would be tacky—but I'd have to slip away from him at the next one and spread the word to a few people. I needed more than just Cornerstone executives to sustain me, and I didn't want to start accepting jobs from creeps on the internet. I preferred to save those creeps for future dating prospects.

On the last day, I bid farewell to the Nemos and the horny seahorses. At least the entire tank had managed to stay alive. Even the eel-looking thing I was certain had played dead a few times just to fuck with me. When Jim cut me a check for the second half of my fee and showed me the door and I still hadn't gotten a hit on my website, I had to admit defeat. I headed to my brother's condo to do laundry while I tried to psych myself up for another night of sleeping under my desk.

Of course, now that Cade knew my secret, I probably could've just stayed at my brother's place until I had a new job lined up, but I felt like I had something to prove. Cade was certain that house-sitting in lieu of having an actual place to live would blow up in my face eventually. I didn't want to give him the satisfaction of being right. Besides, the floor under my desk wasn't that bad. Halfway through a day of mind-numbing data entry, it began to look downright cozy.

I didn't have to stress for long, though. As I was pulling into the parking garage under my brother's condo, my phone buzzed on the passenger seat, letting me know I had an email. Someone named Jillian Stubbens needed a house sitter starting on Sunday night. She'd gotten my contact info from Jim, and apparently worked on the first floor of Cornerstone Enterprises. She wasn't high enough on the ladder to be as recognizable as Alice Bishop, but she had five cats, and she'd found out from Jim that hiring a house sitter was cheaper than boarding them. She also wanted me to sign an NDA that basically stated she had the right to sue me if I told anyone at Cornerstone about anything

I saw in her home. That made me a little nervous, but who was I going to gossip to about her house? I didn't have work friends.

I unlocked the door to my brother's condo, not bothering to make a lot of noise and bang around like last time, though there was no need for me to be stealthy about it. Cade sat on the couch, wearing sweatpants and nothing else. I swear, the man owned plenty of shirts. Why couldn't he ever keep one on?

I dropped my latest load of clothes in the washer, then went over to the refrigerator to snag a bottle of water. I looked out the window, to the building across the street, the clouds in the sky—any place that wasn't Cade's naked chest. Because it wasn't just Cade's chest anymore. Now it was the chest I'd dug my nails into while trying to drag him closer as he ravaged my mouth. Nothing about his body could ever go back to being normal.

Truthfully, things hadn't been normal since the Dropped Towel Incident. Or possibly even since Thanksgiving three years ago. Or if I wanted to go even further back, the Rainbow Bear moment. Maybe things hadn't ever been normal between us. I let that thought hover over me as I took too large a swallow of water and ended up choking and sputtering. Real smooth.

Cade gave me an amused smirk. He clicked off the TV and stood, stretching his arms over his head. "Are you ready for event number two today?"

I glanced at him and mentally patted myself on the back for keeping my eyes above his neck. "You still want to pretend I'm your girlfriend?" I'd gotten the impression after last week's kissing and grinding fiasco, he'd try to avoid anything that would put us in another date-type situation, fake or otherwise.

"Yeah." He gave me a funny look. "Why wouldn't I?"

"I don't know." I couldn't answer that question without violating the unspoken rule of never talking about those moments that skated over the line of our preexisting relationship. "Is there a reason why I never get advance notice on these events?"

"Because I need to catch you off guard."

I paused mid-sip. "Haven't you done enough of that this week?"

"Have I?" The was an edge to his voice and a challenge in his eyes. If he was holding his breath, waiting for me to bring up the kissing, he'd only be suffocating himself.

I set my water on the counter and marched up to him. "I know you're trying to antagonize me on purpose. Why are you trying to catch me off guard? Do you think I'd back out? I made a deal, and contrary to what it might look like at the moment, I'm usually someone who honors my commitments. I thought you knew that too."

"Hey." He gripped my arms as he studied my face. "I thought we were just messing around. I don't think you're a flake, and I'm sorry if what I said suggested otherwise."

"Okay." Maybe I was being extra sensitive, but getting kicked out of my apartment because I didn't keep my promise to pay rent hurt the very core of who I thought I was. Growing up, there were times when I'd been wild and reckless, but I always kept my promises.

Until this year.

He cupped my chin and tilted it so I'd meet his gaze. "We good?"

I nodded.

"And you'd tell me if we weren't?"

I shrugged.

"I guess that'll have to do." He squeezed my shoulder and let me go, taking a step back to give me space. "Do you want to know where we're going today?"

"I'm going to take a shot in the dark and say someplace with water?"

He tapped his nose. "Correct. We're going to the splash pad."

"You've got to be joking." I hadn't been to the splash pad since Gina Martinez's birthday party. In the third grade. "Are your bosses twelve-year-old boys trapped in old-man bodies?"

"Basically." He went around to the opposite side of the couch and grabbed a bag, which he handed to me. "I got you something. It's not exactly a fancy dress, but we're going to be beachside all day, and I promised to provide."

I pulled a sheer dress out of the bag and held it up. It had a solid blue strapless bodice, with see-through white fabric that would fall about mid-thigh on me. The silky material felt like water in my hands. I'd never actually owned a real beach cover-up before. I always used a towel because I never saw the point in having both. I got the point now.

"It's beautiful. Thank you." My voice caught in my throat, and I didn't know where this emotion was coming from. Nobody really bought me nice things. People bought me practical things, things I could use, because that's what I always said I wanted. I hadn't realized until right then that I could use the impractical every now and again too.

"No problem." He had a look in his eyes I didn't recognize, and he shook his head. "It'll look good on you while we're paddleboating."

"Ah, there's the fishing angle I was looking for."

"Don't sound so disappointed. There will be plenty of time for you to run through the sprinklers if your heart is really set on it."

"Are we having dinner there as well?" Priorities and all.

"Yep. Ted and Anton rented the small island at the center of the splash pad lake. It has a grill and picnic tables for corporate events, and you can only get there by boat."

"Sounds like a good setup for a horror movie."

"Almost as good as a young woman who promises to watch over a stranger's house while they're on vacation, but then the phone rings, and the call is coming from upstairs."

A chill went down my spine. Even though I planned to only take house-sitting gigs from people at Cornerstone Enterprises, or Torres-Glasser if I managed to make connections there, the creepy nature of it all snuck up on me while I was alone at night in an unfamiliar setting. I didn't need to dwell on those kinds of thoughts, though. I was careful. I documented all my locations with Cade, and all my business came from referrals. There was nothing to fear in the daylight.

"You're officially banned from talking." I turned away from Cade and headed to the bathroom to get ready for our outing.

His laughter trailed me down the hall.

While I was changing, Neeta sent me a text: *Want to come over to watch a movie? My parents went out with their friends, and I'm bored.*

Neeta wanted to hang out with me outside the library or its immediate vicinity? I texted her back: *Seems like a big step in our friendship.*

We'd done a movie night over text. Meaning we decided to watch *Pride and Prejudice* on the same night, then texted each other through the whole thing. Hanging out with Neeta wasn't anything like the time I'd spent with Quinn and Vera during our peak party days. I felt more comfortable with Neeta. Like I could just be. I didn't have to look a certain way or try to get into certain clubs or even act like I had my shit together. She knew I was a mess, and she wanted to watch movies with me anyway.

> **Neeta:** *You didn't lie on the floor the last time you came to the library. I figured you were ready for more responsibility.*
>
> **Me:** *I think this means we need a portmanteau. Neela? Ista?*
>
> **Neeta:** *I rescind my movie invitation.*
>
> **Me:** *You know I'd just show up anyway, but unfortunately, I have plans with Cade.*
>
> **Neeta:** *The guy you're not dating?*

Yeah . . . Except in this case I was, but I couldn't explain it all in text. *I'll call you later,* I texted back.

I finished changing and exited the bathroom. As soon as Cade's eyes began to scan me from head to toe, I winced and hugged my stomach. My bathing suit was a little (a lot) on the small side, but I'd refused to buy a new until this one literally fell apart. I was regretting that now.

"I'm not appropriate for a work function, am I?" I asked.

His expression was unreadable as he stepped up to me and took my hands, pulling them away from my attempt to cover myself up. "You're perfect."

Uh-oh. This was bad, tingly-toes territory. And exactly the reason why I needed to sleep under my desk tonight instead of here with Cade. It seemed like neither one of us could be trusted to keep things the way they used to be.

Somehow, I managed to unglue my tongue from the roof of my mouth and step toward the door without stopping to rub myself all over him like a cat. "Ready when you are."

A sudden hunger for something meaty hit me. Good thing we were headed to a cookout.

CHAPTER ELEVEN

By the time we arrived at the splash pad, most of the staff from Torres-Glasser Bass Fishing had already assembled on the small island. We walked around the perimeter of the lake, passing lopsided sand castles and kids chasing tadpoles in the shallow water, until we came to a small brick building next to a narrow dock that housed all the park's rentals. There were only three paddleboats left. All of them in the shape of giant swans.

I stood on the dock next to swan number two. "I'd rather spend the day running through the sprinklers than be caught dead on one of these things."

"Come on—where's your sense of adventure?" Cade jumped into the first seat, wobbling from side to side before he caught his balance, and held his hand out to me.

He wore swim trunks in a muted gray with a white linen button-down with the sleeves rolled up. He must've googled "corporate drones at the beach" to get that look, because he was deceptively dressed for an island cookout while still managing to exude an air of capital "P" Professionalism. It was at complete odds with the boyish grin he gave me as he tried to usher me into the swan boat. It was like Work Cade was his Hannah Montana alter ego, but around me he could just be Miley.

"Can't we swim over to the island instead?" When he raised an eyebrow, I sighed and took his hand, letting him help me into the swan. "Though I guess something can be said for making a dramatic entrance."

The water lapped against the side of our boat as we paddled toward the island that was a lot farther away than it had looked from the dock. The sun shone on my shoulders, and I'd soon have a light dusting of freckles to go with my tan. The scent of coconut oil and reedy water wafted on the air.

"Do you have another house to go to tonight?" Cade asked.

"I lined up a new job this morning," I hedged. Which was the truth. He didn't need to know that Jillian wouldn't be leaving town until tomorrow.

He tipped his sunglasses down to look at me. "And when does this new job start?"

I shifted. Water had spilled into the boat, soaking my seat. This was not a conversation I wanted to have anywhere, let alone in the belly of a swan with nowhere to run. "Why are you being so nosy about my house-sitting jobs all of a sudden?"

"All of a sudden? Are you kidding me?" He stopped paddling, which made me realize just how little I'd been contributing to the joint paddle effort. Instead of heading for the island, we sort of spun in a circle. "I've been nosy since I saw you lying by some stranger's pool in a bikini and a fur coat. Why are you being defensive? What are you hiding?"

"I am *not* being defensive." I was totally being defensive. "My next job doesn't start until tomorrow, but I didn't want to tell you because you're already so judgmental. Don't worry—I have a place to stay lined up for tonight. It's not a big deal."

He narrowed his eyes. "What place?"

"My friend's." That didn't sound at all suspicious. "You don't know her. She works at the library. Her name is Neeta. She likes romance novels and lives with her parents."

I wouldn't actually be spending the night at Neeta's. Though I was sure she'd let me stay with her—after giving me a questionnaire, a personality test, and hooking me up to a lie detector—I didn't want to dump my problems at her doorstep. Not when this friendship between us was so new. Even if she knew most of my drama, I still wanted to sell her on my more charming attributes.

Cade's lips thinned as he faced forward and started paddling again. "Jesus, Isla. Remind me never to bet on you at a poker table. If you have a date, you can just say so."

I let out a startled laugh. "I don't have a date."

I hadn't been able to swipe right once since the day I saw Cade naked, so I gave up trying. Until I got this temporary infatuation—or whatever this thing was—out of my system, I'd be measuring everyone against the man sitting beside me in a swan-shaped paddleboat. And none of them would be able to compare. Cade was everything I could ever want, wrapped in a package I was never allowed to have, and that made him irresistibly, impossibly tempting. Which was exactly why I had to spend the night under my desk.

"You don't have a date?" He stopped paddling to study my face. He gave a short nod and starting paddling again once he was seemingly satisfied with whatever he'd found. "Where are you really staying then? Because it's not with your friend Neeta."

I crossed my arms. "She's a real person."

"I'm sure she is, but I know you're not staying with her." Finally, the enormous swan boat dragged along the sand near the island and stopped. "We'll talk about this later."

"We will not." I jumped out of the boat before he could respond.

Cade dragged the swan closer to shore, next to the other, regular paddleboats, while I followed the scent of grilled meat up the hill. The line of thin and scrubby trees broke to reveal a flat piece of land covered in grass and grainy mud. Tiny purple flowers dotted the shaded and calming landscape. I took off my flip-flops, and the wet sand felt like heaven between my toes.

Twenty feet to my left, a cement dais held a few dozen picnic tables. About thirty people milled around, clustered in small groups. Cade had told me that all employees were welcome at these events, and whenever Ted and Anton traveled to their manufacturing sites in other cities, they held similar events to bring everyone together off-hours. Because they genuinely cared about creating a friendly and relaxed work environment. It had to have been why they were so successful. Happy employees produced. Cornerstone Enterprises would do well to take more than a few notes from Torres-Glasser Bass Fishing.

Anton waved at me from where he was manning the enormous grill all on his own. There must've been twenty hamburger patties going, and he already had a stack of cooked hotdogs on the table next to him. My mouth watered as I took in the spread of coleslaw, potato salad, taco salad, tuna salad, pistachio salad, and salad salad. The stuff my mom called "graduation food."

"It's good to see you again. Glad you could make it." Anton leaned down, grabbed a beer from the cooler, and handed it to me.

"Oh, um, thanks." I took the beer but glanced back to where Cade had stopped to talk to a coworker at the top of the hill. He didn't drink at work functions, and I wasn't sure if he expected the same from me. I wanted to be respectful of his choices.

Anton noticed my discomfort and reached back into the cooler. "We also have Coke."

"That would be great." I gave him a relieved smile.

He took a drink of the beer I'd given back to him and set it on the table next to his hotdog mountain. "We have horseshoes and a volleyball tournament planned. I hope I can count on you and Cade to be on my team."

"Not if you want to win." I lacked basic coordination just walking up a flight of stairs, and was a known liability to any sports team. Dodgeball—not to mention the batting cages disaster—ruined whatever happy memories from elementary school I would've otherwise had.

He let out a laugh. "Maybe I'll just take Cade then."

Speaking of the devil, Cade joined us and put his arm around my shoulders. The warm weight of him felt nice. Too nice. Like I was already forgetting that this was all an act. "What's so funny over here?"

"Anton . . . ah . . . he, um . . ." It was hard to concentrate when Cade was stroking his thumb over my skin in a rhythmic motion. "He asked me to be on his volleyball team."

"I don't recommend that if you want to win," Cade said to Anton.

"Hey." I shoved him. It was true. But still. "I'm your girlfriend—aren't you supposed to be talking me up and saying how amazing I am?"

"You are amazing." He ran his hand down my hair and cupped the back of my neck. "At everything except sports."

We stared at each other like we had on mini golf day, with the same intensity shimmering between us. Anton cleared his throat. "Feeling a little hot over here, and it's not from the grill."

That shook Cade out of our heated little bubble. His spine immediately stiffened, and his expression glazed over. Work mode activated. "We're going to make the rounds. Thank you for having us here today, Mr. Torres-Glasser."

Cade took my hand, threading his fingers through mine, as we walked around and said hello to various people. He was polite and friendly with everyone, but in a reserved way. Not at all how he'd acted with me. It was as if he couldn't let the polished and professional demeanor slip for anything. Not even beachside weenies and horseshoes.

I spotted Penny Torres-Glasser standing ankle deep in water, tugging on Jeff's hand, trying to pull him in. He looked both horrified by the prospect of getting wet and delighted by the attention. Eventually he relented, splashing in after her like a smart boy. Resisting Penny seemed like a losing game.

"Are people talking about Penny and Jeff now that you're off the market?" I asked.

"Probably." Cade glanced over at them with an amused expression. "They've been flirting around the office all week. I don't think they're a couple yet, but it looks like it's headed in that direction."

"Good for them."

Neither of us remarked on the fact that once Penny had a steady boyfriend, any rumors about her and Cade would be forgotten. But having me around still stopped his coworkers from trying to hook him up with various family members. Thankfully. I didn't want to stop coming to these functions. As sad as it was to have nothing to look forward to except a corporate event every week, it was almost like having a social life. And spending time with Cade wasn't all bad either.

We headed back to the grill and got in line for the food. I managed to score a hamburger and a hotdog. I couldn't think of the last time Cornerstone Enterprises had provided any kind of sustenance for their employees, unless I counted the wooden cookies from the basement holiday party. Which I absolutely did not.

After lunch, they picked teams for the volleyball tournament. I opted to sit out, since I was also playing the role of Awesome Girlfriend to help make Cade look good to his bosses, and my sports skills wouldn't be doing him any favors. The grass tickled my ankles as I took a seat on the sidelines to watch everyone play. And by everyone, I meant Cade. He left his shirt on while everyone else took theirs off. I was sure the prospect of it getting wrinkled from all that jumping around and sweating killed him, but he still looked good whacking a ball over a net.

Penny approached me, and I did my best to be cool. "Mind if I sit with you?"

"Sure." I patted a spot of grass beside me and tried not to lean in and inhale when she took a seat. Not only was she gorgeous in a fire-engine-red beach wrap, but she smelled like vanilla sugar cookies. It made me a little light-headed. "Are you not a volleyballer either?"

She flipped her glossy dark hair over her shoulder and laughed, which lit up her whole face, illuminating her already captivating eyes. I was ready to write sonnets about that laugh. Jeff didn't stand a chance. "My dads tried to get me to be sporty, but it wasn't ever my thing."

"Your dads are wonderful." I loved everything about how they ran their company and how genuine they were with their staff. And while fangirling over these two CEOs was the most

MBA thing I'd done since I'd gotten my degree, I maybe wouldn't have minded working in business so much if it was for a business like this one.

"They're pretty great." She had enough warmth and affection in her voice to let me know they were a close-knit family by choice. Not because of overprotectiveness or smothering expectations, but simply because they loved and adored each other. She nodded to the players in front of us. "Cade has certainly loosened up since you've come around."

"He has?" He wasn't a complete corporate jerk or anything, but he erred on the side of professional at all times. He wouldn't have a drink, even when offered his favorite brand of beer; he wouldn't address Anton by his first name after he'd been told it was okay; and he wore dress pants to play mini golf on a party barge. That wasn't exactly what I'd call *loose*.

Penny nodded. "My dads want me to bring him out of his shell—that's my area of expertise as the social director, but he's a tough nut to crack. He's very insistent on always being in manager mode."

"It's important for him to be professional." While I thought he could stand to relax a little more too, I understood his position. Penny hadn't grown up like Cade. She didn't know what it felt like to fear any kind of security being snatched away at a moment's notice.

"And he's a brilliant sales manager, but it's okay for him to have fun too." She laid a hand on my arm. "I hope you know we also respect his boundaries. In fact, right before you started coming around, we had to have a talk with some of the employees about trying to fix up dates for Cade. We're a close operation, and sometimes people forget that not everyone wants to mix their business and personal lives."

"You stopped people from trying to set him up? Before I came around?"

"Yeah. We could tell how uncomfortable it was making him, and we're not okay with that." She gave me a brilliant smile that radiated sincerity. "My dads love their company and they care about their employees. They take those kinds of situations seriously."

Huh. That meant I really had no purpose here. My stomach dropped as the idea of never attending another Torres-Glasser event began to sink in and make me sad in ways I couldn't begin to unpack. This wasn't my company, and Cade wasn't really my boyfriend. Even if it had all begun to feel a little too real.

I needed to step away before Penny picked up on my mood and started asking questions that I wouldn't be able to answer. I stood, and I must've looked a little woozy on my feet, because Penny jumped up, placing a steady hand on my arm.

"Are you all right?" she asked.

"Yeah." I just needed a minute to myself. "The sun is a little much. I'm going to take a quick break in the shade, maybe dip my toes in the water."

I glanced over at Cade, who gave me a look of concern, but I couldn't deal with him right then. Last weekend, things had gotten confusing with us, but I couldn't start making that level of confusion a habit. There was messing around and harmless flirting, and then there was this attraction I'd begun to develop. Not to mention these feelings of attachment for a company I didn't even work for. None of it sat well with me. I gave Penny a weak smile and cut through the brush to the other side of the island.

I took a seat, leaning my back against a slim tree trunk and pulling my knees to my chest. I liked coming to the

Torres-Glasser events, but I didn't have the right to mourn the idea of never coming to another one when I had so many other situations in my life that should've made me feel worse. Maybe Cade would keep bringing me just for fun. Anton and Ted were clearly socially oriented, so it couldn't hurt for Cade to have a steady girlfriend.

And what else was I going to do with my Saturdays except hang around a stranger's house and eat all their organic food?

Besides, it hadn't been a hardship for him to have me as a girlfriend. Other than last weekend's detour into kissing and grinding, we acted like we always did. Of course, that didn't mean he always treated me like a girlfriend. Did it? Ugh. This had gotten complicated for no good reason. I let out a groan and buried my head in my hands.

A slight rustling of the bushes behind me had me snapping my head up. Cade knelt down in front of me. "You okay?"

I looked at his stupid, beautiful blue eyes and lost my train of thought, which never used to happen around Cade. Maybe we weren't treating each other *exactly* how we used to, but I didn't know if that was a good or a bad thing. We'd certainly been spending more time together than we normally did, and that felt good. But the tingly, buzzy, wanting-him feeling wasn't so great. Especially when he'd made it very clear nothing was going to happen. And I'd agreed. Totally agreed. Nothing good could come of us hooking up.

I gave him a forced smile. "I'm fine. Just a little dehydrated from the sun."

I had a million questions on the tip of my tongue. Did he know his bosses had put a stop to coworkers trying to hook him up? Did it change things if he knew? Did he still want to bring me to events? Did he still want to play the couple charade? Was it confusing him the same way it was confusing me? In the end, I decided not to ask a single one.

Maybe because I liked the game too much to let it go—and maybe that made me an awful person, or at the very least a dishonest one, but I'd worry about that tomorrow.

CHAPTER TWELVE

After Cade insisted on bringing me two bottles of water and fussed over me while I drank both of them to rehydrate, we played a round of horseshoes. Which—surprise—I was also abysmal at. I avoided Penny because I was a coward. I liked hanging out with Cade, and I liked fishing at his work events with his kind bosses and entertaining coworkers, and I wanted to keep pretending this ruse was actually my life. So that's what I was going to do. And having me around was still good for Cade. Hadn't Penny said he'd started loosening up because of me? That settled it. I was doing the right thing by keeping this going.

There was also more fishing, of course. I'd gotten pretty decent at it, though there was significantly less touching in day fishing. Which was just as well. We'd gotten into enough trouble at the last outing, and if we ended up making out again, Cade would definitely stop bringing me to these functions.

Soon after we started fishing, Cade introduced me to Sam, the top salesperson in his division, while he stepped away to talk to Ted about something presumably boring and work related. Sam turned out to be great company, and they'd be taking a vacation with their partner at the end of the summer and promised to use me for their house-sitting needs. They also promised to pass along my information to anyone else with an upcoming vacation and said they wouldn't tell Cade. It turned out to be a productive end to what could've been a crappy day.

As the sun began to set, everyone started packing up and bringing their paddleboats back to the rental dock. Between the sun, the socializing, and the roller coaster of emotions, I was exhausted. The prospect of curling up in the sand and sleeping on the island had some merit. I barely contributed to the paddling effort as we brought the swan back to its rightful place on the other side of the lake. Not that I'd put in a ton of effort the first time.

The beach had mostly cleared out as the first few stars peeked out from behind hazy clouds. We only passed a few remaining stragglers on our way back to Cade's Jeep. By the time we reached the parking lot, my legs felt like jelly. The thought of sleeping under my desk horrified me. And not for the reasons it should've—like not having a place to live or any kind of plan for after vacation season ended or any idea what I'd do with my boxes once Seb returned from London. I just wanted to sleep in a familiar bed and wake up knowing my surroundings.

I laid my head against the passenger window as Cade drove away from the splash pad. The cool glass felt nice against my sun-warmed cheek. We turned on the road that would take us back to the condo, and I made up my mind. "I'm going to sleep on the couch tonight."

Cade gave me a teasing grin. "What about your big plans?"

With my eyes half closed, I mumbled, "My big plans had been to let myself into Cornerstone Enterprises with my key card so I could sleep under my desk."

He jerked his Jeep to a stop so abruptly, I lunged forward, and he flung his arm out to stop the seat belt from digging into my chest. "I'm sorry—what? You were going to sleep under your *desk*?"

I glared at him, fully awake and pissed at myself for letting that one slip. "It's a temporary situation."

"No, moving back in with your parents, crashing on a friend's couch, or getting a hotel for a few nights is a temporary situation. Moving into your cubicle isn't normal." Okay, he was yelling now. Cars honked and drivers flipped us off as Cade stayed firmly stopped in the middle of the road. This wasn't good. "How many times have you slept there?"

I lifted my chin, meeting his gaze head-on. I wasn't proud of all my choices, but I did what I needed to do. "Just once."

He shoved his hands into his hair. "I swear, I'm going to be bald by the time Seb gets home. Is that where you went that first night, when you moved your boxes in?"

"Maybe."

"I hate that you won't go to your parents'." He ground his teeth together. "However, if pull you that sleeping-under-your-desk shit one more time, I will call your brother."

And Seb would call my parents, so he'd be forcing my hand either way. I had no idea what would be worse: facing my family's disappointment, or the jokes they'd make at my expense for the rest of my life. I really wished I'd kept my mouth shut. "What about our deal?"

"Fuck the deal."

"You're being an ass."

"And you're being a child." He gripped the wheel tight enough to leave finger grooves in the leather, but at least he'd started driving again. "This isn't like that time you strung up a bunch of Christmas lights in your dad's shed and tried to charge all the neighborhood kids an entrance fee to your nightclub. This is real life with real consequences. What if security caught you at work? They would fire you on the spot. Is that what you want?"

I had to admit, the idea had some appeal. Quitting my job, quitting my bills, going off the grid, and just living in other people's houses forever. But my next student loan payment would be auto-drafting from my checking account in six days. The minimum payment on my credit card was due in three days. The meager amount of money I'd managed to scrape up from house-sitting was already earmarked for this bill or that bill. And the fear of falling apart and falling behind clawed at my throat every minute of every day. My debt was a thousand-pound boulder on my chest. No matter how hard I pushed it, scratched it, or pounded my fists against it, it continued to suffocate me.

"I don't know how to get out of this." I stared at my fingers knotted together in my lap. "This wasn't supposed to be my life."

Cade turned into the parking garage, stopped the Jeep, and undid his seat belt. "Come here." He gathered me in his arms and rubbed my back as he held me against his chest. "You're going through some shit right now, but it's not always going to be like this."

I sniffed. No tears, of course. Just a runny nose. "Do you remember the Game of Life?"

"Yeah. I always got stuck with a car full of kids and had to pay for those little bastards on every other turn. It was my first lesson on why condoms are essential."

I pulled back and looked at him in the dim light of the parking garage. "No one ever chose to start a career. It was a guaranteed loss. Everyone picked the college option because you got better job choices with better salaries, and you were able to pay off your student loan debt in, like, three turns. And you know what? Fuck that game."

"I don't know." He rubbed his jaw. "I'm pretty grateful for the lesson on condoms."

"Fine, but the rest is bullshit. And it's not just the Game of Life either. All throughout high school it was just a given we'd go to college. Every book, every movie, every TV show had some minor subplot about picking schools or admission angst. We were led to believe that if we didn't get a degree, we'd never have hope of making more than minimum wage. No one ever talked to us seriously about alternatives. Why?"

"Probably because if you want a specialized career, you need some education."

"Some, sure. But why did I have to pay for algebra and sociology and American Short Stories from 1850 to Present? And why am I sitting in a cubicle next to a woman who doesn't have a degree, working the same job, making the same salary, except she drives an Audi and I'm carrying a plastic Cucci purse and sleeping under my desk?"

He blew out a breath. "I don't have an answer for that."

"I don't either." I opened my door. "And isn't that a damn shame."

We took the elevator up to the condo in silence. Not uncomfortable, but weighted. I'd given Cade some things to think about. College had worked out for him; he had a job that he loved, and even though he also had enormous student loans, he could afford his condo and his bills. That was great. That's what was supposed to happen. But it didn't happen that way for everyone, and I had a feeling there were just as many people like me. People who were barely adults, trying to juggle entry-level pay with a lifetime of debt.

As soon as we stepped inside the condo, I wanted to melt into the floor. There was no way I would've been able to immediately leave again. I also needed a shower in the worst way. Grainy sand stuck to the inside of my toes, my pink shoulders were sore, and I smelled like Miss Tropicana 1995. Cade collapsed on the couch and put his feet up on the coffee table, letting me go first. I grabbed a towel from the hall closet and closed the bathroom door behind me.

Seb had one of those rainwater showerheads, and bless him for it. I moaned as the perfect amount of water pressure washed away the grit from the day and soothed my tired limbs. I was going to have to buy a matching sweater for this showerhead and put it in the yearly family photo. It was that good.

I changed into cotton shorts and a Harry Styles T-shirt with a hole in the boob. After I towel dried my hair, I opened the door. "It's all yours."

Cade sat on the couch, flipping through channels with a pillow over his lap. His gaze tracked my body down to my toes. "Feeling better now?"

The husky tone of his voice made my skin heat. "It's a nice shower."

"You were . . ." He cleared his throat. "Making a lot of noise in there."

I glanced at the pillow on his lap and instantly connected the dots. Everything inside me tightened with need as my skin went from heated to on fire. "It was the water pressure."

His pupils flared. "Fuck, Isla. Are you trying to kill me?"

"No." Oh God. A hysterical laugh bubbled up from my chest, but I managed to choke it down. "I didn't mean it like that. The water pressure was good on my shoulders. It loosened the tension. I didn't use it anywhere else—I swear."

He tilted his head back and closed his eyes. "I need to get in the shower."

"Then go." I swept my hand toward the bathroom door. "I'm done in there."

"Don't look at me when I stand up."

"Why?"

The air in the condo had become thick and heavy. His eyes were darker than the ocean before a storm and twice as turbulent. "I'm hard as fuck and my swim shorts aren't doing a damn thing to keep it contained."

I clamped down on my lower lip, kneading the plump flesh between my teeth. "I'll do my best to be polite and give you proper privacy."

"That doesn't give me a lot of confidence, considering how you've never been polite and proper a day in your life."

"It's cute how you think you're the civilized one between us, when I'm just standing here minding my business, and you're currently hiding a raging boner behind a pillow."

He groaned. "You win. I'm standing up now."

In an effort to give him the promised privacy, I turned around and faced the corner. "This feels like the sexiest version of hide-and-seek ever. Should I count to ten?"

"Please don't." From the sound of his voice, he was only a few feet from me. "It wouldn't be smart for me to be found right now."

"One . . . two . . . three . . ." I smiled as the bathroom lock clicked behind me.

Messing with him was too much fun.

My smile died a few moments later, though, when he started moaning, and I knew for a fact it had nothing to do with muscle tension or water pressure. I clenched my thighs together on the couch. My mind drifted to the image of him in the shower, soaped up, taking his cock in his palm. Maybe he was thinking of me as he stroked his big, calloused hand up and down his shaft. He let out a short grunt, and I *felt* it in my center. A flush crawled up my neck. My nipples were rock hard and poking through the padded layers in my bra and my T-shirt.

As soon as the bathroom door opened, I grabbed the pillow and put it over my chest. He wore loose sweatpants and water dripped down his abs. He took one look at the pillow and gave me a knowing grin.

I ground my teeth together. "Not one word out of you."

He held up his hands. "I wasn't going to say anything."

I leaned back on the couch, holding the pillow against me. I'd been ready to sleep for a hundred years on the way back here, but it was early. I didn't have to be at Jillian's house until after two, and I was all wired up. "What do you want to do?"

Cade took a seat on the opposite of the couch, leaving a full cushion between us. "We could order a pizza and watch a movie."

"Sounds good to me." Just when I'd start to convince myself that I wasn't a real adult, I'd do something old, such as breathe a sigh of relief over staying in on a Saturday night with pizza and Netflix, instead of going out barhopping.

Like most things with Cade, picking a pizza was easy. We both liked pepperoni and mushroom. No sausage. He knew how I felt about balls of meat. Since I'd already been fed at the Torres-Glasser cookout, per our agreement, I offered to pay half. Which was awkward for both of us. I knew he would've refused to let me pay even if I was still living with Quinn and Vera and he thought everything was fine, but now that we had talked about money, it was like he had to think about how he was turning me down. Making sure it didn't come off as a pity supper. On the flip side, even though I didn't have a place to live, and I always appreciated free food, I had to think about how I accepted his offer without it sounding like I expected him to buy for me just because I really couldn't afford half the pizza. The social constructs around money sucked. I had no idea when we, as a society, had gotten to the point where giving and accepting help required a ten-page disclosure. And that was just for a twelve-dollar-and-ninety-nine-cent pizza.

Instead of a movie, we opted to watch *Schitt's Creek* because he still hadn't finished the series. It was nice to sit with someone whose company I enjoyed, and not do anything more pressing than watch TV. Eventually I stretched out and tucked my feet beneath his thigh, because I naturally engulfed whatever space I occupied. I was a nightmare to sleep with. He just gave me a look and wrapped his hand around one of my ankles. Within two episodes, I fell asleep.

I woke sometime around eight in the morning, tucked into a cozy blanket like a caterpillar. It was the best sleep I'd had in over two weeks.

CHAPTER THIRTEEN

Cade tapped on the bathroom door and let me know he was stepping out to get coffee while I got ready for the day. He still hadn't returned by the time I finished, so I left him a note to tell him I was heading out. That was different. I didn't want to overthink it too much, but Cade and I didn't leave each other notes. If we needed to go someplace, we just left. But for the first time, I assumed he would care about where I was going and what I was doing, and that should've been worrisome. It wasn't, though. Just like the pizza and TV binging, it was . . . nice.

Jillian had Venmoed me half my fee that morning. I stopped by the bank to withdraw cash, then headed over to Quinn and Vera's apartment to slide the final rent payment under their door. I had considered leaving it in a box on the sidewalk, but I was better than that.

Since I had a few hours before I needed to be at Jillian's, I stopped by the library. I figured I could keep my not-lying-on-the-floor streak alive by doing something completely out of character, like checking out a book. The scent of ink and paper and half-wilted carnations hit me as soon as I walked in the door. There was nothing better than the smell of the library. I wanted to bottle it and keep it with me always.

I'd have five days at Jillian's. During my week at Jim's, it had taken me by surprise when the one thing I'd wanted to do more than anything else was sit beside the lake and read. It had been years since I'd read just for the pleasure of it. When I'd put aside my dream of being a librarian and stopped blogging, I didn't think I could pick up a book without feeling like some part of me was missing. It had become a small, yet persistent, ache. While I couldn't bring myself to get rid of all the books I owned, I hadn't been able to seek out new stories either. But long before I'd ever wanted to be a librarian, I'd been a reader, and it was well past time to put that old hurt aside.

Neeta waved when she saw me, then looked at her hand like it had betrayed her. "What brings you in today? I hope you intend to stay on your feet."

"Believe it or not, I'm here for a book recommendation."

"Actually? Or is this one of those times where you tell me you're looking for a recommendation, and then use what you're looking for as a thinly veiled attempt to tell me about the drama in your life instead of straight up asking for my advice like a normal friend?"

That's what I liked best about Neeta. She wasn't someone who minced words. I probably would've been better off if I'd listened to her more often, but I'd been making poor decisions my entire life, and it had gotten me this far. "I'm looking for real for a book recommendation this time. Nothing too dark that'll make me afraid while I'm in a stranger's home for five days."

She pulled a book out from under the reference desk and nearly toppled forward from the weight it. A boom echoed through the library when she dropped *Renaissance Paintings: A Complete History* on the counter. "How about this? It's large enough to use as a weapon for when someone inevitably tries to murder you."

"Funny. But that won't happen since I'm only house-sitting for people I know." I might've been shoehorning the word *know* into that sentence, but I knew *of* them. Or in Jillian's case, I knew of the floor where she worked. Good enough. That was more familiarity than I had with most of the people at my last family reunion.

"Right." Neeta pressed her lips together. "But since you're asking for genuine recommendations for once, let me show you two books I've recently enjoyed."

She put Roselle Lim's *Natalie Tan's Book of Luck and Fortune* in my hands and told me to keep a lot of snacks on hand while reading, then handed me Kellye Garrett's *Hollywood Homicide*, which she promised would make me laugh. I'd just checked out my new reads for the week when my phone buzzed. Seeing my brother screaming on the screen, I picked up.

"Hey, Sebastian." I grinned when calm and collected Neeta fumbled a stack of books she'd been sorting, and they tumbled to the ground. "Isn't it around dinner time for you? You must be so sad, being all alone across the pond, with no girlfriend to keep you company on those foggy London nights."

"Are you on drugs?" At the exasperation in my brother's voice, it hit me right then how much I missed having him around. Even though he was a complete pain in my ass. "And since when do you give a shit about my dating life?"

"I have a friend—"

"No." I could practically hear his frown through the line. "Not after last time."

Neeta stared at me with wide eyes, shaking her head, but I waved my hand as I walked away from her. I totally had this. "Listen. I didn't know Quinn was going to bring you to a Naked Bike Ride event. I told her to save that kind of thing for the third date, but Neeta is normal. She thinks *I'm* the weird one in our friendship."

"You're the weird one in most situations."

"Ha. How long are you gone for again? Forever?"

"Why? Are you thinking about turning my condo into an Airbnb for a little extra cash?"

Even though I knew he was teasing me, the constant "Isla is a screw-up" jokes from my family grated on my nerves. I leaned against a shelf in the Mysteries and Thrillers aisle until my butt hit the floor. At least I wasn't lying down. Progress. "You sound like Mom."

"Have you called her yet? She thinks you're avoiding her, which means she's going to start digging into why you're avoiding her, so I'd be careful."

I pulled the phone away from my ear and gave it a nasty look. There was no way Seb could know what I'd been up to the last few weeks. My phone would've been blowing up if my family knew about my side business. "Is that some kind of threat?"

"I'm just saying, you're usually hiding something, so call Mom if you don't want her to figure out what it is."

"Bold of you to talk so much shit when you're over there and I'm here with the key to your condo." I smiled at his audible gulp. "How is business in London anyway?"

He paused long enough for me to wonder if we'd gotten disconnected. "It's not going great. I'm tired of traveling."

My heart hammered against my chest. "Does that mean you're coming home early?"

If Seb was coming home, I needed to get my stuff out. Now. I had a hundred dollars left in my checking account from house-sitting for Jim. I could probably rent a storage unit with that. Or maybe I could sneak into my parents' house at night and move some boxes into the attic and keep what I needed for immediate use in my car. They both slept like the dead. It was doable.

"No. My company is actually insisting I stay another month." The bitterness in his tone seeped through the line. "They think it's only fair if I pick up the extra work on these assignments because I don't have a spouse or kids or anything."

"I'm sorry." My brother had a fear of flying that had nearly cost him this job when he'd first started, and he never liked staying in hotels. He said it always felt like he was being watched. "Is there anything I can do while you're gone?"

"Nah. Cade is staying at my place. He can water my plants."

As soon as he mentioned Cade, I peeked around the aisle, like I really expected his name to manifest him in the library. He wasn't Beetlejuice, for fuck's sake. But of course Seb had to tell me Cade was staying at his condo. That was completely new information to someone who hadn't scared him out of his towel while moving in boxes.

"Neat." I cringed. Had I ever used the word *neat* in casual conversation? I needed a subject change before he started getting suspicious. "What is it you do at work again?"

He huffed out a breath. "How many times do I have to explain this to you?"

As he rambled on about what he did for a living, while I absorbed exactly none of it, I thought about texting Cade, just to make sure we kept our stories straight. But did I really think that was necessary? Or did I only have that thought because I wanted to text Cade? It would probably be best if I just left it alone. He'd already done more than enough by keeping my secret when it must've been eating him alive, and I knew he talked to Seb on a regular basis. I owed him an edible arrangement. Or something equally nice, like a new car.

"You know how it is," Seb said.

"Yep." I had no clue what he was talking about. "I need to go."

"Oh. Yeah. I'm sure you're busy." He sounded disappointed. Which was odd. We were close, but not super chatty on the phone. All the traveling he'd been doing over the last year must've been getting to him beyond the fear of flying and overly occupied hotels. "I'll talk to you later."

Maybe he wouldn't be as lonely if he had someone who could be there for him between trips. As soon as he hung up, I approached the front desk and leaned a casual hip against the counter. "My brother isn't due home for another six weeks, but what do you think about all of us going out to dinner when he gets back?"

"Who is 'all of us'?" Neeta asked.

"Me, you, Seb, Cade."

"As in Cade, the guy you're not dating?"

"Right." I was not dating Cade. Not for real anyway. So why was I arranging a night out that looked suspiciously like a double date? "We'll figure something out."

I grabbed the books I'd checked out and left. Jillian would be gone by now. It was time to find out whatever secret she was keeping that was bad enough to require an NDA.

* * *

Oh. My. Fucking. God.

That was the first—and really the only—thought pulsing in my brain as I took in the scene before me. When she had me sign an NDA, I'd been expecting something like a sex dungeon. Or at worst, a wayward head in the freezer. I had not been properly prepared for the nightmare before me.

The smell reminded me of a retirement home, Lysol and the overly sweet scent of rotting fruit. The entire room was badly in need of dusting. Dolls of all shapes and sizes lined the walls, grouped by specific type. One wall had dozens of porcelain dolls in crinkled satin dresses while another had been decorated in special edition Barbies in extravagant evening gowns. The wall separating the front room from the hall held wooden dolls with no faces, perched on floating shelves. Why wouldn't someone put faces on the dolls? Unless they were waiting to claim the faces of unsuspecting victims. I shuddered and stepped more fully into the rectangular living room, which had crunchy pink carpeting.

On the opposite side of the room, a giant dollhouse had been set up in the corner, stuffed full with miniature furniture and a tiny family with terrifying grins. Three ancient dolls, one with a missing eye and another with a missing hand, sat around a small wooden table with a chipped tea set. A baby buggy had one of those dolls whose eyes closed when it was lying down, and an old highchair held yet another antique doll with kewpie lips, rosy cheeks, and dead eyes. She had a knob on top of her head that you could turn to make her cry.

"You look like a Helga to me." I turned the knob to her sad face and had immediate regrets. "We're just going to keep you happy this week, okay?"

Everything appeared to be well loved, despite the thin layer of dust coating every surface, but the overall effect was unsettling. Who needed this many dolls? I understood collections; my grandmother on my mom's side had a whole cabinet full of commemorative Elvis plates, and my old roommates had once called me a book hoarder, but this went beyond a normal collection. This bordered on obsession.

Not even the hall leading to the kitchen had been spared. Framed photos of advertisements for various dolls through the ages hung from the papered walls. In the kitchen, doll-shaped cookie jars lined the old-school Formica countertops. The room had been outfitted with retro appliances in powder blue. It had a black and white checkered floor, and the ceiling was bordered with ivy and pink roses, which would've been cute in a normal house, but I got the feeling this was all part of Jillian's quest to make her home into an actual dollhouse.

To make matters worse, the contents of the refrigerator left much to be desired. There were a few restaurant containers, condiments, and a moldy block of cheese. The freezer had two frozen pizzas, but otherwise, it looked like Jillian lived on takeout. The dolls I could live with, but the lack of food was intolerable.

After digging through the cupboards in search of provisions and coming up equally empty, I took the stairs to the second floor, which had been decked out with black and gold wallpaper. Brass scones provided the dim lighting for the windowless hall. Jillian had told me I'd be sleeping in the Nutcracker Room, and I could only imagine what fresh hell waited for me in there. The muscles in my back hugged my spine as I pushed open the first door on the left. When I met a pair of large eyes in the dark, I screamed and flung myself backward. Tripping over my own feet, I landed against the opposite wall and hit my head.

"What the fuck? It's just another doll. Get it together, Isla."
The back of my skull throbbed, and I rubbed it as I righted
myself and went back into the room.

I flipped on the light. The eyes belonged to a five-foot-tall
nutcracker positioned in the corner of the room. Shelves upon
shelves of nutcrackers stared me down. All different sizes and
varieties, all with that severe jaw built for splitting shells. I shut
off the light and slowly backed away. There was no way I'd be
spending a single night in that room.

The next bedroom was filled with floor-to-ceiling angels.
Stuffed, ceramic, wooden, papier mâché—it didn't matter; if it
had wings and a halo, it was in this room. Even the headboard
of the four-poster bed was carved with Raphael's cherubs. The
third bedroom had pale blue walls, a queen-sized bed with a
simple navy comforter, and a plain white dresser with a matching nightstand. Not a single picture or knickknack in sight.
The normalcy of this room against a backdrop of utter chaos
gave off major creep vibes and freaked me out worse than the
nutcrackers. The fourth bedroom had an under-the-sea theme,
with tropical beach murals painted on the walls and stuffed
octopuses and fish hanging by clear strings from the ceiling
at various heights. Actual sand had been rubber cemented to
the floor, and the bed was really just a mattress that had been
dumped into an old fishing boat, but it was the room that had
the least number of things that could watch me sleep, so I
claimed it as my bedroom.

This was going to be a long five days.

I went in search of Jillian's cats and found their lair in the
basement. She had already proven to be an all-or-nothing style
of decorator, so I didn't even blink when I discovered she'd outfitted the entire lower level of her house to be a cat kingdom.

Twenty carpeted cat trees of various sizes and colors took up what would otherwise be a family room. As soon as I stepped into the space, five pairs of glowing yellow eyes focused their attention on me. Sadly, not the creepiest thing I'd encountered in this house of horrors.

There were two bedrooms, one which had been converted into a dining hall of sorts, with five dishes and water bowls. The second bedroom had been turned into a cat bathroom, with four-foot wooden cats positioned between each of the five litter boxes, like guards. What they were guarding was anyone's guess, but the room had a surprisingly light, clean smell for essentially being a giant cat toilet.

I refilled the food and scooped some poo, doing my main duty for the day, and went back upstairs. I now had the whole night ahead of me. Just me and about five thousand dolls. Awesome. I started laughing, and the sound was a little too high-pitched for my own ears. How was I supposed to go into work this week and keep a straight face if anyone mentioned Jillian? Never mind that: How was I supposed to sit in this house all night by myself, NDA be damned? Neeta was at work until five, and then she had dinner plans with her parents. The only other person I knew in the city was Cade.

I hadn't texted him all day, on purpose, even when I had a completely (somewhat) reasonable excuse after talking to Seb. Would it be weird if I texted him to come over now? Maybe if I hadn't left that note this morning, I wouldn't be stressing over this. But a note and a text in one day felt like too much. As if I was trying to initiate . . . something. On the other hand, this was Cade, not some random hook-up. Who cared if I texted him fifty times a day? Why was I worrying about this at all? Making it a big deal would just make it a big deal.

Before I could talk myself out of it, I pulled him up in my contacts and sent the text.

You've got to see this place. 3429 Kingman Ave. I can't provide dinner, but I promise there will be entertainment.

CHAPTER FOURTEEN

"There's too much going on here. I don't know where to rest my eyes." Cade leaned against the front doorframe, a bag of tacos in one hand and a six-pack of All Day IPA in the other, as he took in the visual assault of Jillian's living room. "You know one of these has been possessed by a sadistic demon, but the question is, which one?"

"My money is on Helga." I pointed to the doll with the wooden knob on her head. I'd turned her face to happy, but I knew she was crying on the inside.

"You *named* them?" He gave me an incredulous look. "What were you thinking? Everyone knows if you name them, you give them power."

"I'm trying to build familiarity." I stroked the top of Helga's head like she was a good kitty. "If they think of me as a friend, maybe they'll spare my soul."

"That was your first mistake." He pushed off from the doorframe. "We'll eat in a minute. I need to see the rest of this funhouse first."

Having Cade here already made the place feel less spooky, and he'd brought food. Texting him had been a win–win. He peeked in the hall, and my eyes roamed over his faded blue T-shirt pulled tight over broad shoulders, then moved down to the way his worn-in jeans showcased his extremely fine assets. I bit my lip and turned away. While he was nice to look at, I couldn't afford to pay attention to the warm and fuzzy caterpillars that tickled my stomach. If I gave them too much care, they'd be in very real danger of becoming butterflies.

"Let's put the tacos in the kitchen, then I'll give you the grand tour." I took his arm and steered him in the right direction.

"Look at these." He picked up the lid on one of the cookie jars and frowned. Then he checked five more and grunted in frustration. "Who has all these cookie jars and no cookies?"

I put the beer in the refrigerator. "My guess is it's an aesthetic choice."

"It's definitely a choice."

"Wait until you see the rest."

Next I showed him the cat kingdom in the basement, just so he'd know where to look first if I didn't show up at Seb's condo in five days. As soon as I flicked on the light, six gray cat heads peered out of various hidey-holes in the maze of cat trees.

Cade poked his head into the feeding room and bathroom. He counted the food dishes and litter boxes, then counted the heads of the cats. "Who has to share?"

"What?" I tilted my head in confusion.

"There's five food dishes, five litter boxes, six cats."

I swiveled my head between the open rooms and the cats watching us with still and intent eyes. There had been five when I'd come down here earlier. And Jillian had told me she had five cats, not six. Where had the sixth cat come from? "Maybe we should go. Now."

"Yeah, good idea."

We backed out of the room slowly, then bolted upstairs. I flung the door shut behind us, laughing hysterically. "Oh my God. What am I supposed to tell Jillian when she gets home?"

"Nothing." Cade mimed zipping his lip. "If she asks you about it, act like there were five in the basement the whole time."

With any luck, the sixth cat would just go away on its own. I didn't even want to know how it had gotten into the basement. I took Cade through the rest of the house, which he found equal parts horrifying and fascinating. In the nutcracker room, he spent a full twenty minutes just messing with the dolls, making the giant one pretend to crack his hand, and making the others have conversations with each other. He was worse than a little kid. When I took him into the angel room, he just chuckled and shook his head.

All the amusement in his eyes died when I opened the door to the normal bedroom. He placed his hands on my shoulders and squeezed as he gave me a serious look. "I don't think you should stay here alone."

For some reason, it made me feel validated to know he was also creeped out. "You find this room absolutely terrifying too? It's not just me?"

"No, it's not just you." He glared at the room, as if the normalcy of the space was a personal attack. "Why isn't it a gaudy, overstuffed nightmare like the rest of the house?"

"I'm not sure, and I'd really rather not spend any more time in here finding out." I shoved him out of the room and shut the door before he could say anything else.

Now that the normal room had taken all the fun out of the house, I grabbed the comforter from the angel bed, and went back downstairs. Cade didn't say another word, but I could *feel* him working up to something as he walked behind me. Tension crackled in the air, and he had the kind of stiff posture I only ever saw at his work functions. He grabbed the tacos and beer and followed me outside, but still didn't say whatever was on his mind.

Jillian's backyard was so at odds with the rest of her house. Not in a scary way, like the lone normal bedroom in a kaleidoscope of trash, but because the wild overgrowth in the backyard somehow had a pleasing effect. It was a mess, but in that beautiful, untamed way nature was supposed to be. Giant dogwoods, forsythias, and azaleas created bold bursts of color along the border of the eight-foot-high privacy fence. Lilacs and roses scented the air with their heady perfume. Paths of mosaic tiles cut through overgrown bushels of sweet-scented lavender and sage. A small stream running under the gazebo at the center of the yard held a collection of jewel-bright koi fish. Garden stakes in the shape of various butterflies, ladybugs, and dragonflies speckled the lush gardens, and little cherub-cheeked gnomes popped up in seemingly random spots. It was cluttered and charming, and I loved it.

I spread out the blue angel comforter on the floor of the gazebo and split the tacos between us. Birds chirped from under the cover of leafy trees. We ate in silence. Cade mulled over whatever he wasn't saying, and I obsessed over whatever he wasn't saying. He'd gotten really quiet after seeing the normal bedroom. While he hadn't been ready to break out the pompoms for my house-sitting business, he'd been reasonable about it. Meaning, he hadn't told my brother. But I was beginning to wonder if he was having regrets about that decision. Even though we had a deal, and I'd been holding up my end pretty damn well, seeing this place in person was a whole different thing. Maybe it had been a mistake to text him. Of all the houses I could've shown him, this one didn't exactly scream, *"I'm staying safe."*

After I finished eating, I opened one of the IPAs, and kept darting my gaze to Cade as I took nervous little sips. The quiet and the growing tension were slowly killing me. Finally, I set my half-finished beer down with a hard clink on the gazebo floor. "Obviously, you want to say something. Would you just spit it out already?"

Cade took a long, controlled swallow from his beer before setting it aside. "Okay. Let's talk. Why are you doing this?"

"Doing what?" I knew what he meant, but I wanted him to spell it out for me anyway.

"This." He waved a frustrated hand toward the house. "Living in stranger's homes, dealing with whatever the hell is going on in there? Do you seriously think I'm going to be able to leave you here by yourself tonight?"

"It's not your decision. I'm a big girl, Cade." While I understood that I'd fully brought this on myself for inviting him over, I hadn't expected him to have quite this reaction. "I can handle a couple of scary dolls and a squatting cat."

"It's more than that, and you know it. The dolls, the cats—it was funny at first, but there is something wrong with that house. Why are you so determined to see this through when you can just stay at the condo?"

I rolled my beer bottle between my hands, purposely keeping my eyes on the label. "I need the money from these jobs to get back on my feet before Seb gets home. I told him and my mom I'd gotten a promotion."

"Why?" He tilted my chin up to meet his gaze, and I cringed, expecting to find disappointment, but he only looked curious, and maybe a little concerned.

"I accidentally let it slip to my mom that I wasn't living with Quinn and Vera anymore, and when she asked what happened, I couldn't stand to tell her the truth." It was like I was still seven and sprawled out on the sidewalk, gravel stinging my palms, because I didn't want to tell my mom that I couldn't tie my shoes. "You know how she is."

Instead of stories about princesses and dragons, I'd grown up on a steady diet of capitalistic fairy tales. The unwavering belief that any success could be achieved through hard work and a good education. Even though my parents lived every day with the proof that they could work themselves into the ground and still never do more than scrape by, it was like they had to believe otherwise. To face reality meant having to face that they'd broken their backs their entire lives to pad the portfolio of a trust fund baby who'd never worked a day in their life. And yet, knowing all of that, I still wanted my family to be proud of me.

"You won't go to them for help, will you?" A storm of conflicting emotions swirled in Cade's eyes. "Even if it gets really bad."

"No. I'd go back to sleeping under my desk first." Even as I said the words, an alarm went off in my head, screaming the wrongness of it all. And it wasn't just my parents. The don't-ask-for-anything, rugged, individualistic attitudes were ingrained in every facet of our lives. I rubbed my hands over my face. "It's so fucked up. Why is asking for help treated like something we're supposed to be ashamed of?"

"Shame is a luxury. Be happy you can still afford it." There wasn't any judgment in his tone. No anger or bitterness. Only the kind of tired resignation he'd earned the hard way.

As I studied his face, a long-ago memory came into the forefront of my mind. My mom used to Seb, Cade, and me to the grocery store in the summer. For a couple of Popsicles, she'd put us to work hauling bags into the house and putting the food away. One day my dad had come into the kitchen and joked about how hard she was running us kids, and my mom replied that she wasn't handing out welfare Popsicles. They both laughed, but they hadn't seen Cade's face. They hadn't seen the way his cheeks burned so red he looked like he'd gotten too much sun. They didn't see the way he kept his head down and put the crackers and the peanut butter in the cupboard with a shaky hand. I remembered thinking at the time that Cade was going to stop coming over because my parents kept saying things that embarrassed him, and it made me mad on his behalf, even when I didn't understand exactly why.

I understood all too well now.

God, the thought of asking my parents for anything made me want to shrivel up into a ball of self-loathing. What must it have been like for Cade growing up in our house? My parents couldn't even get through one of our birthdays without telling us that the only reason why we had such nice gifts was because they worked so hard, like that was the sole reason why we had nice things when other kids didn't. All while they set a place at our table for a boy who likely wouldn't have had anything to eat otherwise. An enormous amount of anger I'd never been able to work up for myself washed over me for what they'd done to Cade.

"I'm sorry." I laid my hand on his knee. Which I'd meant to be comforting, but he tensed beneath my palm, so I removed it. "You didn't deserve to hear my parents' bullshit growing up."

"I'm not exactly sure what you're sorry for." His expression closed off, like he'd already shut down this avenue of conversation before it could begin. "Your parents did a lot for me."

"That didn't give them license to be assholes."

A muscle in his jaw ticked. "I appreciate the sentiment, but I'm not looking for a pity party, and I'm long past being anyone's charity case."

"You think I pity you?" I choked on the absurdity. "Don't be ridiculous. I'm the failure, remember? If anyone is getting a pity party around here, it's me. But I can still say I'm sorry my parents said a bunch of shitty stuff when we were kids because I *am* sorry, so just deal with it."

He didn't want to talk about it—that much was obvious—but I hated the idea of him thinking he owed my parents something. It was okay for him to be grateful for my parents *and* resent the things they said. It was okay to love someone and admit that they'd been hurtful. Being honest didn't mean he was writing them off.

"You're not a failure," he said quietly.

"Why are you deflecting?"

He held my gaze. "Why did you leave that morning after Thanksgiving?"

I sucked in a sharp breath. *Okay. He really just went there.*

We hadn't talked about that night at all, and I didn't want to start now. Just thinking about it made me feel like I was standing at the edge of a cliff. My stomach flipped. Back then, there had been nothing but free-falling and air beneath me. I'd told him all of my fears, my uncertainty about going into business, how I couldn't even pick up a book without feeling complete and total despair. I couldn't go back after that. I couldn't just be fun and flirty Isla who liked to mess with him anymore.

Suddenly, I'd become someone who had problems. An emotional burden. I didn't want to be that person. I didn't want him to feel obligated to offer me any kind of support. So I left.

"It was easier." That was the simplest way I could put it.

He nodded. "It's easier."

"We're kind of messed up, aren't we?"

"Yep." We finished our beer, and conversation moved on to lighter topics as we enjoyed each other's company in the tranquility of the backyard. As the sky began to darken, he stood and held out his hand out to help me up. "Thanks for texting me. I didn't really want to sit at Seb's by myself all night."

"Sure. No problem. Thanks for bringing dinner." My voice sounded normal, but there was nothing normal about what buzzed around inside me.

I was dazed and half drunk and not a little bit terrified. I didn't know if it was the way he looked at me or the feeling of his hand against mine or the sweet-scented garden, but I was suddenly overwhelmed with wanting him. To stay, to listen, to be someone I could lean on. All those things I'd been so close to having that Thanksgiving night and walked away from because of my own fear. He must've seen something in my expression, or maybe he felt it too, because he cupped my face and held me like I was made of spun sugar. So close to breaking. With aching gentleness he pressed his lips against my forehead.

And that cliff I'd stood at the edge of on Thanksgiving? I went and fell right off it.

CHAPTER FIFTEEN

As soon as we got back inside, I shoved Cade out the door. Which wasn't easy. The guy was huge. He wanted to stay, but that was absolutely out of the question. I couldn't have him here when my body was doing funny things, making me light-headed and breathless. My stomach felt like it was in my throat, and my heart was beating so fast, I could hear it knocking against my breastbone. There was something wrong with me. I needed to lie down.

After he left, I sagged against the door. My entire body unclenched in relief. The six, supposed to be five, cats and creepy dolls would actually be a welcome distraction. I pressed a hand to my chest, hoping this wasn't what I suspected. There was no way I was developing romantic feelings for Cade. Affection? Sure. Attraction? Yes. Annoyance? Always. But I didn't know what to do with whatever was going on inside me now. It couldn't be love. I'd been in love in before. It hadn't made me feel like I was dying.

Unless I'd never really been in love in the first place.

Nope. I would not even begin to entertain that train of thought. I flopped down on the couch and flung my arm over my eyes in true dramatic fashion. That forehead kiss hadn't been anything close to the kind of kissing we'd done on the party barge. It was soft and sweet. The kind of kiss meant to be a comfort between friends, the kind that said "I care about you." *Not* "I want to tear your clothes off." And yet, here I was. A complete and total mess.

None of this would've been happening if I hadn't seen Cade naked that day. I could've gone on pretending he was built like a Ken doll, with little more than a plastic thumbprint beneath his clothes. Just thinking about the Dropped Towel Incident caused my pulse to quicken. Before I could stop myself, I imagined his big hands running up my legs. The brush of his tongue against my clit. His fingers stroking me with the right amount of pressure. His cock stretching and filling me. My nipples tightened, and the second floor groaned above my head. I could only assume it was the nutcrackers assembling to cart me off to horny jail.

As the sky darkened and the streetlights outside lit up, the walls of the house began to press in on me. The dolls were overwhelming in the light of day but had become downright terrifying at night. Not to mention a sixth, unaccounted-for living creature in the basement. I couldn't stay here alone, but I couldn't call Cade either. Not after I'd pushed him out the door with good reason. I needed some time to sort myself out.

So instead, I texted Neeta. *What are you doing?*

Neeta: *Washing my hair*
Me: *Really? Or is that the thing you say when you don't want to be bothered?*

Neeta: *Really. If I didn't want to be bothered, I'd just tell you.*

Fair enough.

Me: *Do you want to come over? I'm a little freaked out right now.*
Neeta: *Is this about the guy you're not dating?*
Me: *No*

Thirty minutes later, Neeta stood in Jillian's living room, completely unfazed. "This woman is in desperate need of some decluttering and an introduction to eBay, but I'm not sure why this is freaking you out."

"You're not sure why this is freaking me out?" I said it slowly, as if I couldn't quite comprehend my own words. Was she messing with me? I turned the knob on Helga's head to make a point, but she only raised her eyebrows like I was the one having an inappropriate reaction. "How is this not the scariest house you've ever been in?"

"My aunt collects dolls. Not this many. No one collects this many. But they're just dolls."

"*Just* dolls?" Was she out of her mind? No one believed dolls were innocent little playthings. Not anymore. Even if their empty eyes and frozen smiles didn't make people's skin crawl, horror movies ruined whatever redemption they might've otherwise had. "Dolls haven't been "just dolls" since *Child's Play.*"

She gave me a blank stare. "I don't know what that is."

"Chuckie? With the red hair, overalls, and penchant for murder?" When she shook her head, my jaw dropped. "How does one manage to walk this earth for twenty-four years without hearing of *Child's Play*? It's the movie that made everyone want to burn their plastic babies and salt the ash pile."

She shrugged. "My parents didn't let me watch R-rated movies growing up, and I don't really like horror. It tries too hard."

Oh no. This would not do. The entire foundation of my being was built on the horror movies Seb, Cade, and I used to watch in the basement on Saturday nights. "I'm sorry, but I can't let that go. We're watching *Child's Play*."

"You want to watch the movie about murder dolls while you're sleeping in a house full of dolls?" She was giving me that "Why are you lying down in the library?" look. "What if this movie scares me away? Then who will protect you from imaginary boogeymen this week?"

"Something tells me you don't scare easy."

"Okay. We'll watch some horror. But don't expect me to be impressed."

I followed her into the kitchen, where she pulled a bag of popcorn out of her purse and stuck it in the microwave. I leaned against the counter next to the empty cookie jars. "Do you just carry popcorn around?"

"Yeah. Doesn't everyone?"

I had no response for that, so I said nothing at all. As soon as the microwave dinged, she pulled out the bag. A warm, buttery scent filled the kitchen. Maybe it wasn't a bad idea to keep a supply of popcorn on hand. She dumped the contents into a large glass bowl decorated with hand-painted teddy bears, and then we went back to the living room, where she logged into her Hulu account on Jillian's TV and loaded up the movie.

As predicted, Neeta rolled her eyes at most of the scary parts, while I watched from between my fingers. Even after all these years, that movie got to me. And though I'd probably end up regretting the decision to watch *Child's Play* at some point in the week, having Neeta here to tell me that my fears were ridiculous made them seem smaller and more manageable. If only that worked on my growing and discomforting feelings for Cade.

*   *   *

Neeta ended up staying with me for the next five days. She said she was doing it for my own good, but I had a suspicion she liked my company more than she'd ever admit. Maybe when vacation season ended, I'd talk to her about the possibility of getting an apartment together. The worst she could do was say no, and I'd be in the same position I was now.

I fed Jillian's cats in the morning on my last day and breathed a sigh of relief when only five pairs of eyes greeted me. She gave me the second half of my payment after work on Friday, and since I no longer owed Quinn and Vera back rent, I could keep the entire amount in my checking account as the start of my new apartment fund. She also sent me a text to remind me of the NDA. As if I could forget.

With my laundry stuffed into the back seat of my Corolla, I headed to Seb's condo after work. I hadn't spoken to Cade since he'd brought me tacos and kissed my forehead. I didn't even annoy him with the usual bombardment of memes I found on Twitter during the week. The longer I stayed away and stayed silent, the more my avoidance had started to take on a life of its own. It felt larger now. Even though I kept my distance so I could sort out my feelings, all I managed to do was stew in them. No resolution whatsoever.

When I opened the door to Seb's condo, Cade was still in his work clothes. He sat on the couch, with his tie unknotted and the sleeves on his shirt rolled up. And fuck me, he was wearing a pair of thin wire-framed glasses. It wasn't fair. He shouldn't have been allowed to sit there and be that hot. The fact that I didn't immediately crawl into his lap and sink my teeth into him should've earned me some kind of medal for restraint.

His jacket was slung over the back of the armchair, and he had a bunch of papers spread around on the coffee table. He didn't even glance up as I walked into the condo. Whatever he was doing, it must've been important, so I did my best to make as little noise as possible when opening the bifold doors to the laundry and dumping my dirty clothes in.

"You lived," he said.

The sound of his voice startled me, and I ended up spilling too much soap in the washer. I scooped some of it out and hoped it wouldn't overflow, then spun around to face him. He didn't look any different from the last time I'd seen him, but everything felt different. It couldn't have been all one-sided. I refused to believe I was the only one falling apart on the inside.

"Don't sound so surprised." I slammed the washer shut. "I've been in worse situations."

"I've never doubted your resourcefulness." He took off his glasses and stood. Glasses or no glasses, he was still hot. Damn it. "Do you have another job lined up for tonight? Or have you finally accepted that it isn't worth it?"

"My bank account says it's plenty worth it, thanks. I don't have another job tonight, but I'm actually going to stay at my parents' place. They've been bugging me to come to dinner for weeks now. Might as well get it over with."

I was not looking forward to answering questions about my promotion. Maybe if I made it sound as complicated as whatever

Seb did for a living, their eyes would glaze over, and they'd stop asking me about it. Worst-case scenario, they'd want a return invite to my new place, and since I didn't know where I'd be living in a few months, that would be a little trickier to navigate. But it's not like they made a ton of trips into the city. It would be fine.

"Sounds like fun," Cade said.

I hesitated for a moment while I debated if it would be weird to ask him to join me. Pre–Dropped Towel Incident, I would've asked him if he wanted to come along without question, so I didn't see why now should've been any different. "You know you always have a standing invite too, if you're not doing anything tonight."

"I have plans, but tell them I said hi. Or don't, since I suppose you can't really explain how you've seen me while Seb is out of town."

Plans? What plans? Oh God, did he have a date? If he had a date, I seriously hoped he didn't bring her back here. Not that I'd be here to witness it, but still, it felt like a shitty thing to do. Even when we'd both emphatically stated nothing would happen between us. Seb's condo should remain a date-free neutral zone. While Cade's plans could've just as easily included those papers he had spread over the coffee table, I would've rather hired Jillian as my personal decorator than ask him about it. No reason to give him any indication that I cared.

I cleared my throat and prayed my voice wouldn't betray me. "No problem. I'm assuming we'll have another event tomorrow? Do you want to prep me in advance, or do you want to keep springing the location on me last minute?"

"As much fun as I have throwing you off your guard, we're going to a brewery on a lake." He moved around the couch and leaned against the back of it, directly across from me. "Before you ask, yes, there will be fishing."

I crossed my arms. "I'm not sure why you're giving me that tone. I like fishing. In fact, I think I'm good enough to catch more fish than you."

He let out a laugh and rested his hands on the back of the couch. "Sure, Rainbow Bear. Never mind that two weeks ago you didn't even know what a reel was."

"Care to make a friendly wager?"

He raised an eyebrow. "What do I get if I win?"

I took a step toward him, then another one. His gaze darkened as I closed the space between us, yet he didn't move an inch. I stood on my toes and whispered in his ear. "If you win? You can have anything you want."

The couch groaned as he gripped it tight enough to leave indents in the wood frame.

I took a step back and gave him a cheeky smile. "Now I get why you have so much fun throwing me off my guard."

Without another word, I grabbed my Cucci purse and flounced out the door.

CHAPTER SIXTEEN

The drive over to my parents' house had been good for clearing my mind. Seeing Cade in his glasses had thrown me—not my fault—but I was proud of how quickly I'd rallied and kept myself in check. For some reason, I thought he'd mention that moment in Jillian's garden, though I didn't know why. What could he have said anyway? *Sorry you might be falling for me?* Probably best if we never talked about it at all.

As I turned into my parents' neighborhood, memories from my childhood assaulted me, and every single one of them included Cade. The three of us running up the sidewalk, chasing the ice-cream truck and paying in the nickels and dimes we'd dug out of the cup holder in my dad's truck. Zigzagging through the neighbor's yards, trying to hit as many of their sprinklers as possible. That one time we ran out in front of passing cars and tried to tell them it was a toll road, until my mom caught us and grounded all three of us, even Cade, to the house for a week. Two days later she let us go back outside because we were driving her nuts.

In all that time, in all those years, I'd never felt for Cade what I was feeling now. How could I go back? And if I could, would I even want to?

I parked my car next to my parents' curb. The browning grass, chain-link fence, and faded vinyl siding were all as familiar to me as my own face. It was good to be back. Promotion lie or not, I hadn't been coming over as often as I should've lately.

My mom stood just outside the front door, waiting for me. I hugged her, and my nose started to run. She made her love harder sometimes, but I couldn't deny there was a certain kind of comfort in a mom's hug that couldn't ever be replicated. "How's business?"

"It's going, same as ever." My mom had cut her hair short in the back, with spiky red layers in the front that flattered her pale skin and round face. She never had the same look for more than six months. As a hairdresser, she was a walking advertisement of her services, and she did her best to stay on top of trends. "Had a coloring this morning. I needed to bleach her hair first, so I'm still airing the house out."

I walked in the front door, and the scent hit me first. Chemicals and products from my mom's business wafting up from the basement. No matter how many Glade plugIns she used, the beauty salon smell never really went away. It was baked into the drywall.

Dusty photos of Seb and me, and even a few of Cade, lined the mint-green walls. The same baby photos from my childhood still hung in the hall, as if my parents never quite found the time or the energy to change them out. The lumpy tan couch, where I'd once covered Cade with a comforter and given him a teddy bear, still sat in the living room. A new table, decorated with Aunt Betty's ceramic dogs, sat behind it. It was comfort and stagnation mixed in one.

I hung my purse on the spindle of an oak dining room chair, and followed my mom into the kitchen. Spaghetti sauce bubbled in the pot on the crumb-stained stove. I closed my eyes and took a deep breath. Oregano, parsley, and a pinch of chili powder. God, I loved my mom's spaghetti. The best part of coming to their house for dinner was that she'd absolutely send me off with leftovers. I really needed to make a point to visit more often.

I peeked out the window to the shed. "Is Dad out back?"

"Yep. Messing with some project or another. I swear, the only thing that man likes more than tinkering around the house is bitching about how much he has to tinker around the house."

I smiled. My dad was a doer. He had to constantly be in motion, building something or fixing something. Maybe it was because he'd had to sit for so many hours driving his big rig up and down the state, but he'd never been able to just be still. Our backyard held the rotting remains of his many projects: Seb's treehouse, my playhouse, a sandbox, and a jungle gym with attached swings.

As I crossed the yard, I glanced next door. If I squinted, I could see the ghost of a little boy with startling but haunted blue eyes peeking between the bushes, the look of hunger etching lines into his too-young face. Meadow's moon-and-stars wind chime clinked and spun in the light summer breeze. I had a strong urge to march over there and rip it down and throw it through her back window. She'd probably offer me a serene smile and a honey-flavored edible, and send me on my way with a pat on the head. Nothing rattled Meadow, which some might've looked at as a virtue in a stressful world, but nothing much made her sit up and pay attention either. Least of all her son.

I followed the bangs and clanks coming from the storage shed–turned-workshop at the back of our property line. My dad had the doors open and Journey blasting from an old boombox he had propped up on a wooden bench. He had a bandana tied around his head, and his shoulder-length gray hair stuck to his neck. He wore a Carhartt T-shirt, and mud caked his work boots. After all my worry about his back, it was good to see him acting like he always had, even as I really wished he'd slow down and let his body heal.

A huge grin split his face the moment he saw me, and a rush of affection welled in my heart. "Hey, hey, look what the cat dragged in. Are you sure you're not too good for us now that you got yourself a big promotion?"

He said that like he genuinely hoped it. As if his biggest dream in life was for his kids to be too important to bother with him anymore. It broke my heart and made me angry at the same time, but I couldn't say anything because I was living a lie and the furthest thing he'd ever think of as "too good" by a mile.

"I'll always come to see you. Who else is going to take an interest in your projects?"

He scratched his chin. "Well ain't that truth. Your mother is going to change her grumbling once she gets a look at what I've put together for her, though."

I couldn't help but laugh. Mom hated his projects, but she had a special place of loathing in her heart for the projects he made for her. He once tried to build her a waiting room in the basement for her customers, but the couch he constructed fell apart in a heap of stuffing and wood when Mrs. Dorsett sat down with a little too much force. I could only guess the new table in the living room was the result of another project gone wrong. He occasionally got it right. Seb's treehouse had managed to stand the test of time, but more often than not we were left with a mess on our hands once he put down whatever he'd been working on while he was home, to sign up for a job that took him away for a week. It was no wonder my mom didn't have any energy left to change out the pictures in the hall.

I took a seat on the spinning stool. "What are you working on now?"

"A nail station for the basement. She's been talking about expanding to nails ever since you kids moved out, and well, with my health what it is these days, it might help." He pushed his hand into his lower back, almost reflexively. "Can't take as many shifts as I used to."

Every time I came back for a quick visit or the holidays, I always found it jarring how rapidly my parents had aged since the last time I'd seen them. They only lived thirty minutes outside the city, but there was always a reason why I couldn't come visit more often. My dad's hair had gone gray in his early forties, so I was used to that, but the leathery lines around his eyes, the stooped posture, and the loose skin around his jaw shocked me every time. How had my parents gotten so old when I still felt very much like a child?

"Is everything going to be okay with you taking some time off?" I asked.

The prospect of being out of work terrified me. I couldn't even take a sick day without losing the very small hold I'd gotten on my finances recently. Of course, it was a little different for my parents. They weren't saddled with student loan debt the size of a beach house mortgage, but they had different struggles.

It was give and take.

And by that, I meant those of us who didn't have anything to begin with kept giving, while those who had everything continued to take. The rich sold the rest of us the promise of a better life as a way of keeping us in line, like everything they had could eventually be ours too if we followed the rules they set for us, all while conveniently forgetting to mention the debt and poor wages that would forever hold us down.

My dad waved away my concerns. He couldn't stand it when we fussed over him, though I also suspected he secretly liked it. "I'll be fine. Just need to walk it off, that's all. My damn sciatica is acting up from too many years of sitting on my ass, but it's nothing you need to fret over."

"Yeah, well, try to take it easy. Don't put yourself out of commission for good by trying to do too much." Though giving my dad that kind of advice was pointless. It was in his nature to do too much. That hard work mentality would put him into an early grave one day, and I had no idea how to make him see things differently.

I took his arm as we went back inside and tried not to show any outward sign of worry about the slight limp to his gait. If I mentioned it, he'd likely try to do more to prove that he wasn't in rough shape after all. Inside, my mom sighed as she looked over my dad. She must've seen something in his tired expression, because she pushed him down in a chair and held his shoulders. Like she could physically force him to stay put for a minute.

"Don't you get up from this chair," she said. "Dinner will be ready in a minute. Isla, honey, can you give me a hand with the drinks?"

I followed my mom into the kitchen and whispered under my breath. "Is everything really okay with Dad? He was limping on the way in."

She shot an exasperated look toward the dining room. "He'd be better off if he stayed out of that godforsaken workshop and rested like the doctor told him to."

"I'm sitting right here," he hollered from the dining room.

I cringed as my mom yelled over my head, "I know. That's why I'm saying it." She shook her head. "Damn fool. Not like he'll listen to a word I say anyway."

I reached in the cupboard and pulled out the plastic souvenir cups we'd gotten from the county fair fifteen years ago. The logo was nothing more than a few blue and red spots after so many trips through the dishwasher. I set them on the table, pulled a two-liter of 7-Up out of the refrigerator, and filled everyone's cups. Then I dumped a bag of mixed greens in a bowl and shook some croutons on top and brought it to the table. Mom already had the spaghetti and bread sitting on oven mitts, ready to go. I took a seat and filled my plate, happy to have a home-cooked meal someone else had prepared for once.

After I'd taken a few bites, I set my fork down and reached for another breadstick. "Dad says you're thinking about adding a place to do nails in the basement?"

"No, I'm not." She shook her fork at him. "So you can forget about building me that desk you keep going on about. I haven't done nails in years, and I don't have the supplies for it. Build that birdhouse Meadow Greenley wants for her tranquil garden instead." She used air quotes around *tranquil garden*, something she did when she wanted to emphasize the truly ridiculous.

At the mention of Cade's mom, my elbow slipped off the table, but I righted myself with the cool efficiency of someone used to being the most awkward person in the room. My mom had a tenuous relationship with Meadow. At best, she could stand five minutes of tight-lipped conversation across the bushes separating our property, before making an excuse to leave. Most of the time, my mom avoided Meadow all together, and I figured she would even more so now that she no longer needed to yell at her to take care of her son.

"Why would Dad build Meadow a birdhouse?" Or do anything for her. She was not a family friend. She wasn't even a family acquaintance.

"It keeps him busy, and it's a neighborly thing to do."

"What your mom is trying to say is, it keeps me from messing with too much stuff around our house." My dad gave me a wink.

"Since when do either of you care about being neighborly to Meadow?"

They looked at each other and did that silent communication thing that two people who had been married forever could do.

"She's been coming around for dinner for a few months now," my mom said.

"What?" It pissed me off to no end that they'd make nice with the woman who had made Cade's childhood a living hell. "Does Cade know?"

He didn't visit, but he still called her once a month. She must not have told him, though, because he would've said something to Seb.

"We didn't think it was worth mentioning to your brother." My dad scratched his back and took a swallow of 7-Up, more, I suspected, to get out of having to talk than out of thirst.

"Meadow's a mess, always has been, but now that she's getting older, she's calmed down some. And she's lonely," my mom said. "I don't think she has any friends, her husband is dead, and Cade doesn't go around to her house anymore."

"Do you blame him?" How could they let her sit at the same table where he'd had to sit because he wouldn't have gotten to eat otherwise. "And what about all your talk about people pulling themselves up by their bootstraps and helping themselves and whatever. Why can't she help herself with her loneliness?"

"Inviting a neighbor to dinner who doesn't have anyone else isn't the same as paying money out of our pockets so people who don't want to work can live off the system."

"If the basic needs of people can't be met because it's more important for a stock to go up an eighth of a percent than it is to feed someone who is hungry, then the system is broken." I threw my napkin on top of my plate. "Burn it the fuck down."

My dad excused himself, mumbling something about needing a tool from his workshop. He didn't do confrontations. It hurt my heart to see him struggling with the stairs at the back of the house. He'd spent his entire life defending the very system that was turning him into an old man in his fifties, and he'd still defend it when it shoved him out the door after his body gave up and he was no longer of any use. I'd never understand it.

"Isla." My mom laid a hand on my arm, and I snatched it away. "You don't care a lick about Meadow Greenley, so what's this really about?"

"It's about all this." I swept my hands around the room. "It's about you and Dad always making comments about freeloaders and living off the system. Do you even hear yourselves?"

"Oh, I get it." My mom settled back in her chair. "You go get yourself a fancy degree at a school where they tell you the generation before ruined your life, but don't worry, you'll be the ones to fix all the world's problems."

"No, I didn't learn that in school." I learned it from trying to survive, when I started adulthood with more debt than every single previous generation accrued in their lifetime. Combined.

"How could you say all those things in front of Cade when we were growing up? How do you think that made him feel?"

My mom huffed. "Don't be ridiculous. Cade isn't like those people."

Except he was. He was exactly like the people my parents talked about. People who struggled through no fault of their own. People who were up against systemic barriers that denied them entry before they were even born. Or people like me, who had stumbled, but were trying their damnedest to get back up. "The only difference is that you know him."

"That's not true." She stood and began clearing plates from the table, her spine stiff and her expression pinched. "I'm not sure what's gotten into you, but I'm sorry that whatever it is has made you feel like your dad and I are such horrible people."

I buried my face in my hands. Hurting my mom hadn't been on my itinerary for the evening, but I wasn't sorry. It was long past time for me to speak up.

"I'm going to go." Staying here would be unpleasant for all of us, and my dad would probably end up sleeping in the shed if it meant avoiding another confrontation.

"I think that would be best." My mom wouldn't meet my eyes.

She hadn't officially kicked me out, but it was clear she didn't want me to stay any more than I wanted to be here. My parents needed some time to cool down and maybe discuss some of the things I'd said. Which likely wouldn't sink in or change their minds, but maybe they'd think twice before making any disparaging comments in the future.

At least I could hope.

CHAPTER SEVENTEEN

My mom handed me a Tupperware full of spaghetti as I headed out her door, because even when she was mad, she'd make sure I was fed. It was her love language. On the way back to Seb's condo, I'd gotten a new house-sitting request through my website. Tempting, since I hadn't booked a Cornerstone or Torres-Glasser executive yet this week, but after some internal back and forth, I deleted the email. There were too many risks in house-sitting for strangers.

Since I hadn't crashed at my parents' house as planned, I was presented with a whole new dilemma once I arrived back at my brother's condo: Cade's plans for the evening. He hadn't been specific, but it must've been a date. Otherwise, why wouldn't he just say he was working or catching a game with some friends or rescuing orphans from a burning building? But instead he said he had plans and provided no elaboration. Probably because my stupid feelings had been written all over my face in Jillian's garden and he was still trying to find a way to let me down easy. Because I was important to him. Cue vomit.

I stood in Seb's hall and pressed my ear against the door. If I heard any suspicious noises, I'd immediately turn around and spend the night under my desk, and I didn't give a damn what I promised Cade. Getting fired would've been preferrable to walking in on him in a hot and heavy makeout session with someone who wasn't me.

When five minutes had passed and I'd been met with silence, I decided to risk it. A dark and empty condo greeted me. I supposed I should've been thankful, but it was hard to muster up any sort of gratitude that they'd decided to take things back to her house. Either way, Cade was probably out with someone and I still hated it, even when I didn't have to witness it.

I put the spaghetti in the refrigerator, then put on a movie I had no intention of watching while I stewed in the hurt I had no business feeling. He didn't know I'd had a fight with my mom, and it wasn't his job to comfort me anyway. It didn't stop me from wishing he was here to tease me out of my sour mood though. The night ticked on and he still hadn't returned. I started checking my phone every two minutes for missed texts, but nothing.

Sometime around midnight, I'd become fully sick of myself and shut off the TV. I changed into my sleep shirt, which happened to be one of the T-shirts that used to belong to Cade, which made me feel worse. But it was an old comfort and I wasn't going to take it off just because I was upset with the original owner.

Since he wasn't going to be here tonight, I saw no reason for me to sleep on the couch. Not when there was a perfectly good, unoccupied guest room up for grabs. That should've been my bed the whole time anyway.

I crawled under the covers and tried to sleep, but I felt impossibly small in this space that had become accustomed to a much larger body, and Cade's scent was everywhere. It enveloped me and wound around my heart, squeezing the life out of it. Though I must've drifted off at some point, because I woke as I rolled into a dip in the mattress. The motion startled me, and Cade's hands caught me around my waist, stopping me from colliding into him. He placed his lips near the shell of my ear and I forgot how to breathe, let alone move.

"Hey there, Rainbow Bear." His soft, nighttime voice was a gentle caress down the length of my body. "I didn't think you'd be back tonight. I'll sleep in the living room."

"No. Don't." I grasped the front of his shirt and pulled him toward me. While I could've blamed my sleep-addled brain for the reason behind my clinginess, the simple truth was I wanted him here with me. "Please. Just . . . I just need someone to hold me tonight."

He hesitated and I inhaled, holding it, as he hovered over his indecision. After a beat, he sank down onto the mattress. I exhaled. As he wrapped his warm, strong arms around me, I melted into his embrace. His thumb swept across my stomach, right beneath my breast. The thin material of his old T-shirt was the only thing that stood between us. My nipples hardened as a damp heat pulsed between my legs. I shifted against him, and he tightened his hold on me. Though I was having a really hard time forming coherent thoughts, a nagging sensation tickled the back of my mind. Like I'd forgotten to turn off the stove or something else of importance.

Oh. Right. "Did you have a nice time on your date?"

His thumb stilled and he leaned up on his elbow. "I wasn't on a date."

"Then where were you?" *Who's the neediest girl in the neighborhood?*

"Contractors wanted me to check on the progress. Got distracted doing stuff at my place and fell asleep on the couch." He paused. "But it's nice to know I was missed."

I didn't know how to respond without completely giving myself away. Could he see the relief rushing through me anyway? Probably. I closed my eyes, afraid of what else I'd reveal. His lips brushed my temple, then he tucked me against him and went to sleep.

* * *

The next morning, I woke up alone, looking like I'd lost a fight with the pillows. I had always been a fitful sleeper, spreading out and taking up all the space I could manage. As a result, my hair hung in limp tangles, the makeup I'd forgotten to take off the night before was caked under my eyes, and my sleep shirt was a twisted knot around my waist.

I got up and crept into the hall. When I didn't see any sign of Cade, I rushed to the bathroom, where I quickly brushed my teeth, washed away the dry mascara, and brushed my hair. I'd just snuck back into bed and clamped my eyes shut as the front door opened.

"I got coffee," Cade said. "And tea because I know you hate coffee. Are you still asleep?" His footfalls stopped abruptly at the guest-room threshold.

He started laughing, which annoyed me enough to forget I'd been fake sleeping. I sat up with a frown. "What's so funny?"

"You. Thinking you need to do the 'sneak out of bed and freshen up' routine." He walked over and handed me the tea.

"Like I haven't already seen you dozens of times with old makeup crusted to your eyes and a drool line on your chin."

I set the tea on the nightstand and got on my knees. Balancing myself on the mattress, I shoved him back a step. "Don't you have a disgusting coffee to go drink?"

"Isn't that my shirt you're sleeping in?"

"It is." I stood and stretched my arms over my head, which revealed just a hint of my pink polka-dot thong. He stared at me, holding himself eerily still as I sidled up next to him. I swiped my thumb under his bottom lip with a smirk. "Who's got the drool line now?"

"I'm going out." He turned on his heel and walked out of the room. "I'll be back at five to pick you up. Don't forget, we're going to a local brewery on the lake."

The front door slammed shut.

Smiling, I headed out to the kitchen to finish my tea. He'd left his coffee behind on the counter. Looked like someone was in a hurry. I stuck it in the refrigerator and pulled out my mom's spaghetti, eating it cold, directly from the container.

Without any pressing obligations on my plate, I spent most of the morning lazing around my brother's condo, happy to have a break from the task of keeping things alive for a day. Jillian sent me a text to ask if I knew anything about an orange tabby in her basement, which I literally did not. How many stray cats did she have in her home? I texted her back to deny any knowledge of an extra cat and to ask for house-sitting referrals. I was left on read. That was the thanks I got for adhering to the terms of the NDA. Not that I would've gossiped about her to the people I never talked to at work anyway.

By midmorning I'd taken a shower, shaved all the important bits, and changed into the strapless lavender maxi dress I'd bought for spring break my sophomore year. I paired it with gold sandals and a collection of golden bangles that clinked together on my right arm. I kept my hair down, letting it fall halfway down my back.

I stepped out for a minute to return the books Neeta had recommended, but she wasn't working. I sent her a quick text to show her I'd grabbed *All the Lonely People* by Jen Marie Hawkins, and she sent a thumbs-up emoji. When I got back to the condo, Cade was waiting for me. Although he looked good in his dark gray dress pants and light blue shirt with the sleeves rolled up, he never wore jeans or cargo shorts to these events. Everyone else did, including Ted and Anton. It was like he'd banned anything that might come off as fun.

"You look good." His gaze swept over me.

"Thanks." I patted his chest. "You look stuffy. Why are you dressed like you're headed to a boardroom rather than a brewery? You know everyone else is going to be way more casual."

"I have a certain image to project as a sales manager."

"At the last event, the CEO of your company wore a T-shirt with a picture of a dachshund that said 'Ask me about my wiener.' What image are you responsible for exactly?"

"They can dress like that *because* they are CEOs."

"If you say so."

Ted and Anton wanted Cade to loosen up a little, but that wasn't something I could share. Not unless I also told him about the conversation I'd had with Penny at the island cookout. He should've picked up on that on his own, though, since every Torres-Glasser function had such a party atmosphere. It was too bad Cade couldn't enjoy it a little more.

He tossed his keys between his hands. "Ready?"

"As I'll ever be."

We took the elevator down to the parking garage and got in his Jeep, where he immediately turned on the heated seat for me. I'd been to Rocky Pointe Brewery on a few dates, so I was familiar with the location, but as soon as Cade pulled out to the street, he drove in the opposite direction. Maybe he had an errand to run first.

My stomach dropped when he pulled into the parking lot of the Red Lobster I'd been banned from a month ago. The scene of the incident I swore I'd take to my grave. And what I suspected had been the final straw in my living arrangement with Quinn and Vera.

I knotted my fingers until the knuckles turned white. "What are we doing here?"

"There's no dinner planned for tonight at the brewery, so I'm fulfilling my obligation to feed you." He opened the door to his Jeep. The overhead lights flipped on, and the key in ignition alarm dinged a warning that rattled around in my head.

"Does it have to be Red Lobster, though?" I tried to swallow, but my throat felt like sandpaper. "I mean, I haven't been fucked good recently. Would Beyoncé approve?"

He shut his door and the alarm mercifully stopped dinging. "What's going on?"

Restaurants tended to have a pretty high turnover rate, at least the ten different restaurants that employed me in college had, but not high enough to have a whole new staff in two months. I kept my gaze on my lap. "I can't go in there."

"Why?" His body rustled against his leather seat as he turned toward me. "And don't try to tell me it's because you

165

don't like seafood. I once saw you take down five plates of coconut shrimp at a buffet. I'm still not sure whether I should be impressed or horrified."

"No, I do like seafood." I loved it. But it was so damn expensive. Even the artificial crabmeat that was made out of random fish guts cost more than I could justify spending. "I'm not actually allowed to go in that Red Lobster. Any Red Lobster really, but I don't think the rest of them are going to be checking up on me."

His eyebrows practically touched his hairline as his eyes widened. "What did you do?"

Oh God. Of course he was going to ask me that. Once I told him, it would be out there, and he'd know just how far I'd fallen. Shame heated my cheeks. "I need to preface this story by saying I'd been having a difficult time for a few months."

An understatement. The few hundred dollars I'd managed to put away in savings before my student loans kicked in had run out within a month. I'd been shopping exclusively off the deep discount rack tucked into the mildew-ridden corner of the grocery store. The minimum payment on my credit card had ballooned when I maxed it out having the transmission on my Corolla fixed. I was working forty-five hours a week for nothing. One day, I just snapped.

"It started when I was driving home from work. I was hungry, and the thought of heating up another bowl of ramen made me want to vomit."

He shuddered. "To this day I can't smell ramen without getting sick."

"Same, except I still have to eat it." Not since I'd started house-sitting, but once vacation season ended, my access to decent food would be over. "Anyway, I don't know what came over me, but my brain just shut off. I didn't think, at all, I just pulled into the parking lot, went inside, and ordered the Ultimate Feast."

I barely got that part of the story out, when all my words backed up inside me. Why was I telling him this? What would he think? Panic seized my heart, causing it to beat so loud against my eardrums, I couldn't think. I couldn't speak. I could only feel constant, burning shame.

"I get that." The tone of his voice had me meeting his eyes for the first time since he'd parked. It wasn't something he was saying to placate me. He really did get it. "My mom once gave me ten dollars for lunch money. She never did that. It was more money than I'd ever held in my life, and it meant I'd be able to pick between the A and B lunches for the first time that week without just being given the free option. But then I went over to the gas station with Seb, and they were selling these giant balls with soft rubber strings all over them."

"I remember those." I'd never had one, but some of the kids at school had.

"I spent the entire ten dollars. It wasn't even something I wanted. I blanked out and bought it. Like it was something I had to get, for once in my life, just because I could."

"What did you do with it?" I couldn't remember ever seeing Cade with a ball like that growing up. I would've remembered because he hardly ever had toys of his own. Most everything he'd played with had belonged to Seb.

"I threw it out. After Mrs. Brisbane, the old lady who lived behind us, saw me playing with it in my backyard. She said if my mom could afford to buy me new toys, maybe she'd stop making the Janes feed me all the time."

"That bitch." I was suddenly very glad I'd tried to scam her with her own flowers.

"Yeah, well." He reached across the console and unknotted my fingers. "If you're ashamed of whatever you did inside that Red Lobster, I can promise you I've done worse."

I lifted one of my hands and cupped his cheek, running my palm over his prickly stubble, and he relaxed into my touch. He didn't have to share that story with me. Reliving that memory had likely been hard and embarrassing for him, but he'd done it anyway. Because I needed to hear it.

"Okay." I withdrew my hand from his face reluctantly, not quite wanting to let go of the warmth that radiated from him. "After the waiter brought the bill, I lost it. I owed over forty dollars. That was more than my weekly grocery budget, and I hadn't even tipped yet. So I pulled out my own hair, swirled it around on my plate, and tried to have the bill comped."

His lips twitched, and an amused smile threatened to break through, which oddly enough made me feel better about the whole thing. "I take it your efforts were not rewarded?"

"No, the manager had seen me do it. He said he'd file charges if I tried to run, then stood next to me as I paid the cashier, while the whole restaurant full of people watched. He wasn't quiet about why he was guarding me either. Then he escorted me out, letting me know that I'd been caught on camera and I was no longer welcome at any Red Lobster."

Quinn had found the receipt in the trash and freaked out, demanding to know how I could afford Red Lobster, but not rent. I didn't have an answer. Every time I tried to explain what had happened, I couldn't get my thoughts together enough to push the words out. I couldn't even make it make sense to myself, let alone Quinn. So I stood there in silence while she screamed at me until her face turned purple. Vera came home soon after and started in on me too. A few days later, I found my boxes on the street.

"Fuck them." He started his Jeep and backed out. "Let's go over to the Italian place across the street and order one of everything on the menu, then tip fifty percent."

The bite in Cade's voice brought me out of my rock-bottom memories. I let out a startled laugh at his suggestion. "Can we make it a *Pretty Woman* moment and bring our receipt over here and tell them kicking me out was a big mistake?"

"Absolutely." He squeezed my hand and peeled out of the parking lot.

CHAPTER EIGHTEEN

We had stuffed ourselves on pasta to the point of oblivion. The waiter brought us a whole basket of breadsticks to take home, and Cade made good on his word by tipping fifty percent. He'd also been serious about bringing our receipt back to Red Lobster, but as much as I appreciated his allegiance, I had to pass. The poor college student manning the hostess stand had nothing to do with my humiliation. It was just one of those things that I had to live with having done, but knowing Cade didn't look down on me helped.

We headed over to Rocky Pointe Brewery, where Ted and Anton had rented out the whole bar for the evening's event. The back deck extended twenty feet from the building, with a long pier stretching out over the water. Waves crashed against slick boulders visible through the slats in the wood planking. Torres-Glasser employees gathered at round iron tables and passed around growlers filled with pale ale that had names like Wheat, Bitch and Bend Me Over Bitters. The reason why so many of my Tinder dates wanted to meet up here really went without saying.

Ted and Anton's interest in this location was all about the fishing, though. Rocky Pointe's pier was dotted with barrels of water branded with their logo. At the end sat a second bar inside a small wooden hut. They advertised themselves as the city's only fishing bar. Naturally they partnered with Torres-Glasser and had their equipment available to rent, as well as a kitchen where you could pay to have your catches grilled or deep-fried with all the fixings.

Cade passed on the beer in favor of bottled water, like he always did, and I followed suit out of respect for the way he preferred to do things. The sky was streaked with orange and pink, and a Rocky Pointe employee set about lighting the citronella tiki torches spread out along the pier. Cade placed his hand on the small of my back as we walked around to say our hellos. Just the tips of his fingers were enough to cause pinpricks of awareness to dance along my skin.

"There you are." Anton shook Cade's hand and then pulled me into a hug like I was an old family friend rather than the girlfriend of an employee he'd only met twice before. And damned if I didn't feel a warm sense of belonging in return. "I'm glad to see you're feeling better. Penny mentioned you might've had a bit of sunstroke at the last outing?"

"Oh, ha. Yeah." I'd completely forgotten about my sudden sickness, that coincidently occurred right when she'd revealed they'd stopped their employees from trying to set up Cade on dates, making my presence at these things unnecessary. "I'm doing much better. Just needed some water and shade."

"Glad to hear it. It would've been a shame if you had to miss all the fun tonight. We have these new electronic lures, very lifelike, that send out pulses of energy to draw fish in."

Ted put a hand on his husband's shoulder, rubbing his thumb over the rise of his neck in an unconscious gesture of affection. "You'll get to brag to all your friends that you got to try this one out before it hit the market."

All my friends were Neeta, and I had a feeling she would be less impressed by my early access pass to the latest in fishing lure technology than she had been by *Child's Play*. But I couldn't say that to Cade's bosses. "I'm looking forward to trying it out."

Cade pressed his lips to my temple, and I sucked in a quick breath. Quiet enough to be undetected by everyone except him. His fingers contracted against my back. "I'm going to go get us some poles. Think you can stay out of trouble for a few minutes while I'm gone?"

"Who, me?" I gave him a wry smile. "I'm the picture of innocence."

He let out a bark of laughter, which he quickly masked as a short cough when he glanced at Ted and Anton. The stern corporate exterior replaced the light that had been in his eyes. With a curt nod, he excused himself and headed inside.

Anton whispered something to Ted, who nodded in return. Then he threaded his arm through mine, pulling me to the opposite side of the open deck. "There's some people I'd like to introduce you to who weren't at the last few events."

Torres-Glasser Bass Fishing employed a lot of people. Not surprising, since they were the fourth-largest manufacturer of fishing equipment, which I was beginning to understand was a very big deal. The surprising thing was that Anton knew every single employee's name and at least one fact about their personal lives. My direct boss still thought my name was Elsa. The people who worked at Torres-Glasser were treated like people, however, and it showed. Everyone was loose and relaxed. Small groups waved Anton over and tried to keep him in their conversation bubbles. Not to kiss ass, but because they genuinely enjoyed his company. He made everyone around him feel important and included, even me.

Anton nudged me and pointed to where Cade was standing with Penny. He wore an amused expression while she waved her hands enthusiastically as she told him some story. "He never used to smile at these events, or laugh, or even stay very long."

"Cade is more of a . . ." I twirled my wrist, searching for a term that wouldn't make him seem like a moody loner to his sociable boss. "He's more of an introvert."

Which was the truth. Cade preferred the company of as few people as possible. Even when we were younger, he hadn't gone to the bonfires and parties and road trips if he could help it. On those rare occasions my extrovert brother could drag him out, Cade sat in the corner like a surly specter who had been conjured specifically to be the ruiner of fun.

A lot of girls at school ate it up because he also had the benefit of being hot. A potent combination. But it wasn't because he was cursed to walk the earth alone, thinking his deep thoughts while being pensively sexy. He was just a homebody with trust issues.

"He's different around you," Anton said with a secret smile. Little did he know, this was all pretend, and Cade was only different around me because I knew how to exasperate him like no one else. "I'm really glad you're here. Don't get me wrong: he's a great sales manager, good with clients, level-headed and fair. But it helps with the overall morale when the managers at least act like they like spending time with their teams."

"Is that why you were always pushing Penny on him?" At Anton's blank look, I stopped and reevaluated what I'd just said, giving myself a mental ass kicking. "Not that he said anything like that; he just mentioned she got paired up with him a lot at games and stuff."

To my shock, Anton let out a cackling laugh. "Perhaps we came on a little too strong. Sorry." He wiped his eyes. "Yes. Penny is our social director for a reason. We had hoped it would help if the employees saw him interacting and having a good time at these events, even though he wasn't obligated to attend in the first place. I probably shouldn't be telling you this. You wouldn't believe how often I get yelled at by our head of HR on a weekly basis."

"Oh, I can imagine." I couldn't help but find Anton's sheepish expression anything other than endearing. He must've been able to get away with whatever he wanted as a little boy.

I glanced at Cade, who was now frowning. Oh no. A sick sense of dread trickled down my spine. If they were discussing what Penny told me at the last event, it would not end well for me. As if he could feel me watching him, he caught my gaze. His eyes narrowed, and he gave me a toothy grin that reminded me of the time he found me hiding in my backyard treehouse, eating the cookies Seb had just gotten grounded for after swiping them from the cupboard. A look that told me I was not only busted, but he absolutely intended to make me squirm.

Instinctively, I hid behind Anton like a proper chicken. If Cade couldn't see me anymore, he couldn't be mad. Simple physics.

Oblivious to the tension crackling in the air, Anton took my arm and led me toward the pier. "Let me stick to a safer topic and show you how the new lures work."

"Excuse me, I don't mean to interrupt." A man in his late forties, with a thick mustache and a candy-floss combover, stepped in front of us and offered me his hand. "Pierce Roding-ton, head of distribution for the Midwest region."

Pierce Rodington who worked for a manufacturer of fishing equipment. That couldn't be real. "Is that your stage name?"

He glanced at Anton, humor crinkling the skin around his eyes, as if this was an old joke around the office. "A happy coincidence. Anyway, Sam tells me you're a house sitter. I know this is short notice, but the kennel I use for my dogs closed due to sickness, and I'm in a bind. Would you be free for the coming week starting tomorrow?"

I stood up a little straighter. This was exactly what I needed. An escape from Cade and whatever retribution he had in store. And that whole thing about making money to put away toward a place to live would be good too. "I am, and I'd be happy to offer my services."

We exchanged numbers, and with a spring in my step, I followed Anton out to the pier. He set me up with their top-of-the-line rod, and didn't so much as smirk when I jumped in the air as I cast, throwing my whole body into the action. Every time a little plunk hit the water, I wanted to squeal in delight. Who knew fishing could be this much fun? I got so caught up in testing out the new lure and learning how to fish without hurting myself, that an hour passed before I began to worry about Cade again.

As I continued to reel in an impressive number of catches for a non-fisher using state-of-the-art equipment, Anton entertained me with stories of his early days with Ted. Back when they were Torres-Hernández *and* Glasser Bass Fishing. They started their business because the company they previously worked for sounded a lot like the Cornerstone of the fishing world, and they figured they could build something better on their own. It took a lot of guts to leave a guaranteed income behind, and it made me admire them that much more. They'd also been ridiculously into each other the entire time, but neither of them wanted to risk the business relationship by making the first move, so they quietly pined for years. After the sun fully set and the crickets came out, Anton excused himself when his head of quality control waved him over. Half the employees had already left. I set my pole aside and turned right into Cade's chest.

I bounced off the hard wall of muscle and wrinkled my nose as I looked up at him. "How long have you been standing there?"

"Not long." He tucked a strand of hair behind my ear. "Miss me?"

"Pssh, hardly." He was acting too normal. Obviously, he was plotting something. I just needed to play it cool until I figured out what he had up his sleeve. "I was busy catching fish. As in plural." I pointed at my Rocky Pointe barrel, where four little babies swam around each other. "I named them Rose, Blanche, Dorothy, and Sophia. They're my new girl gang. Which means I have no choice but to let them go."

"Of course you named them." He slung his arm around my shoulders. "You ready to go?"

"Sure." This wasn't my employer's event, so whether I wanted to stay or go shouldn't have mattered. I lifted the barrel over the side of the pier and said a quiet goodbye to my Golden Girls as I set them free. Then I fell in step beside Cade. As we walked up the pier, I wrung my hands together and worked up the courage to ask about his conversation with Penny. It was better to get this over with. Where there were witnesses. "I saw you talking to Penny earlier."

"Yep." He tucked his hands in his pockets and strolled all casual-like beside me.

"Cool." I choked a little on that word. "Sweet girl, that Penny."

"She seems to think the same about you." The gleam in his eye was reminiscent of the coyote right before he set a trap for the roadrunner. "As a matter of fact, she told me about an interesting discussion the two of you had last weekend."

"Really?" It had suddenly gotten very warm on this windy pier. "I chatted with a lot of people last weekend, so it's a little hard to recall."

"Mm-hmm." He took my hand. "Let's go, liar. We'll talk at the condo."

"Do we really need to talk?" I tried to dig in my heels, but he continued walking, so I had no choice but to keep up. "Wouldn't you rather watch a movie? Or do a puzzle? Hey, you know what? I've always wanted to build one of those ships in a bottle."

He ignored me.

When we got out to the parking lot, he opened the passenger door. He didn't say a single word, but I could feel the tension building like a small colony of bees constructing a hive at the base of my skull. He didn't turn on the radio. He did turn on the heated seat, but I suspected that was more from habit than anything else. I wiggled around, which caused the leather to make weird sounds. Then I kept wiggling because I wanted to make extra sure he knew it was the leather, and not me, making weird sounds. The drive back to Seb's condo was awkward. We didn't talk at all. And aside from looking over at me once with that damned raised eyebrow, he gave no other indication of what was going through his mind.

As soon as we got upstairs, I kicked off my sandals and leaned against the wall. "So. We're here. What did you want to talk about?"

He leaned against the couch directly opposite me, with his arms crossed over his broad chest. "It turns out, no one at work thinks Penny and I were hooking up. My coworkers stopped trying to set me up because Ted and Anton told them to back off."

"Huh. Interesting." I was ninety-nine percent sure he could see how fast my pulse was beating. "That's a good thing, right?"

"It is." He rubbed his jaw. "You knew."

I looked up, tilting my head to the side. "She might've mentioned it."

He approached and planted a hand on the wall, but kept just enough distance to avoid touching me. I squeezed my thighs together. The intensity in his eyes burned hot enough to melt me on the spot. "And you didn't think that was information worth passing along?"

"I did not." I bit my lip.

"Why?" That one word kissed my skin, sending warm flutters down my spine, over my breasts, tightening my nipples. I'd never wanted someone so bad in my life.

"Because I liked the way pretending to be your girlfriend made me feel."

"How did it make you feel?" His voice was barely above a whisper.

I placed my hand over his heart, feeling the steady beat before I wrapped an arm around him and pressed my body flush against his. "So good."

He closed his eyes and exhaled. I reached up to rub my fingertip over the seam of his lips. He took my finger into his mouth, gently sucking as he swirled his tongue. Taking my hand, he turned it over, and brushed his lips against my palm. The sensation spread goose bumps up my arm. We held each other's gaze for a moment, a second, a lifetime.

And then he kissed me.

CHAPTER NINETEEN

Cade kissed slow and deep, like he wanted to memorize the feel and taste of me. His tongue swept over mine in languid strokes. It wasn't the frenzied "I'm going to swallow your face" type of kissing from the party barge. This was soft music and candle-light kissing. "I've been waiting my whole life to be with you, and I'm damn well going to savor it" kissing. It was the type of kissing that didn't need to be rushed because we never planned for it to end anyway.

I clung to the back of his neck, wanting, yet so scared he'd stop. He had one hand on my hip, holding me tightly against him, while the other cupped my face. His fingers skimmed the curve of my neck. With the lightest touch, he held me still while he took his time. His tongue became a patient lover, learning what I liked and adjusting to my responses. It was as if he needed to study the exact feel of my mouth. I whimpered and he smiled against my lips.

He pulled back, holding my face as he stared into my eyes. His gaze burned into mine. I still had all my clothes on, but I felt naked in a new and terrifying way. As if I had stripped down to my very soul and spread it open before him.

My legs trembled and my stomach quivered. The hot rush of fear welled up inside me and logged itself firmly in my throat. I needed him. Wholly. Impossibly. Completely. In a way I'd never needed or wanted anyone. He could've asked anything of me in that moment, and I would've given it to him without reservation. The guy who had always been Seb's best friend. The one who had pushed me away only a few short weeks ago.

I laid my palms against his chest. "You know I'm Isla, right?"

He chuckled lightly as he skimmed his hand up and down my side. "I hope so, or I'm having one hell of a hallucination."

"No, I mean, you're not going to suddenly remember who I am and who you are, and who we've always been, and pull away from me, are you? Because I have to be honest here. If I don't end this night with you inside me, it might literally kill me."

"It's just you and me here, and I'm not pulling away." He brushed his thumb over my lower lip. "Not tonight."

His mouth covered mine, and all the fear left my body as a warm liquid haze swept through me. Somewhere in the back of my mind my consciousness was screaming out a reminder that I was kissing Cade Greenley. As if I should've been in shock. But it didn't feel unbelievable on any level. In fact, kissing Cade felt natural. Instinctual. Like I should've been spending the whole of my life doing this and only this.

My fingers shook as I reached up and undid the buttons on his shirt. I parted the cloth, running my hands over the hard muscle, up to his shoulders. He undid the cuffs, and I pushed it down his arms and to the floor. My mouth went dry as my eyes roamed over his chest and stomach, wanting to sink my teeth into every inch.

"If you look at me like that when you've got your hand wrapped around my cock, I'm not going to last more than a few seconds." The gruffness in his tone turned my insides to liquid.

"How embarrassing for you." I trailed my fingers down his abs.

He groaned. "You're going to be the death of me."

He claimed my lips, taking me with more urgency, stroking my tongue harder and faster. My core pulsed as I pressed against him, but my maxi dress had way too much material, and it was all in the way. I yanked down the straps and the dress pooled at my feet.

His fingers caressed my collarbone and trailed down my chest. "I was going to do that."

"You were taking too long."

His eyes darkened as he took in my purple strapless bra and neon-green thong. If I'd known I was going to get naked tonight, I might've attempted to color coordinate. Though I doubted Cade would've noticed, or even cared, by the way he looked at me now. He hoisted me up, and I wrapped my legs around his waist as he backed me into the wall. He kissed my neck, and the scruff along his jaw left behind a pleasant burn.

I reached behind me to unhook my bra, letting it join my dress on the floor. My entire body strained toward him, hungry for any kind of friction anywhere. "Please."

He eyes met mine. "Please, what? What do you want me to do to you, Isla?"

I didn't think—I just let myself feel. "I want to feel your tongue and teeth on my breasts."

He ground his cock against my center as his lips brushed against my ear. "I love it when you tell me exactly what you want. Keep doing it."

He took my nipple in his mouth, swirling his tongue around the areola before sucking the pebbled tip into his mouth. His teeth lightly scraped over me, followed by a gentle caress of his tongue. My back arched as the sensation shot straight through my core. He did the same with the other nipple, and all my nerve endings sizzled and focused in on a singular point.

His hips moved in a circle against me, the pressure building to a breaking point. My breath came out in short little gasps. "Like that. Right there. Don't stop."

"Is this what you want?" His voice held a low growl. "Tell me."

"I want to come." I gripped his shoulders. "Make me come."

He dropped me to my feet, lifted one of my legs over his shoulder, and ripped my thong to the side. Spreading me wide, he breathed me in. "Beautiful."

His head lowered. He ran his tongue over me and hummed in appreciation before fully diving in and fucking me hard with his mouth. So good. I gripped his hair and tried to hold on as he licked and sucked on my clit. I was strung so tight, already on the brink of going over. I lost all feeling in every other part of my body except for the tight bud where he focused his attention.

He slid a finger inside of me, and my inner walls clamped around him. "Damn. You feel incredible. I'm going to need a little more of this."

"That's so . . ." Oh God. He added another finger, moving them in and out of me as he continued to swirl his tongue around my clit. "Nice."

He stopped and looked up with a raised eyebrow. "Nice?"

"Good? Great? Spectacular?" I was about two seconds away from finishing myself off if he didn't put his mouth on me again. "What word are you looking for here? You can have all of them—I don't care. Just keep fucking me."

He gave me a look that melted me into a puddle of want, then spun me around. I planted my hands against the wall as he tilted my ass in the air. His fingers worked me over from behind as he plunged his tongue into me. The tingling sensation started in my toes and traveled upward at lightning speed. I cried out as I clenched and released all at once. His fingers and tongue worked faster, wringing every tremor of pleasure from my body.

I turned to face him, loose and sated and still, impossibly, wanting more. "That was . . ."

He gave me a warning look. "Don't you dare say 'nice.'"

Oh, Cade. He should've known by now that I could never resist messing with him. I gave him a simpering smile and batted my lashes. "Nice."

"That's it." He hauled me over his shoulder. I squealed and laughed as he carried me into the bedroom and dumped me on the firm mattress. "You're in for it now."

I leaned up on my elbows and licked my lips as I took in his hard body. "What are you going to do with me?"

He bent down, putting his hands, then his knees on the mattress as he crept closer to me. "It's probably better if I show you."

I wrapped my arms around his neck and dragged him on top of me. The weight of him pressing me down had me ready to go all over again. "That's so *nice* of you."

He kissed me, and wow, it was *not* a nice kiss. It was hot and dirty and made me squirm against him. He nipped my bottom lip with his teeth, and I gave it back harder, with my whole being thrown into it, like I did everything with him. I undid his belt, and he stood up to take his pants off. He looked down at me with hooded eyes. The clear line of his arousal showed in his briefs. I'd already seen everything, so I thought I knew what I was in for, but I'd never seen him on full alert before. He took the remainder of his clothes off, and his cock sprang free.

God, he was gorgeous. I wanted to feel him everywhere.

I got up on my knees, rubbing my hands over his chest and stomach, wanting as much of him at one time as possible. As I moved my touch lower, his cock jerked, as if impatient. I gave him a coy smile before taking him in my mouth. He sucked in a sharp breath. I rolled my tongue around the head, then took him down to the back of my throat.

His hands immediately tangled in my hair. "Fuck, Isla. That feels so good." The pressure between my legs began to build again as I sucked on his length. His hips began to move, fucking my mouth, as if he couldn't help himself. "I can't. I have to stop."

I released him and leaned back. "Stop?"

He brushed my hair away from my face. "I want to be buried inside you when I come."

"Then what are you waiting for?"

He gave me a grin and reached into the nightstand, where he pulled out a condom. I lay on the bed, with one knee bent, bearing myself to him as he rolled it on. He crawled over me and settled between my legs. Kissing me with an aching gentleness, he rubbed his hand down my stomach and over my clit. My entire body was on fire. Multiple sensations that I'd never felt before, and couldn't even name, crashed over me in waves.

I'd never really known what it meant to want until I wanted him.

"You're so wet." He lifted his fingers and sucked on them. "I can't get over the taste of you. I'm going to need my mouth on your pussy again before the night is over."

I wiggled against him, impatient now that he was this close. "You can do whatever you want later. I want you inside me now."

He took himself in his hand and rubbed his cock against me, and as he nudged my entrance, I suddenly clenched up. I wanted this. Badly. But once it happened, it wouldn't ever be the same between us. He'd see how much I needed him. Maybe it was because I hadn't ever learned how to need people, but that fear of being too much or not enough—anything except the right amount—ran deep, and I didn't know how to turn it off.

He paused, not moving as he held my gaze. "Are you okay?"

"I don't know." I turned my head away, and when my nose started to run, I wanted to scream at the unfairness of it all. Why couldn't I just cry muted, beautiful tears like they did in the movies? Why did I have to be a snotty mess?

"Hey." His fingers traced my jawline. "Talk to me, Rainbow Bear."

"I don't want to lose you or what we have." I wrapped my arms around him and buried my face in his neck. "I want you so bad, it's all I think about, but I'm scared. I don't want you to see me and find me . . . lacking."

"Do you think I haven't always seen you?" He rested his forehead against mine. "I see your brilliant mind." He kissed my temple. "The things you say that drive me crazy." He kissed the corner of my mouth. "Your incredible heart." He kissed my chest between my breasts. "I know it all, and every part of you amazes me."

I held his gaze. The open tenderness in his eyes caused my heart to stutter. All my stories and memories, the beautiful and ugly parts that made me, included Cade. No one saw me as clearly as he did. Every insecurity, every bit of doubt, fled from my mind.

I leaned up and gave him a soft kiss. "Make love to me."

As he entered me, I gasped. It felt better than I'd been able to picture in my most heated fantasies. He pushed in, little by little, letting my body adjust to him. Once he was fully inside, he threaded his fingers with mine, and with sweet, aching slowness, he pulled back before moving forward again. His rhythm was unhurried, as if determined to pull every moan and soft sigh from me at a leisurely pace.

"Fuck." He gritted his teeth. "You feel so fucking good. I had no idea it was going to be like this. I don't know if I can hold out for very long."

It didn't matter, I was so close anyway. Which I would've told him if I'd been able to form words. The plea for more was on the tip of my tongue, but he was so in tune with my body; he moved where I needed him just from the gentle shift of my hips or the increased pressure of my nails on his back.

He gripped his hand under my ass and tilted me against him, going deeper and hitting that spot. The one that caused little bits of light to burst in front of my eyes. "Come for me." He thrust harder as my body tightened around him. "Good girl. Let me feel you, Isla."

At the sound of my name on his lips, I cried out, every muscle in my body twisting up and then letting go. A complete and total release. Two more thrusts, and he followed me, groaning in my ear as his body shuddered. He kissed my neck, my forehead, my lips as he pulled out. He discarded the condom in the wastebasket by the bed, then collapsed against me.

I trailed my hands up and down his back and smiled when I felt little goose bumps rise. His cock stirred against my thigh, and just like that, I wanted him again. He leaned up on his side, propping his head up on his hand as he stared down at me. His fingers danced around my belly button. The soft light in his eyes looked a lot like something I wasn't yet prepared to name.

I reached up to touch his face. "That was nice."

He gave me a wolfish grin and flipped me over, kissing my spine. "Lucky for you, I've just begun to show you how nice I can be."

He pulled another condom from the drawer, rolled it on, and lifted my hips. I whimpered in anticipation as he rubbed his hand down my stomach, then swirled his finger around my clit. In one thrust, he was fully inside me again. I let out a moan loud enough to give the neighbors two floors down an idea of what was going on in this room. He felt just as good, if not better, than the first time. Like he'd been made to fit me perfectly.

Within minutes, I was crying out his name as I came for the third time. I couldn't move, I couldn't even blink. I was Jell-o. "I'll be fine. Just put me in a mold in the refrigerator."

"What?" Cade attempted to lift his head, thought better of it, reached for my hand instead. He drew it to his mouth and kissed my fingertips. "You okay over there?"

"Yep." My eyelids gave up the fight and closed. "Sleepy."

An hour later, I woke up in Cade's arms, my legs tangled in his and my lips resting against his neck. He must've taken a shower after I feel asleep because he smelled like Irish Spring, while I probably smelled like a truck stop. For some reason, I didn't care, though.

I crawled onto his lap, and his hand flexed against my hip. I kissed his shoulder, his chest, lower. He was already hard. I gave him a slow lick, and he let out a soft and sleepy groan. He woke up with his fingers in my hair.

"Come here." He lifted my chin. "Get up on my face. Let me taste that sweet pussy."

We shifted positions, and I sucked him while he brought me to orgasm again. He tried to move my head to signal that he was going to come, but I wanted to taste him, to feel his hot arousal sliding down my throat. It was the most energy we could work up, and we fell into each other's arms again. At three in the morning, he woke up to a deep rumbling coming from my stomach. And the sound of my soul leaving my body.

"Hungry?" He rubbed my hip and chuckled as I quietly died of embarrassment. "There's an all-night diner on the corner. I'll go get us some food."

I sat up, letting the sheet pool around my waist. "Or we could eat something else."

He licked his bottom lip. "Don't tempt me. Food first. Then I'm all yours again."

He stumbled around the moonlit room, and I laughed when he knocked his head into the wall, trying to pull on his pants. Looked like I wasn't the only one with jelly for muscles. As soon as he left, I lay back on my pillow and stretched my arms over my head.

I couldn't imagine ever being happier than I was in this moment.

CHAPTER TWENTY

Cade brought back French toast, with extra powdered sugar because he knew me best. We devoured the syrupy bread like we'd just been rescued from a desert island. As soon as we filled ourselves, we made love again. Then again in the shower. And once more, slow and easy, in the early hours as the sun began to peek through the blinds. I'd gotten maybe two hours of sleep, but I'd never felt more relaxed. I had no idea why Cade and I hadn't been having sex much sooner than this. Clearly, we excelled at it.

At around nine in the morning, I walked my fingers up his chest as I debated going another round with him. Just as I'd come to the conclusion that we could stand to get a little dirtier before our next shower, a key turned in the lock at the front door. It swung open, knocking against the opposite wall. Cade and I both sat up so fast, we nearly tumbled off the bed.

There was only one other person who had a key besides us.

The owner of the condo.

"Cade?" My brother called his name, and I wanted to die a thousand deaths.

"Um . . . just a minute." Cade leaped from the bed like a cat spooked by its own reflection, which would've been hilarious if we weren't both losing our collective shit. He began tossing clothes at me, half of which were his. "Didn't expect you home so early."

"Yeah. Well." A heavy thunk sounded from the living room. "Things changed. You can still stay here, though, if your condo isn't ready."

"Okay." Cade gestured for me to hide in the closet, but I shook my head. I'd already filled what little space was left from Seb's ski equipment with my book boxes. "I . . . uh . . . it should be ready this week, or at least livable again."

"Cool." The TV flicked on in the living room. "What are you doing in there?" Seb paused, then laughed. "Am I interrupting your alone time?"

"Not alone time, no." He glanced at me as I fell over trying to tug on a pair of shorts.

My brother's footfalls sounded in the hall, and Cade dove for the lock. Seb stopped suddenly, and I bit my lip, sinking to the ground as I realized he must've stumbled on my dress and bra on the floor. "Oops. Sorry, man. Didn't realize you had company." He paused again. "You do have company, right?"

"Sort of." Cade cringed and looked at me with wild eyes. "I mean, I did."

This was it. We were caught in the treehouse with the stolen cookies. If only I was a random cat who had taken up residence in Jillian's basement, maybe then I could figure out an exit plan. Or if my brother was normal, I could've stayed in here until he took a shower or a nap. But if Seb so much as suspected Cade had someone in here, he'd demand an introduction so he could be as obnoxious as possible. It was his way of showing he cared. Or something.

I dove under the bed just as Seb tapped on the door. "I should say hi to our guest."

"She's already gone. I'm just picking up in here." I peeked out from under the bed as Cade opened the door and held it wide for my brother to come in. "See? This room is just like your dating profile. Absent of ladies dying to meet you."

"You made her leave without her clothes?" Seb turned to Cade and shook his head as he clapped a hand on his shoulder. "Dude. That's cold."

I got my first look at my brother in over month. His pasty skin threw me off for a second. Usually, Seb tanned as easily as I did in the summer, but it looked like he hadn't seen much sun in London. Or his job kept him inside and working seven days a week.

Cade rolled his eyes. "She stole one of my shirts and a pair of boxers."

"Women are always taking your shit. What's up with that?" Seb took a seat on the bed, and I slid toward the headboard to get out of the way as the springs dipped closer to the floor. "I think Isla has at least twelve of your shirts."

My cheeks heated. I had, like, three of Cade's shirts. Maybe four. But they were soft and comfortable and had a nice smell. They made great sleep shirts, and they weren't anything Cade still had in his wardrobe rotation. That wasn't the same as stealing his underwear.

"I've missed you, asshole." The grin and easy affection in Cade's voice warmed my heart. Even though it was damned inconvenient right now, I missed Seb too. And I missed him and Cade together. There was something comforting about having the two of them around. Like a security blanket that always felt like home.

"It's good to be back." The springs on the bed creaked as Seb kicked his feet up. "What the hell is with all the boxes? Didn't know you needed so much stuff with you, princess."

"Please. Those are Isla's. She's downsizing."

Seb choked on a laugh. "Why do I get the feeling that's code for running a scam?"

The familiar shame slammed into my gut. As far as Seb knew, I had my shit together. I had my degree, he thought I still had my apartment, and I'd allegedly just gotten a promotion. Yet he took one look at my boxes stacked in his guest room, and his first thought was I must've been running a scam? He was just making a joke and being Seb, and I knew that, but it still hurt. No matter what I did or what I achieved, it would never be good enough for my family. I would always be a screw-up in their eyes.

"Come on, man." There was a chiding edge to Cade's voice. "We've talked about this."

They've talked about what? Did Cade tell Seb my boxes were here? He'd said he wouldn't, and it didn't sound like Seb had already known about them. What had Cade talked to him about then?

"Yeah, you're right. Old habit." Seb jumped off the bed. "I've got to get in the shower and wash about ten hours in coach off me. I'm never fucking flying again."

Seb shut the guest-room door, and I crept out from under the bed. "What's going on?" I kept my voice as low as possible because of Seb's dryer-sheet-thin walls. "Why is he home?"

"I don't know." Cade blew out a breath as he rubbed a hand over the side of his neck. "But we need to get you out of here. Now."

My mind was a scattered mess as I threw a bunch of clothes I'd need for the week in my suitcase, not bothering to see if they matched or if they'd be office appropriate. If needed, I'd always be able to stop by midweek and grab more. If I'd been thinking clearly, I would've slowed down and tried to assess the situation. Such as figuring out why Seb was home. And why was Cade in such a rush to get me out of here if we were together now? Wouldn't Seb find out eventually? Why bother continuing to hide it?

But I didn't stop to ask myself any of those questions because I was focused on other things. Like the fact that Seb now knew I was using his guest room like a storage unit. Which meant it was only a matter of time before my parents found out too, and they were a hell of a lot more observant than my brother. They'd know right away what those boxes meant.

Of course, Seb wasn't completely dense. He hadn't bought the downsizing story any more than Cade had, but unlike Cade, he'd just assumed I was up to no good. How messed up was it that Cade knew me better than my own brother did?

As we took the elevator down to the parking garage, tension radiated off him in waves. He started mumbling under his breath. "It'll be fine. I'll tell Seb I ran out for coffee."

"Everything okay?" My voice sounded a lot smaller than I'd anticipated.

He didn't respond, lost in his own thoughts and quiet panic.

Seb and Cade had always been a unit, and I'd just been the tagalong they put up with because I refused to be left out of their adventures. But over the last few weeks, I'd thought Cade and I had started to become our own unit. Something different and only for us.

Then my brother's unexpected arrival had popped the secluded little bubble we'd been living in. As much as I tried to deny it to myself, I could already feel Cade pulling away from me. It had been so good last night. I should've known it would come crashing down. The knots in my stomach tightened as the air around us became chiller, marking the distance between us with every step toward my car. By the time we reached my driver's side door, I'd already begun to mourn what we could've had if Seb hadn't come home early and thrown us back into our old roles before we really had a chance to explore new ones. I glanced at Cade and couldn't read his expression at all. The wall had gone up. I'd been shut out.

I should've just driven away and blown my nose in private, but I wasn't built to give up. At least not without a fight. I leaned up to give him a kiss, but he turned his head. "I don't think that's a good idea, Isla."

"Not a good idea now? Or ever?"

"Probably." He swallowed. "Not ever."

All that sorrow and loss and hurt that had started to build on the way down here flashed in a pan of molten anger. I'd shown him everything last night, and this was what he chose to do with it? "Are you fucking serious?"

"Seeing Seb . . . hiding you under the bed like some dirty secret . . ." He raked his hands through his hair. "I can't keep doing that. To him or to you."

"Then don't." I should've been happy I didn't know how to cry, except now my nose started to run in earnest, which was even worse. Not only did he get to see how upset I was, but I also got the joy of being disgusting while doing it. "I get that

Seb coming home early was a surprise, and you have this weird idea that you're betraying my brother or whatever, but I thought all that went out the window last night when you put your dick in me." I sniffed, hating myself just a little more. "Or have you already forgotten that you made me come six times?"

"I will *never* forget last night." His fists clenched at his sides. "It was everything I never dared myself to believe I could have."

"So what's the problem?" I threw my hands in the air. "Just tell Seb we're together. He'll be an ass about it at first, because he's Seb, but not a serious ass. He'll get over it."

"And what about your parents?" He crossed his arms. "How will they feel about the dirt -poor neighbor kid they had to feed for over a decade dating their daughter?"

"First of all, I don't give a damn what my parents think. And second of all, you're not anyone's charity case, remember? They'd probably be thrilled I managed to land such an upstanding member of productive society when they think I can barely wipe my own ass."

He shook his head. "You really don't get it, do you? Just because I'm doing well now doesn't mean your parents won't always look at me and see Trent and Meadow Greenley's trash son. Sometimes . . ." He pinched his lips together. "Forget it."

"Oh no." I poked a finger at his chest. "We're not forgetting anything. Tell me what you were going to say. I deserve to hear it."

He held my gaze, and a world of hurt he kept locked inside passed through his eyes. I wanted to reach for him, cover him with a comforter, and give him a teddy bear, but we weren't children anymore. "Sometimes, when we would be sitting on the swings out back, just the two of us, your dad would call you over to help with one of his projects."

"That's a Dad thing to do." The frustration welled up inside of me. It was beginning to sound more like an excuse than an actual reason not to be with me. "It wasn't personal."

"It was personal the night you sat in your backyard with Toby Booker."

I narrowed my eyes. "What do you mean?"

"I'm not doing this." He turned to walk away, and I grabbed his shirt. I'd jump on his back if he took another step. His shoulders slumped. "I don't want to start a war with your parents. They mean a lot to me, and I'm not angry at them for the way things are."

"Tell me about what happened with Toby Booker." I had no idea what night he was referring to, since I sat out back with Toby a lot of nights. We'd dated for six months, and he had only lived two streets over from us. "And whatever you're about to tell me, I'd like to state for the record that guy was a jerk. I'm glad he spent prom night alone with his hand."

The ghost of a smile quirked Cade's lips, gone so quick I was certain I imagined it. "I was in the kitchen, getting a glass of water one night, when I looked out the window and saw you two on the same swings we used to sit on. He leaned over and kissed you, and your cheeks turned this pretty shade of pink."

Probably because Toby had slobbered all over my chin and I was trying to find a polite way to introduce him to the concept of swallowing. "And?"

"And I knew—I think I'd always known, but right then it really hit me. I wanted to be the one who made you blush. That should've been me with you on that swing."

My breath caught in my throat. "Why didn't you say anything?"

If I'd known Cade wanted me like that, it would've changed everything. Maybe I could've confessed the real reason why I watched him and Crista Martin in the basement. Maybe I'd always been drawn to him in ways I'd never let myself admit. Maybe I thought about him when Toby Booker was slobbering all over my face, and wondering if Cade's kisses would've been different. Maybe I wanted to be the one who made Cade blush. So many maybes. An entire decade of regrets could be wrapped around that one word.

"Are you sure you want to hear this?" He used the same tone a doctor might use to ask a patient if they were sure they wanted to amputate. Once you said yes, there was no going back.

I lifted my chin, preparing myself for the worst. "Tell me."

"Your dad came into the kitchen and caught me staring." He lowered his gaze to the ground, as if he couldn't stand to look at me when he said the next part. "He put his hand on my shoulder and squeezed it in that way that looks comforting, where you can almost convince yourself it's comforting, but it's really not. He pointed out the window and said, "Now aren't those two sweet together?" And he looked at me like my only option was to agree."

"Cade." My voice cracked as I reached for his hand and held it between both of mine.

"People used to praise your mom for taking care of me, and sometimes it seemed like she got wrapped up in all those compliments. Like when she used to take us to the Ice Cream Garage. If anyone from the neighborhood was there, she'd ask me what I wanted just a little louder than she'd ask the two of you."

"I'm so sorry." Those words felt hollow, like nothing I could say would ever be big enough to fix a wound that cut that deep. "And I'm so angry for you."

"Don't be." He cupped my face, rubbing his thumb over my cheek. "I'm not telling you this to turn you against your parents or make you think they treated me bad. They didn't. It's just the small things they probably weren't even aware of, but were constant reminders to me. I didn't really belong. And you deserve someone you can be proud to wake up with on the holidays. Not someone you have to sneak away from the next morning when things get too real."

There were many times over the last three years when I'd regretted the morning after Thanksgiving. If I gathered all those moments up, they wouldn't weigh nearly as much as this one right here. "That wasn't about you. It was about me being afraid of my own feelings."

"You don't have to make excuses. I get it." He dropped his hand to his side and gave me a sad smile.

"You really *don't* get it." He had to understand Thanksgiving had been about me being afraid of falling for him and getting hurt, because I'd always put him on a pedestal, not the other way around. "If this doesn't end with you and me together, then you get nothing at all."

"Then I guess I'll have to live with getting nothing."

He turned around and went back upstairs, leaving me alone in the parking garage.

CHAPTER TWENTY-ONE

How did I get here? How did I go from the best night of my life to this? Everything hurt. Things I didn't even know I had hurt. Cade didn't want to be with me. He'd all but confessed he'd been into me since we were kids, and yet he wouldn't stand beside me as an adult. Would it have been better if I didn't know that? What if I hadn't demanded he tell me everything, and instead I'd walked away to save face like I always did? Would this have been easier? I didn't have answers, just an endless loop of miserable questions.

"And we were doing so well."

I rolled over to face Neeta, and groaned as the overhead florescent lights blinded me. I threw an arm over my face. "Can you maybe give me a break today? Feel free to judge me all you want tomorrow."

She took a seat next to me and crossed her legs. Resting her back against the row of romance books on the bottom shelf, she frowned as she looked me over. "What happened?"

"Everything." I gave her a rundown of all the events of the previous night and what happened after Seb came home this morning, without giving her all the precise details surrounding the six orgasms. I was in crisis. There was no need to brag.

"Your brother is back in town?" Neeta's face took on a dreamy expression.

"Hello." I snapped my fingers and pointed at myself. "Friend in need here. Focus, please."

"Yes. Focusing." Neeta shook off her daze and straightened her shoulders. "What do you want? Advice? My interpretation? Or just someone to listen?"

"I get a choice?" I expected Neeta to have an opinion, and I valued her opinion, but until she gave me options, I hadn't realized that I sometimes needed that too. I sat up and crossed my legs, leaning against the opposite shelf. "This is new."

She shrugged. "My gynecologist had an inspirational poster about friendship hanging on the ceiling over her table. I decided to give it a try."

"I'm feeling inspired already." I tapped a finger on my chin as I mulled over what had been presented to me. "You already listened, so maybe hearing your interpretation would be great, and then maybe follow that with some advice?"

"Wow. Leave it to you to take all three."

"Only because I respect your advice."

"If you respected my advice, you would've listened to me last time."

Trying to match wits with Neeta felt a lot like playing tennis. With Serena Williams. At some point you just had to stand there and hope a ball didn't hit you in the face. "Okay, fine. You are the greatest and I'm a bad listener. I'd still love to hear your thoughts."

She perked up when I called her the greatest. "Here's the deal. He's in love with you."

I rolled my eyes. That was so not helpful. "Did you miss the part where he said we're not going to be together? His exact words were that he'll live with nothing."

Neeta grabbed a paperback from the shelf and whacked me over the head with it. When I shot her a glare, she whacked me again. "You need to learn how to read between the lines. If you'd gone for your master's in library science instead, you'd be much better at it."

"Ouch. Way to rub the salt in," I grumbled. "But since I'm lacking that particular skillset, would you like to fill me in on those lines I need to read between?"

She gave a long-suffering sigh, like I was just this side of beyond help. "You're both acting like you have to earn the right to be together. Which is really messed up, but not surprising. Considering you were essentially raised in the same house, it makes sense that you'd have similar hang-ups. He's basically circling you, afraid he's going to fall short, and wondering when he's going to get screwed over. And you're doing the same."

I loved Neeta, truly, but sometimes she got it wrong. "*I'm* not pushing him away."

"No? What do you call what you did that morning after Thanksgiving then?"

"That was three years ago." Was everyone going to hold that over my head until the end of time? "I even admitted to him that I was running away from my feelings."

"And have you shown him anything to suggest that you've grown since then?" She gave me a know-it-all grin. The kind that could only be worn by someone who always ended up being right. "Or did you only speak up when he put the brakes on to protect himself?"

"I hate this conversation." I stood and dusted the carpet fuzz off my butt. "This has been fun, but I have a house to go sit."

She laced her hands behind her head. "My work here is done."

"You've done no work," I called over my shoulder as I walked away. "Don't go giving yourself a cookie just yet."

"I'm ordering another cake." Her nose scrunched. "Drinks on Friday?"

I huffed out a breath. Being besties with Neeta was both the best and worst at the same time. "I'll invite Seb. It'll be good for him to have a night away from work."

She rubbed her hands together. "Excellent."

Seb had no idea what he was in for. The thought of the two of them combining forces both awed and terrified me. I couldn't wait to see the sparks fly on Friday.

* * *

I showed up at Pierce Rodington's house just after noon with my squeaky suitcase. Before I got out of my car, I reapplied my lip gloss and brushed my hair. It turned out I cared more about making a good impression to one of the top executives at Torres-Glasser than I did any of the Cornerstone people. Not that I was looking for a job. Cade had already told me they weren't hiring, and I had no interest in selling fishing equipment anyway. But going to all the Torres-Glasser events had given me a glimpse into what it could be like to work someplace where employees were treated like humans.

"I can't thank you enough for this." Pierce shook my hand with a used-car salesman's level of enthusiasm. "Make yourself at home. Eat whatever you'd like." The best words that could ever be spoken. "If the dogs give you any trouble, you have my number."

"Don't worry. I've got this." I waved at his wife, Melinda, who was another high-level executive at Torres-Glasser, as she wrangled eight-year-old twins and a ten-year-old into a mini-van. "Enjoy your trip."

Once they left, I stepped into what would be my place of residence for the next week. The first thing that struck me was how normal everything appeared, though that shouldn't have surprised me. Pierce seemed like a down-to-earth guy despite his utterly ridiculous name.

The house gave off happy vibes. There were no animals that looked like they'd lost a bet with Mother Nature or elevators or freaky doll collections. It had nicer finishes and more bedrooms than any home from my parents' neighborhood, but it wasn't anything extreme like the Cornerstone executives owned. The living room had an enormous maroon sectional with lots of well-smushed pillows and tons of family photos decorating the walls. Tall bookcases held a collection of political nonfiction, picture books, and clay figurines that had clearly been made by a child's hand. The room had a lived-in, scattered charm to it.

In the kitchen, the refrigerator was covered in torn-out coloring book pages and homework assignments marked with gold stars. It held veggie and fruit trays, plus all the staples. There was cookie dough ice cream in the freezer, half an apple pie on top of the microwave, and a bottle of grape-flavored vodka in the cupboard. It's like Pierce knew I'd be nursing a broken heart this week and stocked his house accordingly. Bless him.

I took my suitcase up to the only guest room. It had a double bed with a creamy floral comforter and a simple wooden dresser. An outdated sewing machine sat on a dusty desk in the corner. The sound of dogs barking drew me to the window, and I gazed down at the backyard. Four chocolate labs romped around in the dewy grass, chasing each other while stopping to leap into the air with open mouths every time the neighbor's sprinkler arched over the fence. I smiled for the first time since talking to Cade that morning.

After I put my clothes away, I plopped down on the couch with the pie and vodka, and dug in for some quality self-pity time. Neeta had been wrong about Cade being in love with me. If he loved me, he wouldn't have walked away. He wouldn't have let some misguided loyalty to my brother or old issues with my parents stand between us.

If only the sex had been bad, dammit. I'd probably still be a mess, but it would've been made it somewhat easier to choke down the bitter pill I was now forced to swallow. The worst part was, I no longer had Cade as a friend either. Not after last night. For me, it had to be all or nothing, and he'd already made the choice of nothing. I poured a generous amount of vodka into a paper coffee cup. It burned my throat as it went down and warmed my stomach. Just a few more glasses of this stuff, and maybe I'd be able to forget for a little while.

Around six in the morning, I woke to the sensation of being slobbered on and wondered if I was having an extremely vivid dream about Toby Booker. Apparently, I'd passed out practically facedown in the apple pie pan, and one of Pierce's dogs was assisting in the cleanup. My head pounded and my mouth tasted like a lint trap. While that feeling of freshly baked death should've been a useful distraction, Cade was still in the forefront of my mind. There was no escape. Not even last night's vodka binge had helped. I'd gone from missing him to drunk and missing him, then woke up this morning nauseous and missing him.

And as much as I wanted to wallow while I lay very still in a cold and dark room until my hangover subsided, I couldn't afford to do more than pop a few Tylenol and chug a glass of water. Between the dogs I had to feed and walk, and the computer waiting to be logged into at work, I had too much on my plate for a sick day. So I forced myself to get up, get in the shower, and find something presentable to wear. All while dragging my heart around behind me.

The next day, I stopped over at Seb's condo to change out clothes, since I had indeed packed a bunch of useless shit in my rush to get out on Sunday morning. Part of me hoped I'd run into Cade. Another part of me hoped he'd contracted some rare but curable disease that would leave him unconscious for a few days. The kind that would make him have fitful dreams and repeat my name in his sleep, like the very thought of me was the only thing that could bring him back from the brink. And when he finally came out of it, we'd have a sexy bedside reunion, complete with a sponge bath.

I had a lot of time to daydream while I was supposed to be doing data entry.

Seb waved to me from the couch, where he balanced a bowl of Fruity Pebbles on his chest while he watched Netflix. It was so reminiscent of Cade, it made my heart hurt. "Just because you have a key, doesn't mean you should use it."

"Shut up." As far as he knew, this was the first time I'd seen him since he'd been back, but we weren't really into sappy reunions. "Why are you here?"

"Work sent me home early."

"I'm glad they didn't make you stay another month." While it would've been more convenient for me, I really did miss my brother. I rolled my squeaky suitcase down the hall.

"I'm just here to grab a few things from my boxes. Is Cade here?"

I mentally kicked myself. Asking about Cade had not been part of the plan. In fact, the plan had been to act like he didn't exist until I forgot about him altogether. It had not been going well so far. Not when everything reminded me of him. Someone said hi to me, and I thought about the way Cade said words. I got a drink from the water cooler, and I thought about how thirsty we'd been after making love for the third time. A pencil rolled off my desk, and I thought about how he rolled his hips while inside me. He was everywhere.

"He went back home," Seb said. "They installed his toilet yesterday, so his house is semi-functional, though he'll be living on takeout for a few more weeks."

"Cool. Not that I care." Because I hadn't spent an hour shaving and moisturizing and flat ironing my hair this morning on the off chance I'd run into him today.

Seb looked up at me with milk dripping down his chin, and I smiled in spite of myself. "Speaking of Cade moving back into his place, why are you keeping all those boxes in my guest room? Is it going to be for long?"

"I don't know." I really didn't want to store my things. It seemed like a giant waste of money, not to mention I'd die if my neon thongs ended up on a storage auction reality show when some other shit inevitably hit the fan and I couldn't pay the rent on that either. "I'm in the process of downsizing. Because I'm getting a place of my own."

"That's right. Your big promotion."

"Yep." I swallowed and ignored the twitch in my nose. "Moving up in the corporate world. Might as well start doing the living alone thing too."

"You'll love it. You can bang whoever you want on the dining room table and no one is going to kick up a fuss about it being 'unsanitary.'" He did air quotes around that last word, a habit he'd picked up from Mom.

"Great." I mimed gagging. "Remind me to decline your next dinner invitation."

He grinned. If my brother were a dog, he'd be one of Pierce's chocolate labs. "Just don't give your key to an annoying sibling who doesn't know how to knock."

"Trust me, I'll be knocking from now on." I glanced around the condo. A stack of newspapers was piled on the coffee table, sweatpants in various stages of frayed were tossed around the living room, a frightening number of string cheese wrappers littered the love seat. Seb wasn't the neatest person. In fact, his condo probably hadn't gotten a proper cleaning until Cade had stayed there, but he picked up after himself. "Is everything okay?"

"Yeah." He glanced around the living room. "I'm off work this week. You know I don't like to do shit when I'm off work."

That was true. Seb often asked what the point of vacation was if you still had to cook and clean, so for three weeks out of the year his condo turned into a war zone of stained clothes and take-out boxes. "I thought you didn't take time off until August?"

Seb hunched down on the couch and hugged his cereal bowl to his chest. "What is this? An interrogation? I didn't ask you to come over here, so mind your business."

I rolled my eyes. "Keep your secrets then. I'll get it out of you sooner or later. And please drag your nasty ass into the shower by Friday. We're going out for drinks."

He shot me a look full of suspicion. "With who?"

"My new friend, Neeta." He opened his mouth to protest another setup, and I raised a hand. "Before you object, this friendship is actually important to me, so I'd prefer if you didn't hook up. We just want to go out for drinks."

"Wait." He set his bowl on the coffee table. "Why would you prefer if I didn't hook up with her? Because I happen to be a pretty great guy."

"You're the best. You'll never hear me say otherwise." My brother was simple. Tell him he couldn't have something, and he wouldn't rest until it was his. Not normally a tactic I'd use to introduce him to a friend, but I had a feeling Neeta could handle Sebastian Jane. "Though she might take one look at all those string cheese wrappers and go running for the hills."

"It's trash. I can take care of it." He stood and scooped up all the wrappers and threw them in the garbage next to his kitchen cabinets. "I'll be there on Friday. I'll even shave. Maybe. Just tell me the time and place."

That had gone much better than I'd thought it would. Asking about Cade had been a mistake, but it had only been a few days since I'd last seen him. I was bound to trip up at some point. Eventually we'd have to see each other, though. Our lives were too intertwined. I just hoped the next time we met, it would be when I looked incredibly hot, and he was drowning in regret. With that happy scenario in mind, I left my brother alone in his pile of vacation stink.

CHAPTER TWENTY-TWO

I trudged through the rest of the week like I was walking up a mud hill. The extra five hours I put in at work felt like fifty. Even my time at Pierce's house crawled by. The only thing that gave me a small bit of comfort was sharing a bed with all four of his chocolate labs. It was hard to be completely miserable while buried under a pile of dogs.

Before I'd started spending all that extra time with Cade, I'd see him once or twice a week at Seb's or out at the bars. We'd joke around and trade barbs and do a little harmless flirting. During the day, I'd send him funny memes, and he'd text back a short "I'm working," but now I couldn't even do that anymore. I'd lost him. Fully. And as much as I liked to say I was an all-or-nothing person, I would've settled for half a Cade. Anything other than this complete and total emptiness. I hadn't even realized how *there* he'd been in my life until he wasn't anymore.

I made it until Thursday without contacting him. I should've left well enough alone, but Cornerstone had just hired five freshly graduated analysts who would all probably get promoted before me, so I was in the mood to punch myself in the face. When I texted to ask if he'd be going to a Torres-Glasser event this weekend for the Fourth of July, he replied back with "no." Nothing else. Not even the customary "I'm working."

Which was fine. I was fine. All this was fine.

One good thing about the holiday weekend, besides the extra day off, was that it set me up nicely for my next house-sitting job. Come Friday, I'd been approached by two executives at Cornerstone who each had a vacation scheduled for the coming week. After some back and forth, with both of them offering to double my pay if I chose them, I made my decision. Hugh Noble had the disposition of a tobacco lobbyist, but he had no pets or plants. He literally just wanted someone to sit in his house while he was gone. A clear winner.

After work, I picked up my phone to text Cade about my small windfall, and dropped it like it had burned me. That had been the hardest part about this week. Texting him random things about my day had become such a habit that not talking to him now made me feel like I was missing key organs. This was getting to be downright ridiculous.

What I needed was a good old-fashioned spite date. Someone who could distract me from all my sad and annoying thoughts for a few hours. I opened Tinder and swiped right on the first guy who popped up. Josh Something-or-Other. I didn't even pay that close attention to his profile. We chatted long enough for me to let him know where I'd be having drinks that night, then I shook out my date dress and got ready.

I stopped by Neeta's to pick her up, and my jaw hit the ground when she stepped out her front door. I hadn't expected her to go out in a cardigan and ponytail, but our movie nights were usually low-key, the yoga pants and old T-shirts type of affairs. I'd never seen Date Neeta.

She wore a skin-tight dress in electric pink that stopped at mid-thigh and pushed her boobs up to her neck. She paired it with six-inch shiny black heels. Her dark hair fell in sleek waves down her back, and she'd done something with her eyes to make them look enormous.

It was like watching a makeover montage in real time, minus the smoke machine and generic empowerment anthem. Seb was going to be a goner.

She slid into the passenger seat, and I couldn't help it. I openly stared. She glanced at me with raised eyebrows. "You're making this weird."

"You're right. Sorry." I backed out of the driveway. "You look amazing."

"Thanks." She sat up a little straighter, a light smile playing across her ruby lips.

My brother preferred bars that had a more relaxed atmosphere, nothing with loud music or dancing, so we ended up at Tavern on the Square. The inside was all dark wood and low lighting. Most of the crowd packed into the place looked like shadowy outlines of people. The last time I'd had a date here, it took me an hour to realize I was sharing a booth with the wrong guy. The outside had a large brick courtyard, though, surrounded by a short iron fence adorned with ivy and a scattering of round tables.

I waved to Seb, then stopped short at the sight of Cade seated beside him. My traitorous heart jumped in an erratic beat, and I placed a hand on my chest to hold it still. He had skipped his morning shave, but unfortunately the stubble only served to make him hotter. His hair stuck up in odd places, as if he'd run his hands through it too many times, and the buttons on his shirt were misaligned.

Instead of looking disheveled, however, the effect was endearing and so unfair. Why did misery get to look so good on him while I got stuck being a puffy, snotty mess? And what was he doing here anyway? Couldn't I have just one night out with my brother without him tagging along? Of course not. Because they were a package deal, and I was just . . . nothing.

Our eyes met, and I stumbled.

Neeta wrapped a hand around my arm. "Get it together. You are a sexy, powerful bitch. Hold your stiletto to his throat and make him beg."

"Wow." I tore my gaze away from Cade and widened my eyes at Neeta. "You should be the one writing inspirational posters for gynecologists."

"All part of the friend package." She nudged me forward. "Now be cool. Act like nothing happened between the two of you. It will drive him insane."

"Right. I can do that." I repeated the mantra in my mind as we approached the table. *Be cool. Be cool. Be cool.* "I didn't realize you'd be here tonight, Cade. I assumed you'd be at home trying to figure out how to remove your head from your ass without making a mess."

Neeta groaned beside me.

"I didn't realize you'd be here either." Cade shot my brother a dirty look. "I didn't get a lot of details before I was dragged out of my condo."

"Quit being a surly bastard. I saved you from a night of jerking off to your high school yearbook pictures." My brother stood and pulled out a chair for Neeta. "Hi. You're really pretty.

Was that too forward? Can I get you anything to drink? Or maybe I should quit talking now."

So Seb was a little rusty in the flirting department. His job made him work some bizarre hours, not to mention all the travel. He didn't get out much. Neeta gave him a bemused smile, like she wasn't sure if she wanted to let him buy her a drink or scratch him behind the ear. Lucky for my brother, most women mistook his cluelessness for charm.

Cade leaned over and his scent enveloped me. "Do you want me to leave?"

"I don't really care what you do." I stretched my neck, trying to catch the eye of one of the servers weaving around the tables with drinks. I needed something strong. Stat.

He lowered his voice. "You look beautiful tonight."

"Stop." I crossed my arms, and if they happened to push my boobs up closer to his face, so be it. I hoped he suffered. "You don't get to say stuff like that to me anymore. You forfeited that right when you chose nothing."

Cade frowned into his beer. "Can we talk?"

I glanced at my brother, who was telling Neeta some story about work. Maybe she'd understand what he did for a living, and then she could explain it to me like I was five. At least Seb was fully occupied and not paying attention to Cade and me. "Have you changed your mind about us?"

"I don't know." He looked like those three words were slowly killing him from the inside. Good. I hoped it ate away at him until he realized how utterly idiotic he was being.

"Until you know, we have nothing to discuss."

The tension brewed so thick between us, not even Seb could continue to miss it. He pulled his attention away from Neeta with stars in his eyes, and glanced at me, as if I was automatically the culprit for any unrest at our table. "Did something happen while I was in London? I feel like I'm missing something here."

"Just more of the usual." I stood. "I'm going to the bathroom."

When Neeta didn't move, I kicked the back leg of her chair. She startled and jumped to her feet. "Right. I'm going to the bathroom too. Because that's what girlfriends do."

"You didn't need to overexplain." I hooked my arm through hers as we walked away. "You're worse at the friend cues than my brother is at flirting."

"No one is worse at anything than your brother is at flirting."

We pushed open the bathroom door. It had the same dark wood as the bar, but bright enough lighting to move around without bumping into people. The sound of someone retching in one of the stalls echoed in the chamber-like room. This so wasn't my scene anymore.

A hoard of college-age girls stood at one end of the long counter. They smoothed their hair and picked mascara blobs out of the corner of their eyes, and their biggest worries were who they'd hook up with tonight and how much they had left to write on a paper due on Monday. They had no idea what waited for them on the other side of graduation. I wanted to scream a warning at them—to run, to get out now before their debt piled so high, they'd never be able to scale it. But I knew how they would react, because I used to be them. Fearless and certain in my future. And it would've taken a hell of a lot more than the incoherent ramblings of a stranger in a bar bathroom to convince me otherwise.

I went to lean against the wall while Neeta reapplied her lipstick, then thought better of it and stood up straight again. "What do you think of Seb, poor flirting skills aside?"

"He's okay." Neeta zipped up her clutch. She didn't seem as dreamy about him anymore, but much like myself, it took people time to see the real Seb. Once he got over his initial awkwardness, he was actually quite loveable. "We'll see how the night goes, but he's cute in a leg-humping way. Did you actually have to go to the bathroom?"

"No." And even if I did, between the puker in stall one and the spray left behind by a hoverer in stall two, I'd hold it until I got back to Pierce's. "I can't think when I'm around Cade. I just needed a minute to get away from him."

"I'd need a minute too." She fanned herself. "The way he was looking at you—whew. I nearly caught fire just being in your proximity."

"That's not at all what I meant." I paused. "Wait. How was he looking at me?"

"Like you're his favorite flavor of ice cream, and he's dying for another lick."

Oh boy. Flashes of his head between my legs and his hard body pressing me into the mattress as he thrust hard deep strokes into me passed through my mind, and a warm flush crawled up my neck. I tamped down on those images. It wouldn't do me any good to relive them. Neeta didn't know Cade the way I did. He might've been stuck between what he wanted and what he thought I needed, but he'd always take what he considered the responsible route.

"It doesn't matter how he looked at me." It didn't help that I knew he wanted me. In fact, it made his refusal to be with me that much worse. "I just need to get through this evening."

"People who are in love are hopeless." Neeta's lip curled. "If it ever looks like it might happen to me, do me a favor and remind me why it sucks."

We went back out to the courtyard, and part of me hoped Cade had left while we'd been gone, but no such luck. He still sat there, looking rumpled and hot as ever. Neeta whispered encouraging words to me on the way back to our table. I only needed to survive for the next hour; then I could make an excuse about needing to feed the dogs and leave. I had this.

Before I could sit down, a vaguely familiar guy with short blond hair, a crooked nose, and an arrogant expression approached me and touched a hand to my elbow. "Isla? Hey. Josh." He said his name as if I should've already known it. "Sorry I'm late—traffic was a nightmare on the expressway. You look better than your profile pictures. How is that possible?"

Oh God. I'd forgotten about the Tinder guy. "Josh. Right. Great to meet you."

"Are you kidding me? You have a *date*?" Cade's chair scraped across the brick as he got to his feet. The fury on his face made me feel about two inches tall while I simultaneously bristled at his gall. He had no right to be angry.

I lifted my chin, challenging him in a way I knew would get under his skin. Daring him to do something about it. "It's none of your damn business."

"The fuck it isn't."

"Is someone going to tell me what the hell is going on?" Seb stood, his brow furrowing as he glanced between me and Cade. "The two of you have been acting strange all night."

"It's nothing." I glared at Cade. "Isn't that right?"

He didn't answer. He didn't need to. I already knew where he stood.

"I think I'm going to go." Josh touched my arm, then shrank back from the look Cade gave him. "Clearly, I've walked in on something I didn't sign up for here."

"Sounds good. I'll go where you're going." I didn't care that Cade's head was about to explode, or that I didn't find Josh the least bit attractive. I needed to be anywhere but here.

"No, thanks. You're cute. We probably could've had some fun." He glanced at Cade and gulped. "But I like my face. I'd like to keep it intact. Have a nice night."

Josh practically tripped over his feet as he ran from the courtyard. While he definitely hadn't been car-sex material, he'd made for a great excuse to get away from this shit show, and now he was gone. I turned around and shoved Cade. "What's wrong with you?"

"I'd like to know that too." Seb eyed Cade like he'd never seen him before. "I know being the fifth wheel sucks, but why do you give a shit about Isla's date?"

"Oh no." Neeta—the best friend, but the worst actress—fell against Seb, twisting her leg at an odd angle that was so obviously fake. "My ankle. I think I sprained it."

There was no way Seb would fall for—

"We need to get ice on it before it swells." Seb leaped into action, and I stood corrected.

He pushed past a gathering crowd at the entrance, making his way into the bar with comical speed. It only mildly offended me that he moved a lot faster for Neeta's fake injury than he ever had for one of my real ones. As he disappeared from view, I waited to see what she wanted me to do next, since I had been her ride here.

She gave me a smirk as she plopped into her seat and gestured to the parking lot. "Go before he gets back. I'll catch an Uber home."

That was all the permission I needed. "Love you. I'll text you later."

I hoisted the strap of my purse over my shoulder and booked it toward my car. Cade gave me a meaningful look, but I was so furious with him, I refused to acknowledge it as I brushed past him. His heavy footfalls sounded behind me. I should've known he'd follow.

"Isla, wait." He stopped beside my car. "I'm sorry."

"Oh, you're sorry?" I didn't want to hear his apology. I didn't want to hear anything from him at all. "That's so *nice*. Great, I mean." I cringed, and he looked away. Awesome. Cade had officially ruined the word *nice* for me too.

"I don't know what happened back there. That guy was so smug, and when he touched you . . ." He ran his hands through his hair. "That's not me. I'm not like that."

I put my hands on my hips. "You mean a possessive asshole?"

"Yeah." He raised his head, meeting my gaze. Misery rolled off him, permeating the air, and all I wanted to do was soothe his heart and heal my own, but I couldn't do that alone for either one of us. "You have no idea how sorry I am."

I got the feeling he didn't just mean how he'd acted with Josh anymore. We needed to talk, but I was so tired. Of everything. Missing Cade so bad it physically hurt had taken its toll on me. Now Seb knew there was something going on with us, and I'd have to deal with that too. It was too much. I'd been completely emotionally drained, and all I wanted was a hot bath and a bed full of dogs. I didn't have the bandwidth left for anything else.

"I can't do this right now," I said.

He stepped aside to let me in my car, shoving his hands in his pockets. I started the engine and drove away without looking back. My nose ran the whole way to Pierce's house.

CHAPTER TWENTY-THREE

On Saturday morning, I ignored Seb's calls as I lay on Pierce's couch with my feet propped up on the back cushions for proper blood flow. I was now "high heels cause uncomfortable swelling" years old. It was all downhill from here.

I texted Neeta, but I didn't hear back from her. Cue anxiety. The hardest part about only having one friend was suspecting she'd wake up one day and realize you weren't worth the trouble. And to be honest, I was a lot. I exhausted myself all the time. I hoped she wasn't mad at me for leaving last night, though. She'd been the one who'd told me to go.

Last night. Ugh.

My dream scenario had happened. There was no groveling or sponge bath, but I'd looked fantastic while Cade had looked like a rumpled mess. And yet, it still felt like he had gotten the upper hand. Probably because I couldn't see him in any state without wanting him to wrap his arms around me like my own personal Cade cocoon. Why?

"I'm in love with him." I slapped a hand over my mouth. As soon as I said the words out loud, I wanted to force them back in with a crowbar. It was terrifying to call what I felt for Cade by its name. Everyone knew that's how you gave it power.

But whether I said it out loud or not, the fact would remain the same: I was in love with Cade. And I could either let it ruin me or use it to make myself better. The choice was mine.

Usually when faced with a dilemma like this, one that seemed too large or too important, I coped in one of three ways: lying down in the library, drinking too much, or partaking in some unique form of self-sabotage that caused my family to give me the Classic Isla head shake. But not this time. Maybe this was a sign that I was at long last growing up, but I didn't want to sit around and get steamrolled by my feelings. I was in love with someone who didn't want to love me back. It was scary as hell. But I was also a smart, capable, independent woman with a goddamn master's degree. It was past time I started acting like it.

My brother called again, and I sent him to voicemail. I had my day planned already, which didn't include dodging questions about what had happened between me and Cade. My mom called soon after, and I sent her to voicemail too, though with significantly more guilt. We hadn't talked since the disastrous dinner. If I'd thought she was ready to have an honest conversation, maybe I would've picked up, but I knew my mom. Just as I suspected, she left a message that suggested she planned to go on as if nothing had happened.

I wasn't willing to do the same anymore.

Feeling at peace with that decision, I got up off the couch and got ready for the day. After I showered, threw on a pair of cotton shorts, and put my hair in a ponytail, I updated my

CV and applied for every job within a twenty-mile radius. The gut-clenching fear of rejection hit me hard, but I couldn't keep letting that hold me back. Even if a lateral move was my only option, it was clear Cornerstone had no interest in nurturing whatever dormant talent I had for business, and I was tired of letting them determine my worth. An MBA wasn't a cakewalk. I'd earned that degree, and I deserved to see just what I could do with it.

I ate a quick lunch of avocado toast and tomato slices, then leashed up Pierce's four labs and took them over to the dog park. I let them chase ducks in the pond for over an hour and splash muddy water all over me because it made me laugh. It also gave me a sense of calm to know I could find joy on my own.

I'd still have to face Cade, but not yet. Today, I'd take care of me. Starting with those little decisions to be better, to do things that were good for me. Because how could I truly love someone else if I didn't love myself first?

That night, I cooked a dinner for one. Roasted chicken, asparagus, and red potatoes. I poured myself a glass of wine and sat out on the balcony, where I had a decent view of the city fireworks show. Bright bursts of red and blue and purple lit up the night sky. One of the neighbors was grilling out, and I tucked my feet underneath me while I breathed in the smoky-scented air. For the first time in a long time, I was proud of who I'd decided to be today.

*   *   *

On Sunday morning, Pierce and his family returned home, with his skin baked to a leathery crisp. Turned out, they'd spent the week on their boat up north. Fishing. Which seemed to me like a waste of a vacation considering where he worked, but those Torres-Glasser employees could never be accused of not loving their jobs. As soon as the labs heard their owners enter the house, they plowed through the doggie door and jumped all over them. The kids fell into a pile of loud barks and wagging tails. I'd miss those crazy dogs.

Pierce set his suitcase in the entry way and took off his "I'd Rather Be Fishing" ballcap to wipe his brow. He handed me a check for the second half of my fee. "Any issues?"

"None." I tucked the check in my purse. "I think this is my first issue-free house. It's almost as if everyone outside the company I work for is normal. What's that like?"

He laughed. "Boring, but in a good way." He scratched the head of one of the labs that was currently drooling on his boat shoes. "My kids were sorry to miss the water park event, but we told them we'd take them next weekend, to make up for it."

"The water park event?"

"Yeah." He gave me a funny look. "You didn't go?"

"Oh." My heart dropped to my stomach. Cade must've lied to me when I asked about an event this weekend, even though he knew how much I loved a lazy river. Before our argument at the bar. Because he didn't want to see me. "No. I . . ." I swallowed and smiled hard enough to make my face hurt. "I had some work to catch up on."

"On Fourth of July weekend?" He shook his head. "Brutal."

The Cornerstone offices were closed for three days. I opened my mouth to reply, and a noise that sounded suspiciously like a sob came out instead. But I should've been prepared for this. While it would've given me the greatest pleasure to watch Cade attempt to keep his professional veneer while riding a giant inner tube around a cone-shaped slide, if he didn't want me at his work functions, what could I say? I wasn't a Torres-Glasser employee, and he didn't owe me an invitation. Our deal was over. We'd both fulfilled our conditions.

I thanked Pierce for hiring me and for passing my name to other Torres-Glasser executives, and then I wheeled my squeaky suitcase out to my trunk.

The sun streamed in through the windshield as I sat in my car and gripped the wheel. The engine was running, but I'd yet to pull away from the curb. Hugh texted to let me know the key to his house was tucked under a blue planter by his front door. The idea of spending another week in a stranger's home didn't quite fill me with relief like it had previously. It just made me feel adrift and alone, without an anchor to hold me steady.

With a heavy sigh, I made the trek out to the same gated community where everything had started. Hugh lived five houses down from Alice. The fact that they were friends made me vaguely uncomfortable in a way I couldn't put my finger on. The same way I used to avoid the kids in high school who allegedly tripped people in the halls for sport, even though I'd never seen any of them do it.

I drove past Ted and Anton's house, and ducked down, afraid they might peek out their windows and see me. Would it matter if they did? For all I knew, Cade had already told them we'd "broken up," and they'd have no reason to associate with me in any capacity again. Maybe we'd see each other on the street one day and wave, and I'd recall that one summer when it had almost felt like we'd been friends.

Hugh's house was just as imposing as Alice's, with the same gray siding and jutting roofline. His shutters were red, though—the only sign of individualism in a neighborhood that required approval from an entire board before anyone could plant a garden.

The inside was more understated than Alice's, but it had a laminated vibe. The plants were artificial, the candles on the bookshelves and mantle were flameless, and everyone in the portrait hanging over the fireplace wore plastic smiles. Every room was in perfect order, with just enough personal items to keep it from looking like a catalog, but not enough to make it feel like a home. Even the teenager's rooms could probably be found in a Google image search. It was like being in the residence of a robot who had been programed to mimic humans. But who was I to judge the authenticity of Hugh's life? I'd fallen in love with my brother's best friend while we were pretending to date, and the bulk of my summer social activities consisted of attending multiple corporate events for a company that didn't employ me while I lived in a series of homes that didn't belong to me. We all had shit we kept hidden in plain sight.

I dumped the clothes in my suitcase in the washer. At some point before the weekend was up, I'd need to get over to Seb's to swap out my wardrobe again. With no plants to water or animals to feed, I had nothing to keep me occupied. Raiding the liquor cabinet and trying on expensive clothes had lost all appeal to me now that I was on the path to becoming a better person. I needed an outlet for all my restless energy. Which began and ended with my feelings for Cade. Our deal might've been done, but we were far from over.

With more determination than sense, I drove over to his condo and banged on the door. As soon as his footfalls sounded through the wall, I put my finger over the peephole. It wouldn't have surprised me if he refused to answer, but I came here with the intention of having it out, and I wouldn't be leaving until he saw reason. He had fears, and I got it. I had them too. But we could face them together. We didn't have to do everything on our own.

He flung open his door, and the sight of him threw me off. His scruff had become a full beard—which I didn't mind, if I was being honest—his shoulders slumped, and dark purple shadows smudged his eyes. He looked like he hadn't slept in days.

"Are you sick?" I asked.

He let out a humorless laugh. "Do I look that bad?"

I shoved past him and took in his living room. Black couches, bookshelves lined with historical nonfiction mixed with Stephen King paperbacks, and not a speck of dust to be found. He'd always managed to keep his entire condo cleaner than I could keep my purse. "Don't try to make me feel sorry for you. Maybe you just got too much sun at the water park yesterday." I peeked over my shoulder. "Yeah. I know about that."

"I didn't go to the water park."

"Oh my God. You are sick." I turned around and put my hand on his forehead. He felt normal, but that didn't mean anything. Cade wouldn't miss a work function unless he was dead, and even then, he'd probably request to have his wake be one of the weekend events.

"I'm fine." He pushed my hand away. "Why are you here?"

Ah, yes. The question I'd been waiting for. I adjusted my features to my mad face and straightened my spine as I balled my fists at my side. "I came to fight with you."

"Is that so?" He rubbed his jaw as he circled me. I eyed him warily, and his serious expression cracked. "Fuck me, you're adorable when you're trying to look pissed off."

I rolled my eyes. "I don't know why I bother with you."

"I think you know exactly why you bother with me." He stood close enough for me to feel the heat radiating from him. Maybe he had a fever after all.

"Cade . . ." I laid a hand on his chest.

"Come on, Rainbow Bear. Give me a fight."

The intensity in his gaze caused every thought to empty out of my head. I wanted to fight. The plan had been to march in here armed with righteous anger, and there would be lots of yelling before we reached an understanding that hopefully ended in some truly spectacular makeup sex. But I hadn't counted on my need for him burning too bright.

I grabbed the front of his shirt and pulled his lips to mine.

He backed me against the wall and pressed his body fully against mine. I plunged my fingers into his silky hair, gripping his head, pulling him into me. I thought I'd kissed Cade in all the ways a person could kiss. The first time was wild and frenzied. Like if we didn't do it right then, we'd never get the chance again. The next time we kissed, it was soft and sweet, as if we had an entire lifetime to do nothing else. But I'd never kissed him like this. It was a soldier going off to war, a captain going down with his ship, a bank robber going down in a hailstorm of bullets kind of kissing. Like this would be the last kiss of our lives, and we needed to take it with us.

It was equal parts desperation and absolution, and it consumed me.

Buttons went flying as he tore my shirt open. I didn't even know shirts could do that outside the movies. Cade lowered his head and pulled my bra aside with his teeth, sucking my nipple into his mouth. My back immediately arched in response. He hoisted me up, and I wrapped my legs around him as he carried me to the couch.

My nails scraped against his abs as I rushed to take off his pants. We wasted no time stripping each other bare. He rubbed his thumb over my clit, and I ground my hips against his hand, desperate for any sort of friction. The urgency to have him inside me drove me to the edge. He grabbed his wallet from the coffee table and pulled out a condom. The moment he rolled it on, I climb on top of him, and let out a satisfied moan as I sank down on his cock. There was no hesitation on my part. No achingly slow buildup. I moved hard and fast right from go, wanting more, needing to feel that delicious clench around him. I rode him to the point of forgetting everything except his name. Within minutes, I came so hard my entire body shuddered.

As the high wore off, I buried my face in the crook of his neck and just breathed.

His hands skimmed my sweat-slicked back. "Good fight."

I laughed, and he picked me up again, carrying me to his bedroom. It briefly registered with me that I'd never been in Cade's room before. He had dark wood furniture and silky cream-colored bedding, and the only thing hanging on the wall was the black-and-white portrait of downtown that I'd gotten for him two Christmases ago. I wanted to go through all his drawers and rub anything that smelled like him against my face like a genuine creep. But I'd have to do that later. I had more pressing things to attend to first.

He put a knee on his mattress and laid us both down on the bed. As he settled down beside me, it felt right and whole, like this was exactly how we were supposed to be always. And because it was so good, I naturally expected it to fall apart. I didn't want to ruin the moment or dig into anything heavy. I was in Cade's arms. I wanted that to be enough. But the last week had been hell for me, and amazing sex didn't erase appalling communication.

I reached up to cup his face, swallowing my insecurities and doubts. "I realize it might be a little late to ask this after what just happened, but are we going to be okay?"

"Yeah. I think we'll be okay."

"I need more than that." Again, the urge to let it go and stop pushing and just be happy with what I could get rose to the surface, but his rejection and distance had been devasting. I was terrified he'd offer to walk me down to my car, and I didn't mind confessing that I needed some reassurance on his end. "What happened last weekend?"

"It's complicated."

I stiffened at his vague reply. If we were ever going to work, he'd have to let me in on his own thoughts at some point. "That's it? Nothing else you feel like sharing?"

"I'm working on it." He took my hand and gave it a quick squeeze. "Growing up, your family became my family. I don't know what would've happened to me if it hadn't been for your parents, but I wouldn't be where I am now."

"You don't know that." While I understood he'd always have a certain amount of gratitude toward my parents, I couldn't help but notice how much credit he gave them and how little he gave himself. "You're the one who got you where you are."

"I didn't get there alone. The first time I stayed in your home and watched the way the four of you were with each other, I thought that was what happiness looked like."

"Not always." Just because my parents did better by me and Seb than Cade's parents had done for him didn't mean they were without flaws. Lifting a bar off the ground didn't automatically make it high enough. "I think your perception is a little off."

"I don't doubt it, but didn't you want inside my head?"

I kissed his nose. "Smartass."

"Here's where it gets complicated," he said. "I never wanted to ruin the happiness in your home." When I gave him a look, he sighed. "Happy by my perception. But those little things I told you about your parents last weekend? The things you didn't realize? There is no way you'd be able to be with me and not see it. If we tell them we're a couple, it will become obvious to you too, and I never want to be the cause of any problems between you and your family."

"That's sweet but misguided as hell." In case he hadn't noticed, I had plenty of problems with my family all on my own. What were a few more sticks on the bonfire?

"Like I said, I'm working on it." He rolled on top of me and settled between my legs as he brushed my hair back from my face. "But even when I tried to keep my distance, I couldn't seem to stop loving you."

Everything stopped the moment those words left his lips. A warm glow spread through my chest, even as I searched his eyes, looking for a contradiction. Like I was afraid to believe he meant it. His gaze held a mix of things I knew he kept under the surface, things I hadn't seen since we were kids, when he hadn't yet learned how to mask his emotions. Vulnerability, awe, doubt, but most of all, a question. Did I love him too?

I ran my hand over his jaw. "You love me?"

He kissed my cheek and each corner of my mouth before skimming his fingers over my jaw, tilting my chin, and gently pressing his lips to mine. "I've always loved you, Isla."

I exhaled and held him tight against me. I couldn't quite say the words out loud. This thing between us was so fragile, and I wasn't above admitting it scared me. But I'd never been able to hide myself from Cade. Tears blurred my eyes, and their presence startled me so much, I wiped my hands over my lids, smearing my mascara. There weren't enough real tears for them to make it past the rim of my eyes, and my nose immediately started running, but it was a start.

Once I pulled myself together, our kisses became a slow seduction. Every touch an appreciation, every sound a vocalization of how we made each other feel. He rested his forehead against mine and held my gaze. And when our fingers threaded together, and he moved inside me, I understood why they called it making love.

CHAPTER TWENTY-FOUR

The next morning, I woke up sprawled across Cade's bed with one leg hooked over his, an arm flung over his chest, with the other stretched out on my opposite side. I slept like a starfish. The desire to spend the rest of the day snuggled up against Cade was overwhelming, but I needed to get back to Hugh's house. I shouldn't have stayed. Not when it caused me to completely disregard my house-sitting duties. While I didn't have anything living to attend to, and there were so many things I couldn't stand about the Cornerstone executives, I had made a commitment to Hugh. It was my responsibility to honor that.

Cade's even breathing let me know he wasn't fake sleeping, but he'd probably wake up soon. He loved me. We were going to be okay. I let myself marvel over that for another minute before I carefully extracted myself and put on one of his shirts and a pair of his boxers, fully understanding why women stole his clothes. They were soft and smelled like him. It was a wonder he didn't have to replace his wardrobe monthly.

I peeked in the hall, forgetting for a moment that we were no longer in Seb's condo, then headed to the bathroom. Even though he'd seen me at my morning worst a million times, I owed it to us both to at least brush my teeth before I kissed him goodbye. I also washed my face and attempted to brush my hair with the tiny black comb I found in a drawer. By the time I went back to the bedroom, Cade had woken up. He sat on the edge of the bed with his head in his hands. When he turned, there was no mistaking the guilt that clouded his expression.

It was like being punched in the gut, and the pain nearly doubled me over.

The touches, kisses, and shared whispers from last night crystalized and hung suspended in the air between us. And right when I thought it might be safe to hold everything I ever wanted, it shattered apart. The first time he'd rejected me, I'd accepted it. The second time, it almost broke me. I flat out refused to do this with him again. There weren't a lot of things in my life I could take pride in—not my job, my living situation, or my overall aesthetic—so I damn well didn't have any self-esteem to spare on getting rejected by Cade Greenley for a third time.

I ran my hands to the back of my neck. What was wrong with me? Why was I getting so worked up? Cade hadn't even said anything yet. One look on his face, which I could've easily misconstrued, and I was ready to shut down. Was this what it was going to be like from now on? Worrying and waiting for him to throw up his walls again? How long would it be before I began to resent him for it? I needed to check on Hugh's house, but I really needed to take a minute to breathe and clear out the jumbled mess in my head.

"I have to go," I said.

Cade stood. "I'll walk you down."

Oh God. There it was. The acidic bite of fear flooded my system as I was flung into last weekend and what had happened the last time he'd offered to walk me to my car. I backed up a step. "I don't need you to come with me."

He looked confused, and I nearly faltered. Panic and pain sunk their claws into me. I wanted to believe he meant everything he'd said last night, but I couldn't even trust myself right now. How was I supposed to trust him? My insides felt like a toothpick house built by a third-grader, and I was one soft breeze from blowing over. I had to get out of here. I was too wrapped up in him, too afraid of my feelings, to think rationally.

"I need to make a coffee run anyway." He stood and pulled a T-shirt over his head.

"Please don't." I swallowed. I'd never been all that skilled at making good choices, so it was no wonder this went down like a pack of razor blades. When he stilled at my tone, I tore my own heart out. "What I mean is, I need a little bit of space."

His face hardened as he crossed his arms over his chest. "You want space?"

"Yes." I hated the way he was looking at me, but I couldn't lie to him and act like I was fine when I clearly wasn't. "I've got a lot on my mind that I need to sort out, about us, and I can't do that when I'm around you."

"Wow. I'm surprised you said it to my face this time, instead of trying to sneak out when I was in the shower or something." He gave me a slow clap. "You must be growing up."

A direct hit. He might as well have ripped a page out of my family's playbook, and I had no doubt he was aware of that too. It was the worst part of knowing someone your entire life. They'd always know exactly how best to hurt you.

"I guess you've got me all figured out." I spun around and marched toward his front door.

My bottom lip trembled, and I pressed a hand against my nose to keep it from running. Even as every step away became more painful than the last, I made myself leave. He didn't follow. Which only reenforced that I'd been right.

But it didn't feel anything like winning.

*   *   *

I drove to my brother's on autopilot. At one point, I was pretty sure I ran a stop sign, based on all the honking that followed, but it wasn't the first time I'd missed some very key signs. The urge to drive directly to the library tapped against my mind. An incessant rhythm demanding me to fall back on old comforts and bad habits. I didn't know if Neeta was working—she still hadn't texted me back—but being a good friend meant not being a pain in the ass or making her job harder. The only reason I'd be going to the library anymore would be to check out books. And if I needed to lie down somewhere, they made beds for that. Which I'd have to get around to buying. Eventually.

It wasn't until I'd gotten into the elevator and looked up at the mirrored ceiling that I realized I was still wearing Cade's shirt and boxers. All of my clothes were upstairs.

If things had gone differently this morning, maybe I wouldn't have cared if Seb saw me in Cade's underwear, but now there was no reason for him to ever know I'd hooked up with his best friend. Even when I was angry at Cade, I still respected what he meant to my brother.

I only needed to make it to the guest room, and then I could change. I'd just have to be sneaky about it. Seb was probably sleeping anyway. It was a holiday weekend. He had told me to knock from now on, and despite telling him to shut it—because he was my brother and that was the only reasonable response when he told me what to do—I had intended on respecting his wishes. But that would've messed up the whole sneaking-in part of my plan.

I slid the key into the lock like I was trying to extract the funny bone in Operation and one wrong move would set the buzzer off. Once the deadbolt clicked, I pressed my ear against the door. No footsteps. No sign of Seb preparing to accuse me of being an underwear-stealing friendship ruiner. I exhaled and pushed the door open. The living room was empty. No lights on. Huh. Maybe he really was sleeping. I'd just change and pack up what I needed for the week, then be on my way. I tiptoed toward the guest room, across from his dining nook, where . . .

Oh God. There wasn't enough bleach in the world for my eyes.

Seb and Neeta were going at it on his dining room table. Neeta's skirt was around her waist, and Seb's pants hung off his ass, as if they'd been in a serious hurry. The salt and pepper shakers I'd gotten him as a housewarming gift two years ago were shattered on his laminate wood floors. Those roosters had deserved better.

"What the fuck? I told you to knock from now on." Seb turned away to cover himself and helped Neeta sit up. She pushed her skirt and sweater back into position, her cheeks stained with a fierce blush. "Why are you here? And why are you wearing Cade's underwear?"

It was painfully awkward for all of us. Neeta wouldn't look at me. Seb probably wanted to murder me. And I would've been just fine with a sinkhole opening beneath my feet. The void would've been a welcome escape. I couldn't answer a single one of his questions, so I stood there with my mouth hanging open, unsure of how to proceed.

"I just . . ." I waved my hands around. "I'm so sorry." I gave Neeta horrified look and backed into the guest room, promptly shutting the door behind me.

No wonder she hadn't texted me all weekend. Seb must've been keeping her pretty occupied. I'd gotten the impression at the bar that she hadn't been as into him, but I probably should've expected this. Much like myself, Seb had a way of growing on people when they least suspected it. I definitely wanted the rest of the story, but not yet. I needed a minute to process what I'd witnessed before I attempted to scrub the memory from my brain forever.

A tap sounded on the other side of the wall. A small voice. "Isla? Can I come in?"

I opened the door for Neeta and grinned at her as I sat on the bed with my hands clasped under my chin. "Are we going to talk about this? Or do you want to pretend it never happened?"

She gave me a crooked smile. "I get a choice?"

"I learned friendship tips from the best." I patted the mattress beside me, and she took a careful seat on the edge. The situation was the kind of embarrassing that would probably be funny later, but I had no idea why she looked so nervous. "Are you and Seb a thing now?"

"Maybe? I think we might be anyway." She stared down at her hands in her lap, one folded over the other. "We haven't really talked about it. We haven't done much talking this weekend, period, to be honest."

"Nope." I plugged my ears. "I do not need those details."

She let out a short laugh. "You're not upset, are you?"

"Why would I be upset? I introduced you two, but even if I hadn't, I'd still support your choices." As I said those last words, I couldn't help but think of how Seb would react if he caught me with Cade. Would he really care that much? Or would he just be hurt we didn't tell him? "Seb is my brother, but between us, I think you might be too good for him."

"I can hear you," Seb yelled. "You know how thin my walls are."

"I'm not so sure I want my best friend attaching herself to someone who listens in on private conversations," I said loud enough to make a point. The distinct thunk of a shoe hitting wood sounded against the door. "But if you're happy, I'm happy for you."

Neeta darted a glance at the door. "I'm pleasantly surprised with how it's progressing."

"Fair, but if you two have an ugly breakup, I'm a hundred percent taking your side."

"As you should." She stood and smoothed down her skirt. "I need to get to work, but I'm sorry I didn't text you back earlier this weekend. I was a little busy."

I made a face. "Really don't want to know."

Neeta promised to call later, since we couldn't exactly discuss her and Seb with him right there. Then she went back out to the living room and said her goodbyes. There was some low whispering and kissing—all stuff I'd have to get used to. Though it didn't bother me to see Seb and Neeta together. Fully clothed anyway. They actually made perfect sense.

After the front door shut, I steeled myself for the discussion I knew was coming. Sure enough, not two seconds later, Seb leaned against the guest-room doorframe with a shit-eating grin on his face. "Do I need to take back my spare key?"

"Consider what I saw in there an airtight deterrent from ever using it again."

He nodded once. "I see you've stolen more of Cade's clothes. Is this because of your weird fixation on him, or is there something going on that you're both not telling me?"

"I do *not* have a fixation on Cade." At least I didn't used to. "Why do you even care? Weren't you just getting busy with my best friend on your dining room table? Which I'll never eat another meal on, by the way."

"Let's see." Seb tapped a finger to his chin. "You move all your crap into my guest room but don't sleep here. Then show up in Cade's clothes, minus Cade, after you two acted suspicious as fuck at the bar on Friday. Either you're hooking up, or one of you is dying."

"We're not hooking up." Cade appeared in the doorway beside Seb.

My heart leaped at the sight of him, even though I was still hurt and angry about his growing-up comment. But at least he'd answered any lingering questions I might've had about our status. We weren't hooking up. Message received, loud and clear.

"Oh my God." Seb clapped a hand over his mouth. "One of you is *dying*?"

I shook my head. My poor brother. Brilliant in so many ways, and yet . . . "Have you considered neither as an option?"

A stunned look crossed his face, as if he truly had not considered that. "Then what is going on with you two? Have you roped my best friend into some kind of scam?"

"Knock it off with the scam accusations," Cade said. My eyes widened as I glanced between the two of them. I'd never once seen Cade raise his voice or lose his temper with Seb.

I didn't know how to process it. "Why don't you give Isla a break? She's had a rough month, and she doesn't need shit from her family on top of it."

"How rough of a month?" Seb's gaze darted to my boxes, then back to me, and I watched in horror as all the gears clicked into place for him, one by one. "You got kicked out of your apartment, didn't you? What happened?"

"I stopped paying my rent."

An old but familiar disappointment marred his features, and I couldn't do anything but sit there. Helpless. While every bit of respect I'd worked so hard to earn slipped away. My nose started to run, and I squeezed my eyes shut, begging for tears instead. Of course they wouldn't come. I turned my attention to Cade, who just stood there with his hands in his pockets and his shoulders hunched forward, looking part ashamed and part relieved he didn't have to keep my secret anymore. As I glared at him, the betrayal shredded me apart from the inside out. Even though I should've known better. He had always been Seb's best friend. Never mine. My fault for assuming he might've had any loyalty to me.

"I'm sure you can't wait to get on the phone with Mom and Dad, so the three of you can discuss all the ways I continue to let you down." Before Seb could say another word, I grabbed a plastic bag full of clothes, and pushed past the two of them. I had one foot out the door when Cade took hold of my elbow to stop me. I yanked my arm free. "Are you happy? Now you don't have to lie to my brother anymore. Good for you."

"I didn't mean for it to come out that way, but I'm not sorry it did."

"That makes one of us."

His expression was unreadable. The electric current between us was present and buzzing, though neither of us reached out for the other. "Stay. I'll go. You need help, and you've made it clear you don't want it from me."

"I think you've already done enough." Everything throbbed as I walked away and took the elevator down to my car.

On the drive over to Hugh's, I replayed the entire morning in my mind. The outcome didn't change, and reliving it didn't help. Seb knew the truth now. Or at least most of it. The rest he'd be able to piece together easily enough with Cade there to fill him in on the finer details. It would only be a matter of time before my parents started blowing up my phone, demanding answers. Then every lie would come crashing down. Just like Cade had predicted.

I parked next to the curb in front of Hugh's enormous house, but before I got out of my car, I paused. Something felt off. Like I'd forgotten to unplug my straightener, even though I hadn't flat ironed my hair in almost a week. The blinds in a window next door lifted, then quickly snapped shut again. Not a single bird tweeted from the trees. It was as if the entire neighborhood held its collective breath while I approached the front door.

The entrance appeared the same, but disturbed somehow. An air bubble in the laminate. My internal danger sensors blared as I strained my ears to listen for any odd sounds, which only resulted in a pulled muscle in my neck. Carefully, I tip-toed into the living room and stopped short. The back window had been broken out. Shards of glass were scattered across the plush carpeting like glittering splinters of ice. The flat screen still hung on the wall, but the laptop on the office desk and the tablets in the decorative cabinet were gone.

Clutching my phone in my sweaty hand, I ran back outside to call 911.

CHAPTER TWENTY-FIVE

The police arrived with their lights flashing so everyone could be informed of their presence. Though no one stood in their yards to gawk. They probably thought they were above such behavior around here, but I didn't miss the movement of curtains and blinds from every occupied house around me. It was probably the most exciting thing to have happened in this neighborhood since they broke ground on the development.

A guy who looked like Yogi Bear on steroids exited one of the vehicles while a woman with a firmly defined jawline stayed in the other car and observed. They looked at me like I was both guilty and wasting their time. This would be fun.

"Are you the one who called?" Yogi Bear flipped open a small notebook. "Isla Jane, is that right? Are you the owner of this home?"

He gave me a once-over, taking in my stolen briefs, dollar-store flip-flops, and Cade's faded T-shirt with a loose string on the hemline that hung down past my hips. A smirk tipped the corner of his mouth. *I get it, buddy. I couldn't possibly own this place.*

"I'm actually the house sitter." Once I explained who I was and why I'd been inside a home I didn't own, Yogi Bear asked me to give a statement and wrote down the minimal details I'd been able to provide in his tiny notebook. Or he'd just been drawing stick figures while I talked. It's not like I would've known the difference.

The other police officer finally exited her vehicle. She was short and hard everywhere, like a small boulder. "You're lucky you weren't here, ma'am. There have been a string of burglaries in this neighborhood, and a gentleman who cancelled his vacation last minute was beaten pretty badly when the robbers stumbled on him by surprise."

My pulse froze and a heavy weight dropped in my stomach. Yogi Bear gave me a look that suggested any panic on my part would continue to be a waste of his precious time. "This can't be unexpected news. Why do you think people hire house sitters?"

"To feed their animals and water their plants," I said weakly.

Small Boulder snorted. "We've learned that the residents in this neighborhood have been targeted after they've posted about their vacations on Facebook, giving the exact dates of when they won't be home and how long they'll be gone. We've sent out several warning fliers, but it looks like the owner of this home decided to ignore us."

Of course Hugh posted about his upcoming vacation on Facebook. From what little time I'd spent in his house, it was clear he was a man who valued appearances over people. So, while it ended up being a good thing I hadn't been there during the robbery, I had a feeling he wouldn't see it the same way. I'd literally been hired to do one job: sit in the house and be a warm body to deter burglars. And I couldn't even do that.

Before the police left, they contacted Hugh. He was at his cabin, a little over an hour north of here on Lake Luna. He expected me to be there when he arrived home.

It felt wrong to wait for him inside, like I'd lost the right to be there. Once the neighbors got bored and stopped staring at me, I ran back inside to stuff the half-wet and wrinkled clothes I never got around to drying in my suitcase, and wheeled it out to my trunk. I sat in my car and made it through a bunch of levels on Blossom Blast before Hugh screeched into his driveway. With his pointed eyebrows, angry expression, and brutal sunburn, he resembled a vintage devil.

He got out of his car and just stood there with his hands on his hips. I was surprised he didn't point at the ground by his feet, like I was a misbehaving dog in need of a scolding. "What happened here, Isla? Didn't I pay you to sit my house?"

"Yes." He wasn't really asking, but I felt obligated to answer him anyway. I had to take responsibility and face this head-on. There were no excuses. I hadn't done the job I'd been paid for, and I'd pissed off a high-ranking executive at Cornerstone to boot. "I'll of course refund you what you've paid me so far and sit the rest of the week for free."

"Oh no." He let out a laugh that sounded as dead and dry as my promotion prospects. "You're not sitting the rest of the week. What's the point? My house has already been robbed."

"I'm sorry." There wasn't anything else I could say. There was no going back, and even if I could, I was glad I hadn't been here last night. Maybe I would've been a deterrent, but maybe not. It was the "maybe not" scenarios that caused a chill to burrow in my bones.

"*Sorry* isn't going to fix this." He turned up his nose. "Alice posted about her vacation on Facebook, and she didn't have any trouble because you were there. She trusted you, and because of that, I trusted you."

My palms began to sweat as my internal warning bells wreaked havoc on my nervous system. "You knew the break-ins were happening because of Facebook?"

He narrowed his eyes, which somehow made his eyebrows pointier. "I don't like what your question is implying."

"I didn't mean—"

"Why do you think I hired you? Why do you think Alice hired you?"

"I thought Alice needed someone to water her plants and walk her dog." As I said it out loud, I recognized how foolish I sounded. Hugh didn't even have plants or animals.

He waved a hand, dismissing me entirely. "Just go. There's no reason for you to be here anymore. And believe me, Alice is going to be hearing about this."

I nodded and left without another word, completely dejected. The engine on my car choked and coughed as I turned the key. As if it wanted to send me a message. My house-sitting career was over—no one at the office would hire me after this; my ten-year-old car was on the verge of another bank-breaking problem; and I had run out of options. My job at Cornerstone was secure, there was no way Hugh could get neglected house-sitting duties to fly through HR, though that didn't feel much like a victory.

And I did feel terrible that Hugh had gotten robbed, but I felt even worse that he was genuinely pissed I hadn't been there while it happened. He knew his neighborhood was being targeted through Facebook, and he chose to post about his vacation without telling me about the risk. Because bragging about his second home to a bunch of old high school acquaintances was more important than my safety. But maybe that was just part of being a house sitter. I had no idea because I didn't really know what I was doing. I'd been faking my way through this for weeks.

Still, I posed no threat to him. I'd already Venmoed back the money he'd paid me. Yet with his parting shot he'd implied he'd come for my job at Cornerstone, even when he had everything and I had nothing.

With nowhere else to go, I drove back to my brother's condo. I sat in the parking garage and debated which way the misery scales tipped between sleeping in my car and asking Seb if I could crash at his place for the night. Swallowing the urge to scream and beat my fists against my steering wheel, I got out of my car and took the elevator up. Cade had once told me shame was a luxury. I finally understood what he meant when I could no longer afford it.

Seb answered a second after I knocked. He took one look at me and wrapped me in a hug. "I swear, I won't tell Mom and Dad without your permission."

"Thank you," I mumbled against his arm.

He let go of me and ushered me toward the living room. "Sit down. I'm going to get us both a beer, and then we're going to do some talking."

"Okay." There was so much to say, so much I'd been keeping from him, and it was long past time for me to be honest. "I hope it's not the cheap stuff we drank in college. I refuse."

"Please. Don't insult me." He came back to the living room and set a bottle of Oberon in front of me. The hint of citrus hit my tongue and went down smooth. I should've known my brother would have the good stuff on hand. "So. You and Cade, huh?"

"There is no 'me and Cade.' We're not hooking up, remember?"

"He said what you two are doing isn't hooking up because he's in love with you."

I took a drink at the wrong moment. It went down the wrong tube, and I beat on my chest to clear my throat. "He told you that?"

"Duh." He gave me the kind of goofy grin that belonged on a gumball machine. "I know him better than I know myself. You think I haven't seen this coming for years?"

"I doubt that. You're terribly unobservant."

"Pot." He pointed at me. "Kettle." He pointed at himself.

I rolled my eyes, but smiled anyway, because he wasn't wrong. "Fine. Cade is in love with me, and I'm in love with him. Wouldn't it be great if that were enough?"

"Why isn't it though?"

"We have a lot of problems. I'm not sure if we can fix them." Just thinking about Cade hurt. We both had enormous walls and used them against each other more times than was right or fair. I didn't know how to stop being defensive or how to stop worrying that he would throw up his defenses against me. "I'd rather not discuss it. Can we move on to something else?"

"Let's make it a drinking game. It'll be more fun that way." He finished off his beer and set it aside. "One drink for every time you change the subject."

"I have to work tomorrow."

"Then do yourself a favor and try to stay on topic." He gestured at me to drink up, then went back to the kitchen to get us two more Oberons.

While I appreciated his not-so-sneaky attempt to keep me from shutting down every time he hit a little too close to home, I really did have to work in the morning. And so did he. Why wasn't he as concerned about being hungover?

He set another beer in front of me. "This one is for your house-sitting business."

I buried my face in my hands. Looked like Cade hadn't held anything back. "I don't think my house-sitting business is going to survive after this morning."

I gave him the rundown on everything that had happened at Hugh's. Seb's eyebrows rose higher and higher until I got to the end, where Hugh had dismissed me from his driveway. Seb held up a finger. "First of all, fuck him for treating you like that. Second, it sucks his house got robbed, but who the fuck cares? I'm sure he has insurance."

"He does." Seb's anger on my behalf threw the situation into sharp relief. Even though I could never wish I'd been there during the robbery, I had started to convince myself I deserved to be spoken to like that. "Anyway, he'll tell the other execs at Cornerstone, and no one else will hire me to watch their homes. Not that I'd want to after this anyway."

"There's just one thing I don't understand." He peeled the label on his beer with the corner of his thumbnail. "Why did you feel the need to start a house-sitting business in the first place? Why didn't you just stay here until you got back on your feet?"

I wasn't drunk enough for this conversation. I tipped my beer up, preparing to guzzle it down so we could talk about something else, but Seb snatched it out of my hand. Beer sloshed down the front of my shirt. "Hey. What the hell?"

"You're not changing the subject this time." He set my drink out of reach. "I want you to tell me to my face why you wouldn't stay here."

I took a deep breath. I loved my brother and I knew he had a good heart, but once I told him how I felt, it would likely change things between us. Maybe he'd feel like he had to be more careful about the things he said to me. But maybe that wasn't such a bad thing.

"You know how growing up Mom and Dad always made jokes about my screw-ups or implied that I wouldn't amount to much? And you would sometimes get in on the act too?" I lifted my gaze to meet his, not wanting to shy away from this part. "It hurt."

"Fuck." He ran his hands over his head. "Cade has been riding my ass about that for years, and I thought it didn't matter because I was just messing around, but I never intended for you to feel like you weren't welcome in my home for as long as you needed to be here."

I hated seeing my brother uncomfortable, even when it was necessary. It was in my nature to soothe and tell him it was okay, but it really wasn't, so I wouldn't say it. "Now that you're aware, it would be awesome if you could think about the things you consider jokes."

"Absolutely." He held out his pinky, a sacred swear we hadn't done since we were kids. "I'm sorry. And I hope if I slip up, you'll call me on it. You don't have to, and it's not your job to keep me in check, but I would still appreciate it all the same."

I hooked my pinky around his. "Deal."

He asked me more about the house-sitting, and I told him all about Jillian's house while he roared with laughter. I'd always been close with my brother, but after tonight, I felt like he genuinely had my back too. It didn't have to be me versus the rest of my family. And I didn't have to compete with him or try to be more like him for my parents' approval either. I deserved to be appreciated as my own person.

He gave me my beer back. "Do you want to drink to skip talking about your promotion, or have we gotten past trying to avoid the hard stuff?"

"I'm not avoiding. I'm just thirsty." I took a drink. "I lied about the promotion. It started when I accidentally let it slip to Mom that I wasn't living with Quinn and Vera anymore. I said it was because I was getting a place of my own. She was so thrilled. And so proud of me." I looked down at my hands. "I just couldn't bring myself to tell her the truth after that."

"You'll have to tell them eventually. You know that, right?"

I gulped. "Yeah."

"I think I know how to make it a little easier for you, though. And I owe you one." He picked up his phone and thumbed through his contacts. "Hey, Mom. Are you sitting down? Good. I just wanted to let you know I quit my job, and I've got nothing lined up." My jaw dropped, and he winked at me. "That's right. I'm just kicking it at home. Might lose my condo too. Who knows?" He paused. "Yep. Gotta run." He ended the call and tossed his phone on the coffee table. "And that is how it's done."

"You quit your job?" That explained so much, but at the same time explained nothing at all. "Why? What happened? I thought you loved . . . whatever you did."

"I'm not going to miss trying to explain what I do for a living to you, that's for sure." He smirked at me. "I got sick of the traveling. When they said I'd be staying in London for another month, that was pretty much the last straw."

"All right." I swiped his beer and kept it out of reach. "Why didn't you tell me?"

"I don't know." He scratched his back, the same way our dad did when he got nervous. "I guess I thought you looked up to me. And I liked being that person."

"I do look up to you." I set his drink in front of him. "But not because of where you work or what you've accomplished. You're my brother and I love you."

"Aw, shit. Are we going to have a cry together now?"

"Don't get too carried away."

We spent the rest of the night drinking—Seb more so than me since he didn't have to work the next morning—and sharing stories about growing up. I finally confessed to stealing the cookies he'd gotten grounded for. Turned out Cade never told him about that. Every anecdote, every memory included Cade. It was impossible to separate him from any aspect of my life. Our tangled threads created the fabric of our mutual history.

Sometime around midnight, I stumbled into the guest room and fell face first into the pillow. It smelled like Cade. I held it close and burrowed my nose against it, like I could trick myself into believing that he was here.

Just last night he'd been murmuring declarations of love while he brought my body to new heights. So much had happened since then. It seemed like a lifetime ago now.

I closed my eyes, and my last thoughts as I began to drift off were, of course, about Cade. Had I been too much of a mess this morning, too scared, too worried about protecting myself? I was new to this self-love thing. I was bound to overcorrect. Didn't accepting love also mean accepting that it could fail, and taking that leap anyway?

What was love without trust, after all?

CHAPTER TWENTY-SIX

The next morning, I woke up to find Seb sleeping in front of the open refrigerator. He had a stick of butter in one hand and nail polish remover in the other. I really didn't want to know what he'd gotten into after I'd gone to bed last night.

I only had a mild headache, thanks to my wise decision to switch to water after my third Oberon. I mentally high-fived Past Isla, and stepped over a snoring Seb to grab the carton of orange juice. A little toast and I'd be good to go for the day.

The first day back to work after a holiday weekend hit a little harder. My body had been duped into a state of relaxation, and it screamed against the muscles in my neck and shoulders clenching with weekday stress. Humans were not built to live in cubicles for nine hours a day. I said hi to the person I shared a partition with, but she was tapping away on her phone and either didn't hear or didn't care. And I wondered why I didn't have any work friends.

Alice Bishop exited the elevator, and the sound of phones being shut in desk drawers pinged around the open cavern we called an office. She glanced at me. A barely visible turn of her head. While her expression didn't change, I felt her judgment as surely as if she'd openly yelled at me. I felt more vulnerable than I had when I'd first seen her holding the genuine version of my knockoff Cucci.

She couldn't fire me, though. Not for blowing off my house-sitting duties for her friend. The only good thing about working for a soulless corporation was their airtight HR department. It was actually incredibly hard to get someone fired as long as they showed up when scheduled and did the bare minimum, which I excelled at.

"What did you do?" The disembodied voice floating over the partition startled me.

"I didn't do anything."

Sharon, my Audi-driving cubicle neighbor had put away her phone and found me worthy of speaking to again. "You sure? She's pissed at you for some reason."

"How can you tell?" I could tell Alice was pissed at me, but only because I knew she must've spoken to Hugh. If I saw her on the street, I wouldn't have thought anything at all. "Doesn't she always look like she's just stepped in shit?"

"We were friends forever ago." Sharon stood because it was a little weird talking to someone through a fabric and plywood wall. "Alice used to sit where you are now."

"Wow." I had no idea Alice had once been a cubicle dweller. I'd just assumed most executives were assembled in factories before being placed in their offices. "You were friends? Does that mean you're not anymore?"

Sharon laughed. "No. We stopped being friends when her uncle decided she'd paid her entry-level dues and moved her on up the ladder. She said it was for HR reasons, since she became my boss, but we all know how it goes."

I thought about Alice's cold and impersonal house, freakish dog notwithstanding. How she seemed to have so much, but it was all so empty. And to think, just a few short weeks ago, I'd actually been jealous of her expensive but lonely existence. "I'm sorry that happened."

"It is what it is." Sharon shrugged. "I knew she wasn't long for this position when she started. Most of the MBAs move up pretty fast."

"I have an MBA."

"You do?" She pursed her hot-pink lips. "I never would've guessed."

"I'm a little short on rich uncles paving my way."

"Ah. Yeah. The other piece of the puzzle." She turned her attention back to her phone as she sat down again, her voice already taking on a dismissive and distant quality, letting me know our brief conversation was over. "Don't worry—you probably won't be here long. They'll either get around to promoting you, or you'll get sick of the long hours and shitty pay and some other company will offer you fifty cents more an hour. Either way, you'll be out of here."

I'd shared breathable air with Sharon for over a year and knew nothing about her other than that she hadn't gone to college, drove an Audi, and liked to blast screaming death metal on her way out of the parking lot on Fridays. She never worked more than forty hours, which I respected. It was too bad we'd never been friends. Now that she knew I had my MBA and assumed I was already gone in one way or another, we probably never would be either.

Right before lunch, Alice stepped out of her office. The look she gave me immediately dropped the temperature in the room by ten degrees. Several heads popped up over cubicle partitions like stock-photo jack-in-the-boxes. All of them seeking out the source of the big boss's wrath with gleeful voyeurism, all of them secretly relieved Alice's attention was directed elsewhere.

"Isla, can I see you in my office?" It was framed like a question, but it was not.

I stood and Sharon didn't even glance up from her phone. As I made the long walk of shame between the gray boxes, I kept repeating that she couldn't fire me, couldn't fire me, couldn't fire me. I stepped into the office with a nice view and a door, and a strange buzzing noise hummed in my ears when my direct boss and a man I didn't recognize looked at me with stern frowns.

"Close the door, Elsa." My direct boss, the man I'd reported to for over a year, still couldn't be bothered to learn my name, even for what appeared to be a very serious meeting. The insult of it stung more than usual.

The man I didn't recognize gestured for me to have a seat. "My name is Mitch Clarke, I'm an HR representative here at Cornerstone Enterprises."

All the color drained from my face. "You can't be serious." I turned to Alice, hating the pleading in my voice and the measured chill in her expression. "I'm sorry Hugh's house got robbed, and I'm sorry I wasn't there to get murdered for a couple of iPads, but you can't fire me for that. It has nothing to do with my work here."

Mitch furrowed his brow as he looked between me and Alice. "I'm not entirely sure what you're referring to, but I assure you, this meeting is strictly about an incident that took place on Cornerstone property just over four weeks ago."

He turned the computer screen monitor toward me, and there I was, caught on camera. Sneaking into the Cornerstone offices after hours to sleep under my desk. He fast-forwarded the security footage to the morning, where I'd woken up, tried to get out without being seen, then backtracked to talk to Alice once I overheard her phone conversation. It was all there. There was no way I'd be able to talk myself out of this one.

I glanced at Alice. She gave me just the hint of a smug smile, and I knew. Right then, I knew she'd been aware that I slept under my desk the whole time. She couldn't technically fire me for what had happened at Hugh's house, but those with means always found a way.

I couldn't defend myself. I had nothing left but the truth. "I got kicked out of my apartment. When I didn't think I had anywhere else to go, I came here to sleep. My student loan debt is more than I can handle, and I haven't been able to get a promotion."

"Excuse me." Alice held up a red-tipped finger. "Don't put that on us. I've seen your employee reviews, and it's no wonder you've never been promoted. You display a complete lack of initiative and have no one to blame but yourself."

"That isn't what we're here for," Mitch said. "Your past reviews aren't my concern. If you were in trouble, we have resources."

"Oh yeah, right." I snorted. "Fill out a form and get a list of local charities that might be able to help. It wouldn't have solved my immediate need for shelter. But you know what might've? Being paid a living wage."

"This building employs over five thousand people, yet you're the only one treating it like a bed and breakfast," Alice said. "I don't think the problem is our wages."

It was easy for Alice to say that from her position, but I watched the guy two cubicles over from me make lunch out of beans from a dented can. A woman who sat five rows over from me wore the same dress every single day, and just swapped out two different cardigans to make it look like she changed clothes. Another one who sat three rows over had ripped a seventy-five-cent A-line skirt out of my hands at Goodwill, and I nearly tackled her in the store before we both realized we worked together, and it got really awkward. I wasn't the only one who had an issue with their wages; I was just the only one who'd thought to use this empty building in the off-hours for something other than grinding data. And they said I lacked initiative.

"Regardless. You committed a very serious violation," Mitch said. "I'm afraid we have no choice but to terminate your employment, effective immediately."

* * *

As I took the elevator up to my brother's condo, with my "just been fired" box in hand, I glanced up at the mirrored ceiling. I'd become the world's worst sad girl cliché. I even had a half-dead plant hanging limply over the side of the cardboard box. For over a year, my desk had been my home away from home, and for one night my actual home, yet I had so little to show for it.

I'd already sent out my CV over the weekend as part of my quest to better myself, and I could only hope one of those places called me for an interview before the gap in my employment became too large to ignore. What surprised me more than anything else was the sense of calm I felt when I probably should've been freaking out. Maybe I was in shock, and it hadn't yet set in that I'd been fired. Or maybe Cornerstone had never been a great place to work, and I was too at the end of my rope to give a shit anymore.

Standing in front of Seb's door, I balanced my box of personal effects with one arm while I dug out the key, unlocked the door, and pushed it open with my butt. I headed to the guest room to change clothes, and at the dining nook, I got another eyeful of something I really didn't want to see. For the second time in as many days. Neeta screamed when she saw me, and she and Seb did the mad scramble to cover up. Again.

"For fuck's sake, you two. The bedroom is right there," I said.

"Beds are boring. I apologize for nothing." Seb buttoned his pants, then turned around to face me. "Aren't you supposed to be at work?"

"I got fired."

"What?" Neeta shoved Seb aside and rushed to me. "What happened? Are you okay?"

"I'll be fine." It was a comfort to know I actually believed that. I hadn't been fine in a very long time. The pressure to hold all my fraying strings together had been eating me alive, and it was such a relief to just . . . stop. "I've never been happy there anyway."

Seb put his arm around Neeta and rubbed her shoulder with his hand. "Do you want to go out and have some 'fuck you' drinks anyway? I'll buy."

"No. I'm good."

I glanced between the two of them. They were in a new relationship, and I fully understood how engrossing it could be when you wanted someone twenty-four hours a day. To think about them every second you weren't together and how your hand itched to touch them every second you were together. My brother deserved to have his privacy. This was his place, and he didn't need his sister around when he wanted to have sex on his dining room table. No matter how disgusting I still found that.

"Are you sure? I have a short shift today, and I'll be off by six," Neeta said. "We could even hang out here and watch a movie if you don't want to go out."

"I'm actually going to my parents' for a while." I looked over at Seb, hoping he would understand that I did feel welcome in his home, but I couldn't use that as an excuse to avoid the truth any longer. "There are some hard conversations I need to have with Mom and Dad, and then I'll figure out what my next steps are going to be."

I promised Neeta I would text her for a movie night this coming weekend, then I loaded up as many boxes of necessities as I could in my car. I told Seb I'd have the rest of the guest room cleaned out by Friday. While he made it clear again that I could stay with him and we'd eat string cheese and be unemployed together, that wasn't what I wanted for him or me. Part of becoming an adult included being honest with my parents and not avoiding them because it was easier for all of us. If it all went well, I'd ask for their help. There was nothing shameful about moving back in with them while I made a plan and got back on my feet. And if it didn't go well, then I'd have to make a different plan.

On the drive to their house, I thought a lot about what I'd undergone in the last month and how I'd chosen to respond.

I'd made some poor decisions, but I wasn't going beat myself up over them. Desperation did strange things to people. They acted in ways they might not have otherwise. I'd also learned some things about myself that I didn't necessarily like, but I was trying to do better, trying to be better, and that's really all anyone could do.

I parked along my parents' curb. My mom's car was missing, and when I knocked on their front door, no one answered. I went around to the back, but my dad's workshop was empty too. He might've had a doctor's appointment. They'd come back soon enough. My mom worked from home, and my dad was supposed to be resting.

The sound of chimes dancing in the breeze caught my attention, and I glanced at Meadow Greenley's back porch, where a hollowed-out moon and stars clanked against each other. I stepped into the yard I'd never spent much time in, growing up, despite it being right next door. The plastic pool that had been Cade's still sat in the backyard, sun faded and overgrown with weeds. Meadow still had her herb garden, but it was covered in so many stinging nettles, I doubted she'd done anything with it in years. Unless that was the so-called tranquil garden she wanted the birdhouse for. In which case, yikes.

The windows in the house were dark. My mom had told me a few years ago that Meadow's new-age shop had been doing well thanks to a feature in a local newspaper. It was tucked into a trendy part of town that featured a few head shops, tattoo parlors, smoothie bars, and a local bookshop and gallery. But I truly didn't care. All the success in the world couldn't absolve what she'd done to Cade.

I took a seat in the overgrown yard and tried to view my surroundings the way Cade would've all those years ago. The parents he must've loved, who let him down time and time again. The found family he had next door, who often made him feel ashamed of the circumstances that were out of his control. How hard he must've fought to make something of himself when he had so much working against him from the start. It was no wonder he had so many walls in place to protect himself. It had been as necessary to him as breathing.

He'd opened up to me the other night, taken some of those walls down, and let me in. And I'd thrown it back in his face the next morning because of my own issues. My chest twisted painfully as I played over yesterday morning again and again. The things I'd said, the hurt in his eyes, all of my mistakes. I shouldn't have walked away. And I shouldn't be hiding out here, telling all this to myself, when I should be having this conversation with the person who mattered.

I jumped to my feet, intending to unload my car in my parents' driveway before heading over to Cade's condo. Gas would be an issue. Maybe my dad had a handful of quarters mixed in with the screws and bolts he kept in an old coffee can in his workshop. Either way, I needed to get to Cade's and sit outside his place until he came home from work. He could tell me to leave or fight with me or whatever, but I'd stay there until we fixed what I had broken.

I pushed through the overgrown bushes, back to my parents' property, and stopped short at the sight of Cade standing in their yard with his hands in his pockets. His hair stuck up in the back at an odd angle, like he'd slept funny, and the shadows under his eyes had returned. He looked miserable, and I wanted to cry. Of course my nose started running instead.

"Hey, Rainbow Bear."

That was all I needed to hear. Before he could say another word, I ran to him and threw my arms around his shoulders, knocking us both backward. He let out a choked laugh as he regained his balance. And when he held me tight against him, I buried my face in his neck and breathed in the scent of finally finding my home.

CHAPTER TWENTY-SEVEN

I still couldn't believe Cade was in my parents' backyard. The man I loved, with everything that I had, wrapped his arms around me like I was his lifeline in a chaotic sea. I squished his face between my hands and kissed his forehead, nose, lips—everywhere. He wore a dazed and slightly confused expression, but he didn't push me away. That's all I cared about.

"What are you doing here?" I asked.

"I went to your brother's first—I'm never eating dinner at his place again, by the way—and he told me you got fired. He said you were moving back in with your parents?"

"It's true. The house-sitting business is no more, but we had a good run. You were also right about sleeping under my desk leading to termination." It didn't even pain me to tell him he was right. Was that called growth?

"I'm sorry."

"I'm actually not."

I had nothing but opportunity in front of me. I could start over and do something I liked or work for people like Ted and Anton. I'd become comfortable and apathetic at Cornerstone, knowing full well I'd never want to be there for the long term. Getting fired might end up being the best thing that had ever happened to me. Second best thing. After my now defunct house-sitting business that had, in a roundabout way, finally gotten me and Cade to figure out the feelings we'd been having our entire lives.

And while I'd never be a librarian—my student loan debt was still a monster I'd never be able to escape—maybe I could find a new passion and use my degree in a meaningful way. Not getting my first choice in careers didn't mean I had to give up the joy I got from reading. Not everything I loved was out to hurt me.

"Speaking of jobs and things," I said, "shouldn't you be at work?"

"I called off. I had some vacation time built up." He rubbed the back of his neck and gave me a sheepish look. "I, uh, came here to win you back, but you kind of ruined my grand gesture."

"I'm amazing at ruining things. I should put it on my résumé." I grinned because my face literally could not do anything else. He had come here for me. We weren't over. I hadn't broken us. "I'm so sorry for yesterday. All of it. I love you. I should've said it sooner, but if you still love me too, I swear I'll spend the rest of my life showing you just how much every single day."

"Isla." He held my chin and brushed his thumb along my jawline. "There isn't a damn thing in this world that could ever make me stop loving you."

Unable to hold out any longer, I kissed him, slow and toe-curling deep.

This. This right here was what I'd been missing. The feel of him against me, the soft press of his lips, the need for him that I hoped would never go away. If we'd been anywhere other than my parents' backyard, I would've shown him exactly how much I missed him and how it made me feel to have him here with me. He tipped me back, kissing me with the kind of urgency that made me forget everything except him and me and the way we fit together. I gripped the collar of his shirt to drag him closer, when someone let out a short cough. We broke apart, breathing heavily through swollen lips, to find my parents gaping at us.

No matter how little I cared about their opinion these days, it was still awkward as hell to get caught in the middle of some serious making out by them.

"Mom. Dad. Hey. You know Cade." I patted his chest. "Boy next door who became a man and is now my boyfriend, probably."

Cade squeezed my shoulder as a gentle reminder that I was free to quit talking at any time. "Good to see you both. I hope you don't mind that I'm here."

"You're always welcome in our home, Cade." My dad said this with a certain formality that had Cade stiffening beside me. When he told me all that stuff about my parents that I'd never seen before, this was what he'd been talking about. And maybe I hadn't noticed it before, but I damn well did now, and it wasn't going to fly with me.

"Do you have a problem with me and Cade together? Because if you do, I'm telling you right now that I choose him. Every time." I glanced at Cade, who looked devasted we were even in this position, which only made me more furious. "I think we need to talk."

My dad kicked at a loose rock while Cade stared at the ground like he hoped it would swallow him up. A soft breeze blew through the yard, carrying the scent of Mrs. Brisbane's flowers, which only fueled my anger. The tension between the four of us thickened.

My mom cleared her throat. "I think talking is a good idea. Cade, honey, why don't you come inside and help get some glasses for lemonade from the tall shelf."

She steered Cade into the house, leaving me alone outside with my dad. I crossed my arms and glared at him. "What was that?"

My dad averted his gaze. "Not sure what you're talking about."

"Stop. You just used the same tone with Cade that you do with anyone who knocks on the front door because they want to sell you window treatments or tell you the good word of the Lord. Like you were about two seconds away from spraying him with a hose."

He scratched his back. "I just wasn't prepared to come home from a quick run up to the Home Depot to find my only daughter making out with someone in our backyard."

"Are you upset that it was 'someone'? Or are you upset that someone was Cade?"

"I don't know." A stricken look crossed my dad's face, as if it was just now dawning on him what type of person he was, and it didn't match who he thought he'd always been. "Don't get me wrong; Cade is like a son to me, but I guess I never considered how I'd feel if you two started dating. It changes things."

"Not really." The other night Seb said he'd seen me and Cade coming for years, and the truth of that statement hit home. We had always been endgame. It just took us a lot of years to get there. "And I think, deep down, you've known we'd be here someday too."

My dad frowned and turned toward the house. "I imagine your mom has the lemonade set up by now. Maybe we should get to it before it gets warm."

I knew what he was doing. Passing the problem off to my mom because he hated confrontation, but I wasn't going to let him get away without at least hearing me out. What he chose to do afterward would be up to him.

Inside, my mom and Cade sat at the dining room table. She had a hand on his arm, their expressions serious, but not in an unsettling way. It was a humid day, and even with all the windows open and the fans going, a stifling wet heat hung in the air. The pitcher of lemonade on the table dripped with condensation. I took a seat next to Cade and touched his knee under the table. He gave me a reassuring smile in return. We both watched as my dad limped into the living room, and that pang that came from watching him get older hit me again. Even when my parents frustrated me, I loved them and hated to see them in pain.

My mom poured my dad a glass and fussed over him a bit before taking a seat. "I know you had some stuff you wanted to talk about, Isla, but I thought you should know going in that I completely support you and Cade getting together. In fact, I think it's lovely."

"Thank you. I appreciate your saying that." Though what they thought about my relationship with Cade wasn't my primary concern when I had several other, much larger, hurdles to address. "But that's not why I came here today."

"We saw the boxes in your car," my mom said. "Is there something going on with you that you haven't been telling us?"

"Yeah. There's been a lot actually." I ran my finger over a divot in the oak table that was worn and scratched from decades of family dinners. "I got fired today." At my mom's gasp, I looked up. "I never got a promotion either. I only told you that because I didn't want to tell you I'd been kicked out of my apartment for not paying rent."

"Isla, honey." My mom reached across the table to grip my hand. "Why didn't you come to us if you were having trouble? We could've helped out."

Here I was again, in the exact same position I'd been in last night with Seb. Except this one was harder. Because I knew exactly how my brother had learned all his jokes. "I'm going to say some things that might upset you, but I really hope you'll listen to me anyway." I glanced at my dad, who had been purposely quiet the entire time. "I hope you'll both listen."

"Okay." My mom sounded hesitant, as if she was remembering my last visit and her defenses were already going up. "Go on."

"I didn't ask for your help because I'd finally gotten to the point where you no longer treated me like I'd already failed at life. You make these insensitive comments all the time, calling people 'freeloaders' and judging anyone who struggles, and I didn't want to go back to enduring that. It's hurtful and I want it to stop."

My mom looked at my dad. "Maybe we took the jokes too far sometimes, but to say that's some kind of proof that we don't love you or wouldn't want to help you is pretty extreme, and I'm not sure what to do with that."

I'd expected her to have a much worse reaction, but it still stung. "And turning it around on me by saying I just took it too personal is a pretty awful way to respond."

"I'm at a loss." She lifted a shoulder. "If I had known college was going to brainwash you into thinking we're the enemy, I might not have pushed so hard for you to go. This isn't right. I feel like no matter what I say, you'll twist up my words."

My face fell. If that's truly how she saw this, as an attack, then what hope did I have of her listening and making any sort of meaningful change? I didn't like telling my parents they'd hurt me. I didn't want to sit here and explain to them why I couldn't just take a joke. I did it because I loved them, and I did it because I loved myself too.

"I'm not sure what you think is happening here," Cade said. I hadn't expected him to say anything, and the shock must've been written on my face, because he reached for me under the table. "But Isla has been through hell this last month. I'm not going to tell you the things she's done, but I will say, all of it was because she felt like she couldn't ask you for help. And she's here today telling you why, hoping this will repair your relationship. I think the least you can do is listen without flinging around accusations that border on gaslighting."

Under the table, he squeezed my hand. Another memory from years ago rose to the surface. Seb and Cade were ten and I was nine the summer we pretended to be explorers. The flatland at the end of our neighborhood had been dug out to make way for a new development, with piles of rocks and sand just waiting to be discovered. The ridges of dirt were steep. Seb had run to the bottom without a second thought, but I stayed near the top, afraid to go down but also afraid if I didn't go down, Seb and Cade wouldn't let me be an explorer with them anymore. Cade had gotten about three feet down the side before he realized I hadn't followed, so he made the slippery trek back up and offered me his hand.

"I've got you, Rainbow Bear. I won't let go. Promise."

The only reason I'd made it to the bottom of the hill that day was because Cade had held my hand the whole time. If I'd gone down, he would've gone down with me.

"Cade, son, this is more of a family matter." My dad's scolding tone brought me back to the present. "Why don't you head on home while we sort things out with our daughter?"

"Am I no longer family then?" Cade asked.

He'd never spoken up to my parents, even when they'd said some truly appalling things in front of him. The debt and gratitude he felt toward them had always come at the expense of his dignity, and it never should have been that way. Help not given freely was no help at all.

The only reason he said anything now was because he'd been holding me in some capacity my entire life, but this was killing him. I couldn't stand it. Wouldn't stand for it.

"That's enough." I stood, still holding Cade's hand. "You don't get to decide Cade is family enough for the Christmas card, but not family enough when he says something that makes you uncomfortable. That's on you. And like I already told you, if you make me pick, I choose him. Is that family enough for you?"

"I'm done here." My dad started to get up, running away from conflict like always, but he sat back down when I aimed a glare in his direction.

"Things are getting a little heated here." My mom's brow crinkled in concern. "Isla, I'm sorry you feel the way you do, but the only reason you seem to come home anymore is to tell us how terrible we are. Can you blame me for getting defensive?"

"I never said you were terrible. That's what you chose to hear when I asked you to stop making hurtful jokes and comments at my expense." I looked between my parents, but both of them had already turned away from me. "We're going to go. I hope you'll at least try to process what I shared and do some honest reflection. I believe you love me, and I hope you'll try." I steeled my spine for the hardest but most important part. "But I can't see you until things change. Because I need to take care of myself too."

I got no response in return.

No one said this road to self-love would be easy. I'd been swinging the pendulum in wild directions since I started, but I think I'd finally found a balance that suited me. It was okay to ask for better treatment from the people I loved. It was okay to walk away from them if they wouldn't change. It was okay to forgive those who slipped up but were trying. It was okay to forgive myself for the same.

In silence, I left my parents' house, still holding tight to Cade's hand. It wasn't the outcome I'd been hoping for, but I didn't regret taking that step, for myself or for Cade. As we walked toward his car, he murmured something about sending Seb to get mine.

At the passenger door, he stopped and cupped my face, worry taking over his expression as his gaze focused on my eyes. "Are you okay?"

I tilted my head as I gave his question honest consideration. Standing up to my parents, telling them how they made me feel, and putting my needs first had been scary, but a good, necessary scary. One thing that didn't scare me anymore was giving the whole of my heart to the beautiful man in front of me who had always held my hand, no matter the risk of falling. With Cade, I'd found something I didn't think I'd ever have again: hope for the future.

I grinned as I placed a soft kiss on his lips. "I've never been better."

EPILOGUE

I ran a brush through my hair and smoothed a hand down the side of my navy lace cocktail dress. Torres-Glasser had held their end-of-summer reception tonight to mark the final weekend event of the year. A black-tie affair at a fancy hotel downtown, and the only get-together that didn't include fishing in some capacity. It promised to be a dazzling party with champagne, a live band, and plenty of networking opportunities. Anton had been adamant about this one topping last year's.

The door opened behind me, and my heart, my soulmate, my partner in every adventure life had to offer threaded his arms around my waist and kissed my neck. "You clean up nice, Mrs. Greenley."

"I try." Cade had been my husband for two months. The novelty of being called "Mrs. Greenley" still hadn't worn off, and I hoped it never would.

The day we'd walked out of my mom and dad's house just over a year ago had been a hard one for both of us. No matter how many times I told Cade it wasn't in any way his fault, a small part of him felt responsible. But he supported my decision not to call or visit my parents unless they were willing to apologize and commit to making changes. It was still a work in progress. At least they'd attended our courthouse wedding after declining when they'd first gotten the invite.

We'd started making headway at Seb and Neeta's engagement party. It was difficult for the photographer to place us all when there was clearly tension in the room, but my mom and I got together for lunch soon afterward, and we talked some more. I apologized for my part in our rift, and she did the same. We were both trying. My dad was a little slower to come around.

We were getting there, though. Little by little.

Issues with my parents aside, Cade and I had done a lot of healing over the last year. It didn't happen easily or all at once. We still had tough days. But we'd made a promise to love and care for each other, and we honored it always.

I stood on my toes and pressed a quick kiss to his lips. "I need to view this video one last time, and then we should be good to go."

In my office, which used to be a guest room back when this was just Cade's condo, I took a seat on my plush leather chair and fired up my laptop. I kept my space relatively sparse. Just my desk, a few skinny bookshelves filled with plants, and a print on the wall from a local artist.

I had turned my website back into a blog last year and rediscovered my love for reading, posting the occasional review when I had time. My YouTube channel kept me pretty busy. I'd started it soon after I moved in with Cade. It began as an outlet for me to document the summer I spent as a house sitter, and it eventually evolved into tips, advice, and hacks for anyone trying to survive their first year out of college. I named my channel Avocado Toast. I'd recently passed half a million subscribers. It was my baby and I loved it.

After one last viewing of my latest vlog, I uploaded it and sat back. I watched my views roll in for a second, proud of what I'd built. Then I closed my laptop, tipped my head back, and smiled. I'd come a long way from Cornerstone Enterprises.

All those businesses I'd sent my CV out to right before I got fired ended up snagging me two interviews. The first was for an entry-level business data-entry analyst position at Ridgeway Inc., a stuffy corporation with various divisions across thirty-nine states. They had marginally better pay than Cornerstone and better tea options for the breakroom Keurig. The second one was a bookkeeping job for Rosewater and Pine, a small packaging company that employed just under fifty people. They paid a lot less to start, but it was work from home.

In the end, I took the pay cut to work from home and moved in with Cade to cut back on expenses. Within two months, I was able to monetize my YouTube channel and draw people to it through TikTok, putting away enough money to start my own business selling affordable gift baskets full of do-it-yourself projects for people on a budget. I'd never been happier.

I wasn't going to change the world one gift basket at a time, but I was my own boss, and I enjoyed what I did for a living. It was amazing the things I could accomplish when I was betting on myself. I started building relationships with other small business owners in the community, and we traded ideas and strategies. Some of them became friends, but Neeta was still my bestie.

Money was tight. That probably wouldn't change anytime soon. Having a dual income helped, but Cade had taken out a sizable loan to pay for his fancy work wardrobe and the renovations he'd had done on the condo, thinking he needed to keep up a certain appearance, and we'd both probably carry our student loan debt until we died. Though things weren't nearly as dire as they'd been for me a year ago. I was able to pay my bills on time, and we didn't have a single package of ramen in our cupboards. To me, those things meant everything.

Cade leaned against the door, his hands in his pockets. My husband was ridiculously sexy in a three-piece suit. On our wedding night, I made him leave it on while I rode him to my first of several orgasms. I bit my lip at the memory. If we didn't have somewhere to be, I would've been more than happy to relive that moment all over again.

He stepped into my office, his eyes heating as he leaned down with his hands on either side of the armrests. "You keep looking at me like that, Rainbow Bear, and we're not making it to the hotel on time."

"Oh, really?" I wrapped a leg around him, my short cocktail dress riding higher up my thigh. "What did you have in mind, Mr. Greenley?"

He groaned and rested his forehead against mine. "What am I going to do with you?"

"What if I said whatever you want?"

Taking my hands, he pulled me up from my chair and against his hard body. "We'll revisit this conversation after the event."

I rubbed my hands up his chest. "Can't wait."

While I wouldn't have minded being late, it was incredibly important to Cade to make a good impression. He took his job seriously, which I understood and respected. He had gotten better at loosening up and having fun at the summer events, though he wouldn't be wearing cargo shorts any time soon. Maybe one day.

At the front door, Cade lifted the handle on my squeaky suitcase and wheeled it into the hall. After the event, we had plans to meet Seb and Neeta at a cabin we'd all rented up north. It was on a private lake with a small pebble beach. It had two bedrooms on opposite sides of an expansive living room, and an updated kitchen. Our first real vacation as a couple. We hadn't been able to afford a honeymoon, though neither of us minded much. We probably wouldn't have made it out of the hotel if we had gone anywhere.

On the way over to the Torres-Glasser event, Seb texted us pictures of the steaks, potato salad, and snap peas he'd gotten at a local market for tomorrow night's dinner, and I sent back a warning that the communal dining room table was for food only. Just in case.

Cade parked his Jeep, and when he came around to meet me on my side, he lifted me up on the hood and kissed me deep enough to cause a moan to rise up in my throat. Lost in the moment, I ran my fingers through his hair and wrapped my legs around him, kissing him until I became breathless. He pulled back and rubbed his thumb over my lower lip.

"What was that for?" I asked. "Not that I'm complaining."

"Just wanted to give you a reminder of how much I love you."

"I love you too." I ran my hand over his jaw. "Every minute of every day."

Occasionally I'd play this game where I'd try to trace our time line back to all the different times when we had so obviously been in love but hadn't realized it yet. There was the moment in Jillian's garden when he had given me a kiss on the forehead meant for comfort. Thanksgiving night when we'd split a bottle of Jack Daniels and said things we couldn't ever take back. On the swings in my parents' backyard, when he'd seen me kissing a boy that should've been him. The treehouse, where he'd caught me eating stolen cookies. At the top of a dirt ridge, when he took my hand and promised to hold it. Or when it all had started, with a comforter and a teddy bear.

Every memory I had included Cade, and I loved him in every one. While we'd had plenty of ups and downs, I never took for granted that we had a lifetime ahead of us. Because through it all, one thing always remained true: we never let go of each other.

ACKNOWLEDGMENTS

I hope you enjoyed Isla and Cade's journey! This book has been with me for so long, and I'm thrilled it's finally out in the world. I had the idea for this a long time ago, but because of other commitments, wasn't able to fully dive in until 2021. And this story just poured out of me. Pieces of my own struggles are embedded in different parts of this story from times in my life when everything felt hopeless and I laughed so I wouldn't cry.

My own student loan debt was so insurmountable to me that I had to go back to school after getting my degree because I couldn't afford daycare and my loans and needed that six-month deferment again. So I took on more debt just to keep my head above water. I froze credit cards in blocks of ice, tried to buy gas with cans, didn't eat meat for months because I couldn't afford it. I wanted to write a book that was honest about how hard it can be out there, about how people don't always make what those in more comfortable positions would consider wise choices, and how society as a whole doles out certain promises to those who "work hard and get a good education" while also breaking those promises over and over again. And while I aimed to tell a lighter story with plenty of humor sprinkled in, I also wanted to put something real on the page too.

Thank you so much for reading. As always, books are nothing without their readers, and I deeply appreciate every one of you.

A huge thank-you to my amazing agent, Rebecca Podos, who has been through nine years and five contracted books with me, as well as a few manuscripts that weren't so lucky. I literally don't function without you.

To everyone at Alcove Press, I'm so thrilled I got to work with you on this book. It has my whole heart, and I'm so fortunate to have a team behind me that feels as strongly about Isla and Cade's story as I do. To my editor, Holly Ingraham, thank you for your enthusiasm and insight. Dulce Botello, Madeline Rathle, Thai Fantauzzi Perez, Doug White, Melissa Rechter, Rebecca Nelson, and my publisher, Matthew Martzcover, thank you so much for everything that you've done to bring this book into the world. It means everything to me. To Stephanie Singleton for your cover illustration and Meghan Deist for your cover typography, thank you so much for capturing the fun and flirty vibe of this book so well. I absolutely love it.

My coven, Andrea Contos, Annette Christie, Auriane Desombre, Kelsey Rodkey, Rachel Lynn Solomon, and Susan Lee, what can I say that I don't tell you every day? I'm so thankful for all of you, even when you send me TikToks of a certain Wiggle.

Thank you to Madison Molenhouse. You know why. I miss your face.

To my early readers, Alicia Thompson, Courtney Kae, Diana Urban, Jenny Howe, Emily Thiede, and Jen Hawkins, and my dancing ladies Kellye Garrett and Roselle Lim, I'm unsure how I've managed to convince all of you wonderful humans to be my friend, but I'm so lucky to have you.

Erin E. Adams, I'd hoped to send this to you during revisions, but I had a pretty tight turnaround time and wasn't able to. I still want you in my acknowledgments because I adore you, and really, what better reason is there than that?

To Mr. Sonia and my incredible girls, thank you for all your support, even—maybe especially—during the lean times. We're finally starting to come out on the other side. I love you so much. I couldn't do any of this without you.

ABOUT EMBLA BOOKS

Embla Books is a digital-first publisher of standout commercial adult fiction. Passionate about storytelling, the team at Embla publish books that will make you 'laugh, love, look over your shoulder and lose sleep'. Launched by Bonnier Books UK in 2021, the imprint is named after the first woman from the creation myth in Norse mythology, who was carved by the gods from a tree trunk found on the seashore – an image of the kind of creative work and crafting that writers do, and a symbol of how stories shape our lives.

Find out about some of our other books and stay in touch:

Twitter, Facebook, Instagram: @emblabooks
Newsletter: https://bit.ly/emblanewsletter